"A delicious treat for readers . . . Like a master chef, Judith Fertig takes the tale of a gifted baker starting all over in her old Midwestern hometown and layers it together with an intriguing mystery buried deep in the community's Depression-era past."

—Beatriz Williams, *New York Times* bestselling author of *Tiny Little Thing*

"In a small town where secrets run deep and over generations, Fertig shows friendship, family, and food can bring people together and heal old wounds. A novel that is a true treat for the senses."

—Jill Shalvis, *New York Times* bestselling author of *Still the One*

"This delicious debut will leave your mouth watering and your eyes moist . . . A heartwarming story of community, love, and food so delectable you want it to leap off the page into your mouth."

—Linda Rodriguez, award-winning poet and author of *Every Hidden Fear*

"A dash of complex romance stirs up a cast of characters linked through time by a precious bauble in a delicious setting. This sweet charmer of a story made me hungry for more."

—Jeanne Ambrose, award-winning writer, cookbook author, and editor of *Taste of Home* magazine

"*The Cake Therapist* is charming, captivating, and crave-worthy. Not only do I want to meet (and be friends!) with Neely after reading her story; I want to taste every one of her deliciously therapeutic treats. How I wish I knew what flavor she would choose for me!"

—Denise Mickelsen, cooking, baking, and gardening acquisitions editor at Craftsy

"Fertig expertly weaves a redemptive tale of then and now, of sweetness and pain, all while slowly unraveling a mystery that had me flipping pages faster and faster until its surprising ending."

—David Leite, publisher of Leite's Culinaria

the Cake THERAPIST

JUDITH FERTIG

BERKLEY BOOKS, NEW YORK

BERKLEY

An imprint of Penguin Random House LLC
375 Hudson Street, New York, New York 10014

This book is an original publication of Penguin Random House LLC.

Library of Congress Cataloging-in-Publication Data

Fertig, Judith M.
The cake therapist / Judith Fertig.
pages cm
ISBN 978-0-425-27732-4 (paperback)
1. Women—Fiction. 2. Bakers—Fiction. I. Title.
PS3606.E78C36 2015
813'.6—dc23
2015002608

PUBLISHING HISTORY
Berkley trade paperback edition / June 2015

PRINTED IN THE UNITED STATES OF AMERICA

10 9 8 7 6 5 4 3 2 1

Cover photo by Edward Djendrono / Getty Images.
Cover design by Rita Frangie.
Interior text design by Laura K. Corless.

This is a work of fiction. Names, characters, places, and incidents either are the product of
the author's imagination or are used fictitiously, and any resemblance to actual persons,
living or dead, business establishments, events, or locales is entirely coincidental.

Penguin
Random
House

For my family,
who make life sweet
and help me practice real-life cake therapy

ACKNOWLEDGMENTS

Where to start? At the beginning. First of all, to my parents, Jean and Jack Merkle, whose love and support have been constant and who raised me in a very interesting place, as it turns out. Many thanks to my sister, Julie Fox, and her family for uncorking the champagne. *Merci beaucoup* to Le Cordon Bleu in London and Ecole de Cuisine La Varenne in Paris for my culinary education. You can't write without a life, and I'm so happy to have daughter Sarah, son Nick, daughter-in-law Jessica, soon-to-be son-in-law Eric, and little Anya Sofia in mine.

The Cake Therapist wouldn't be here if not for my friend and BBQ cookbook coauthor Karen Adler, who listened to me blab about this idea for years as we drove to teach classes at cooking schools around the country. A dose of cake therapy to Deborah Shouse and Mary Lane Kamberg, who read a very early chapter in which nothing much happened. A tip of the chef's toque to Kelly Dwyer and "The Plotters" at the Iowa Summer Writing Festival for getting the plot going. Thanks to the amazing Vivien Jennings of Rainy Day Books and the judges at the Kansas City Pitchapalooza, who put me in touch with Arielle Eckstut and her great advice. I'm indebted to the Writers' Colony at Dairy Hollow for the deep time in which to write the first draft. Warm thanks to Dee Barwick, Mary Ann Duckers, and my cookbook agent, Lisa Ekus, who read an early draft.

Many, many thanks to Linda Rodriguez, who brought me into the Kansas City Novel Writers Group, which also includes Jacqueline Guidry, Robin Silverman, and Deborah Shouse. I'm grateful to my delightful cookbook editor, Kristen Wiewora at Running Press, who put her stamp of approval on the title over ice cream in Philadelphia.

Once *The Cake Therapist* was ready to go, I had the great fortune to sign with the talented Stefanie Lieberman of Janklow & Nesbit. She led me to editor Kate Seaver, of the keen eye, warm sensibility, great sense of humor (and superb taste)—plus everyone at the Berkley Publishing Group of Penguin Random House. It truly does take a village.

And all of this has led me to you, dear reader. Enjoy! Let's stay in touch at judithfertig.com.

Prologue

DECEMBER

The windows at Macy's were dressed in the usual high-wattage holiday fanfare, and the Christmas tree at Rockefeller Plaza twinkled as valiantly as ever. But for me, December had been gray and blah, like suffering through the end of a cold when you couldn't taste anything.

Instead of hurrying down Fifth Avenue with shopping bags full of gifts, I was hauling my life away from Brooklyn in a rental truck.

Good-bye, New York.

Slow and steady, careful not to take sharp turns, I made my way out of the city. Past the brownstones in my neighborhood and the concrete, glass, and steel downtown. Past the stone barns and Victorian farmhouses in Pennsylvania. Up and down the stark hills of West Virginia.

When I finally hit I-70 at the Ohio border in the ink-black

night, I pulled off at a truck stop, just to rest my eyes, and ended up sleeping for a few fitful hours.

When I woke up, groggy and stiff, the light was gray again.

I filled the gas tank and poured bad truck-stop coffee, the kind that was so weak that someone could have just murmured "coffee" over a cup of hot water and it would have tasted the same. But it was better than nothing.

At the next Starbucks in St. Clairsville, I got a triple-shot latte and one of their cinnamon scones. Even the jolt of coffee and spice couldn't nudge my taste meter off "Dull." I guess I had to accept that for now.

Driving through the rolling farmland of central Ohio, I let my mind wander as I kept my eyes on the road.

It wasn't often that I had difficulty tasting *something*. Flavor was the way people like me made sense of the world.

We knew that there was a flavor that explained you—even to yourself. A flavor whose truth you recognized when you tasted it. A flavor that answered the question you didn't know you had.

Perhaps it was a voluptuous vanilla that your sharp-edged self could sink into like a pillow. Or a homesick pomegranate, each seed like a ruby slipper that would take you back to the place where you were loved and where people had missed you.

That's where I was going. If only I could taste it.

By the time I reached Columbus and headed south on I-71, I knew I was only two hours from home.

Unlike other aging factory towns around it, Millcreek Valley was reinventing itself as a bridal district. Now in the small 1840s brick cottages, two-story Italianate storefronts, shotgun-style houses, and smattering of nondescript sixties modern brick-and-

2

chrome buildings, you could find lingerie, bridal gown, tuxedo, and honeymoon travel shops. Wedding planners like my high school friend Roshonda Taylor had customers who traveled from three states away. The old brick five-and-dime had become an upscale boutique, selling Vera Wang and Monique Lhuillier gowns.

And that was why I was opening my bakery there. Well, one of the reasons. I wanted a destination place with a ready-made market.

In the bridal business, everyone knew that December was the biggest month for engagements. In January, those happy brides-to-be would start planning their weddings, so we had to be open by the first Saturday, when hordes of mothers and daughters would crowd the sidewalks, shivering from shop to shop.

And the second reason? I needed a project. A big project.

Anything to help me forget I had nowhere else to go and nothing else to do.

When I finally pulled up to the stoplight on Millcreek Valley Road, ready to turn down Benson Street, I gave myself a long, hard stare in the rearview mirror.

I had inherited my father's dark auburn hair along with his green eyes. But I also got my mother's unruly curl, so my hair had a tendency to escape a topknot or ponytail every chance it got. Today was no exception.

I was only thirty-two, but I thought I looked older. Much older. Sleeping in a truck stop in the middle of nowhere on a cold night will do that to you. I pinched my cheeks for color and put on a quick swath of lipstick. I was no primper, but there was something really depressing about looking as drab as you felt. As my aunt Helen often said, "Fake it till you make it."

That was the corollary to Millcreek Valley's unwritten rule:

Work hard and don't complain. People here put a premium on niceness and disapproved of moaning and groaning. Especially on Sunday.

As I pulled into the parking lot of my soon-to-be bakery, right next to my soon-to-be house, I saw Roshonda across the street, opening the front door of Jump the Broom. I waved at her, thankful that my good friend was now my business neighbor, then jumped out of the truck.

We met in the middle of Benson Street in a big hug, then walked arm in arm back to the parking lot.

"Well, you still look like the same Claire O'Neil I knew in high school, thank goodness. I'm so glad you didn't go all big-city glam on me. I really missed you, sweetie," she said, holding on tight. "And now that you're back for good, we can remind the people in this one-horse town how sophisticated thinkers have fun."

"Yes, of course." I nodded with mock solemnity. "Like the time we wrapped ourselves in Christmas tree lights, plugged ourselves in, and danced in front of my house?"

"People still keep asking me, 'When is the next Festival of the Dancing Lights?'"

"Or when we bribed the opposing women's softball team with coffee-toffee bars?"

"Strike out, fly out, just get yourself out; *then* you get a cookie. That was the deal."

"I'm surprised *we* didn't get kicked out."

"We saved that for later. We can get ourselves kicked out of lots of places now."

We both laughed and knew that wasn't about to happen. We talked a good game, but we were both Goody Two-shoes at heart.

When other people in your family chose to be bad, somebody else had to be good. That didn't mean we didn't have a yen for bad boys who always messed us around. You'd think Goody Two-shoes would be smarter than that, but then they'd have to call us Smarty Two-shoes, and have you ever heard of one? No.

"I got you a welcome-home gift," Roshonda said. "It was too heavy to carry, so I had them put it on your front porch."

We walked past the bakery to Gran's old house, the one that I was fixing up for myself since Gran now lived in Mount Saint Mary's memory care wing. A fresh coat of dark gray paint and cream trim had the shotgun-style house looking pretty good. I spotted Roshonda's gift on the wide front porch, right by the black front door—one of the concrete geese that everyone around here wanted as yard art so they could dress them up in outfits for almost any occasion or season. This one wore a chef's hat and a baker's apron. There was a gaggle of concrete geese in the parking lot of Hodapp Hardware on Millcreek Valley Road keeping watch over the town, but none of them ever laid that golden egg as far as I could tell.

Maybe mine would be different. I checked underneath.

"Bad news. No egg," I told Roshonda.

She looked, too. "Good news. No goose poop."

I unlocked the front door. Roshonda and I went inside the house, which was just waiting to be filled with all the stuff I had in my truck.

We walked from the front parlor to the dining room and back to the kitchen, then upstairs to see the two bedrooms and home office on the second floor. The new bed and upholstered headboard that I had ordered online were already set up in the largest bedroom.

"It's beautiful. Fresh and quiet and calm. It feels good in this house," Roshonda said.

"I can't wait to move in. Gavin did a great job." Our high school friend Gavin Nichols had begun his career in the art department of a large advertising agency in Chicago and then quickly charmed his way into a coveted in-house marketing vice presidency at Quaker. But after spending some time climbing the executive tree in brand management, Gavin began to feel hamstrung by corporate life. A couple of years ago, he announced to us he was chucking everything to start his own space planning and interior design business back in Millcreek Valley. Oatmeal's loss was my gain. Of course, the rumor was that Gavin had also left a serious relationship. Still, we knew not to pry; he'd tell us if he wanted us to know.

When I called Gavin to tell him I was closing things up in New York, he shouldered the massive renovation of Gran's house without missing a beat. And he was also helping me revamp the Rainbow Cake building. I couldn't wait to see that, either.

"Let's bring in a few things, just to get you started."

Roshonda helped me unload the handcart from the back of the truck and wheel a few boxes into the kitchen. She also wheeled in my two suitcases.

"When are the guys coming to move you in?"

"Not for another two hours."

"Well, then let's take a look at the bakery, shall we?"

Although Gavin had texted me photos as the work had progressed, it still wasn't like seeing it in person. I hoped it looked as great as my house.

The simple truth was that I owed Gavin, big-time. While my

New York life was melting down as fast as buttercream frosting on a hot day, he took charge of my escape plan, which included renovating the vacant old library building for me.

I found the front door key in my purse, and we stepped inside the revamped storefront.

When I turned the lights on, I felt like I had stepped inside a Tiffany box.

"Oh, Neely!" Roshonda said.

The walls were painted a robin's-egg blue. Antique wood-and-glass display cases had mottled milk chocolate–brown marble countertops. Antique iron-and-glass stands would make the future little cakes (under their glass domes) pop up and down on the counter like jaunty hats.

From the top of the left wall of the bakery, Gavin had hung a canvas curtain and arranged a display area in front of it. Both the curtain and display would change each month—as would, of course, the colors and flavors we showcased. The idea was to sell not only cakes, but also cake stands, serving pieces, plates, paper napkins, and other goodies, so once your little cakes got home, they'd look as good as they did in my bakery. One-stop shopping.

On the right, Gavin had arranged a seating area with dark bentwood chairs and café tables. It looked like a tea salon in Paris.

I sighed with delight.

But I wanted to see where I would spend most of my time.

The work and storage areas were screened off in the back, although I would have been happy to show off my two Vulcan convection-ovens-on-wheels and the big stainless steel worktable with the cool marble slab at one end for chocolate work.

The calm milk-chocolate plaster walls, stainless steel, and white marble made the workspace look like a shrine to the cake baker's art. And I liked to think it was.

"Does this start to make up for everything else?" Leave it to Roshonda to get right to the point.

I nodded yes. I was too tired, too frazzled, to cry.

She offered to help me put things away, but I knew she was busy, too. And I wanted to get into this new life without distraction.

"I'll leave you to it, then," she said. "Just text me if you need anything."

As I unloaded the smaller boxes of bakery gear from the truck and started putting everything away, I had that soothing sense of making order out of chaos. Like reading a mystery novel and having everything tied up at the end.

But no matter how many whisks I hung on hooks or metal cookie cutters I put in plastic bins, there was still a hole in my heart. Two holes, in fact.

The old one had been shrinking. The new one was still ragged at the edges.

1

JANUARY

Dark Chocolate and Rich Coffee

I didn't know until I licked the mocha buttercream from my third devil's food cupcake that this was the flavor of starting over—dark chocolate with that take-charge undercurrent of coffee.

I could actually taste it, feel it. And now I craved it.

Slowly, I was coming back to myself.

The past two weeks had gone by in a flash: packing up on a drizzly December day, driving from the East Coast to the Midwest, getting my house and then my new business set up. I yearned to curl up in front of my fireplace and just stare at the flames.

But here I was on yet another Sunday, getting ready for a soft opening by next weekend. Everything was a fast-paced blur on the outside of my life, but inside, where it counted, I was back in working order. I could taste.

At the moment, I needed a quick break from the sensory overload in the bakery, which held every color, aroma, and flavor of the past few days of frenzied production. I had once read about a Montreal baker who developed a perfume she called "Wheat Siren," inspired by the aroma and flavor of sweet things baking. Even though my own muse seemed to be plodding in chef's clogs rather than sashaying in Jimmy Choo's, the full-body allure of the kitchen had returned to me with emphasis. Years ago, during my very first weeks of pastry school, I had learned that too much of a good thing was still too much. So over time—and with some difficulty—I'd trained myself to step back and reassess at regular intervals. If only I had been as wise in my personal life.

Today, I decided I should step outside, even if it was January. Maybe the shock of the cold and a blast of winter wind would sharpen my focus.

I opened the front door of Rainbow Cake and, like a genie from a bottle, the warm bakery air escaped with me. All of those aromatized esters, the flavor bouquet that wine geeks described as they swirled and sniffed a glass of wine, spiraled out above the sidewalk along Benson Street.

I looked up to see the sun struggling behind a gray mass of snow clouds.

I could relate.

And then a beam of sunlight found a way through. A sign? Maybe.

But what was this? I gasped. The bakery esters had refracted into visible bands of flavor.

Red raspberry, orange, and the yellow of lemon and butter.

Pistachio, lime, and mint green.

The deepest indigo of a fresh blueberry.

The violet that blooms when crushed blackberries blend into buttercream.

The Roy G. Biv that a baker loves.

And then the darkness: chocolate, spice, coffee, and burnt-sugar caramel.

Every flavor, I knew, was a shortcut to a feeling. Sorrow. Joy. Anticipation. Fear.

And every feeling was the heart of a story. And we all had a story.

Above me was a rainbow of stories. Maybe I could have a quick taste of one right now. . . .

Something purple. Mmmmmm. Plum.

Could a flavor be pleased with itself and its position in the world? That was plum. Not the sharp-flavored skin and the sweet flesh of a fresh plum, but more the concentrated flavor when the fruit was cooked down for a tart filling. Like the taste of port. In fact, I liked to pair plum and port together.

You won't be able to wear your pretty gloves and eat one of Mrs. Skillman's crullers; I can vouch for that.

Who said that? I turned around to look for the old-fashioned gentleman who had just spoken, but he wasn't there. Never mind. My imagination was in overdrive, so I didn't see what was coming.

"Watch the dog!"

Tiny, low-to-the-ground Mrs. Amici almost bowled me over as she walked her dog, Barney, down the sidewalk.

"Good morning to you, too, Mrs. Amici." She looked deceptively sweet with her cotton-candy hair, faded pink parka, and aqua velour pants. But we all knew her bite was every bit as bad as her bark. Barney, half dachshund and half beagle, practically toppled over as he angled his long, tubular body to christen every parking meter and streetlight pole.

"Hope you got enough people around here who can afford those fancy cakes," she grumbled, and nodded up to Rainbow Cake's colorful sign.

"I hope so, Mrs. Amici."

"You're not going to make it if you go around looking like that. You've got blue hands," she pointed out. "And your hair hasn't seen a comb since I don't know when."

"You're right, Mrs. Amici," I had to admit, wiping my hands on my white baker's apron, for all the good it did. "A little frosting, that's all. Robin's-egg blue is our signature color."

She tut-tutted, and her gaze went up to my face.

Did I have buttercream there, too? Probably. I quickly patted my face. I knew I still looked tired, as I had been working nonstop.

"If that's how you ran around in New York City, no wonder you had to come home with your tail between your legs," she added, with a mean chuckle. "Little Claire O'Neil. Or is it still Claire Davis? Miss I Can't Wait to Get Out of This Dump. Oh, wait a minute—it's Mrs. Big Shot running back home to her mother. Only thirtysomething and you're already washed up. Don't look so shocked. It has happened before, believe me."

I gasped. Her sharpness started to work its way inside me like a splinter.

Lemon. I could just taste it. Above her head, a band of yellow seemed to separate from the rest of the flavor rainbow. As it went into free fall, enveloping us both, I could taste the crumb of a buttery lemon bar that got more and more puckery. Ehhhh.

"Whatever," Mrs. Amici grunted at me, oblivious, and then hobbled along as Barney did his funny arabesque down the sidewalk.

The wind picked up.

Roshonda opened the front door of Jump the Broom to get the newspaper from her front stoop. "Whatever you're baking up in there, Neely, it sure smells good," she said. "Reminds me of my auntie's tea cakes."

"I'll bring you something later," I promised.

"Neely! We're ready for January," Gavin called from the bakery doorway.

The flavor rainbow was gone, and I went back inside where Gavin and the photographer were setting up the first digital shot. For the grand opening next weekend, I'd gone all out. My signature rainbow cake—layers of lavender, coral, lime-green, lemon-yellow, and raspberry-pink cake frosted with our robin's-egg blue buttercream—provided the logo for the bakery sign, brochure, business cards, and website. We took that photo yesterday.

Like any bakery, it would have the standard stuff—breakfast pastries and muffins, cinnamon rolls, coffee cakes, cakes, cookies, and more. But it was the monthly, flavor-themed specials that would, hopefully, bring customers back to try something new. It was a marketing idea that ice cream makers had been all over for years.

At Rainbow Cake, January's special flavors would be dark chocolate and coffee, those pick-me-ups we all needed to start the day—or a new year. To me, their roasty-toasty flavors said that even if you only had a mere handful of beans and your life went up in flames, you could still create something wonderful.

A little trial by fire could do you good. After all, if it worked so well with raw cacao and coffee beans, it could work for others, including me. Or so I hoped.

I ran back to the workroom, where I had everything ready to go on my rolling cart of vertical shelves. I brought out the sweet, little pillowy kisses—the version of French macarons I call "polka dots" because they sort of dance in your mouth. Every month, our polka dots will highlight a new set of signature flavors and colors.

Same with the éclairs, which would be a weekend special. January's éclairs would be filled with a coffee-flavored pastry cream and finished with a chocolate icing.

Gavin arranged the paper-frilled mocha cupcakes with robin's-egg blue frosting and chocolate sprinkles. Sugar cookies individually decorated like snowflakes—each in a unique pattern of turquoise detailing dusted with a flurry of sugar crystals—as well as cookie mittens and ice skates. Chic bridesmaids' sugar-cookie dresses painted in mocha and espresso. And a five-tiered wedding "cake" display of individual petit fours in pale aqua fondant dotted with dark chocolate.

I thought, again, how lucky I'd been—really. Rainbow Cake was the bakery I'd never have been able to afford in Manhattan, Brooklyn, or the Hamptons. At least, not on my own. While it was true that I had access to money back East, and lots of it, I never felt it was mine enough to spend.

I couldn't have afforded Gavin in New York, either, so I'm doubly lucky he hasn't accepted one of those job offers he's always getting from either coast. His arrangement of platters, plates, and stands holding these little works of Rainbow Cake art against January's chocolate-brown canvas backdrop looked as good as I knew everything tasted.

"We'll have different color and flavor themes every month and use social media to announce them," he told me a few weeks ago, visual and marketing genius that he was. "We'll take all the digital photos at once, so you can use them for advertising and your website and for showing all those clients who will be lined up as soon as you open." He talked even faster. "Then Williams-Sonoma will be calling. . . ."

It would take a village to get all of this done in time, in addition to the village already working at Rainbow Cake.

Jett Patterson was going to make all our specialty decorations, from piped roses and ribbons to marzipan fruits and sugar-paste flowers, based on my designs but with her own special flair. She was the high school art student I hired to work for me afternoons and Saturdays when school started again. I was starting to think of her as "the Goth Van Gogh" on a good day or "Vampira" on a bad one. She took a little getting used to.

Maggie Lierman, my other close high school friend and now a much-put-upon single mom, would run the business.

Norb Weisbrod, tall, pale, and quiet, would be my baker, back of the house. He used to work at Gateaux, the European-style bakery in Queen City that specialized in elaborate cakes and petit fours. But he came out of retirement to work for me—and get away from Bonnie, his bitchy wife. He was also going to help with deliveries when I needed him.

I'd do everything else—meet with clients, do wedding cake tastings, design and assemble the specialty cakes, generate new business, and oversee it all.

"Charming, utterly charming," the reporter from *Queen City Weddings* said when she got a preview on Friday.

"Genius," I wanted to correct her. Rainbow Cake was better than I could ever have imagined it. I sighed and gave Gavin a watery smile.

"Don't say it," Gavin warned. Like every guy I'd ever known, he was unsettled by the imminent threat of tears, especially female ones. "I owe you, remember? You don't owe me."

Gavin and I always looked out for each other. I had come to his aid several times in the past, especially in high school when his slight build occasionally made him a target for abuse from bigger guys. And while I wasn't in the habit of keeping score between us, Gavin was the sort of person who remembered every kindness.

I smiled fondly at my old friend as he slid the curtain off the pole. Gone was January's dark chocolate and coffee. Next up was February's blood orange and raspberry.

Gavin climbed down the ladder and started arranging February's display. "Before I forget and we're too far into this, I've got something for you," I told him. I ran to the workroom and brought out a pale turquoise box tied with a chocolate brown ribbon— Rainbow Cake's signature wrapping for our high-style cakes.

"This doesn't match our color scheme for February," he grumbled.

"It's a gift, you dope." I pressed the box into his stomach. He read the card that said, "Thank you for helping me feather my new nest." He opened the box and saw a tiny cake shaped like a bird's nest in three small round layers of tender, browned-butter vanilla cake with an apricot filling. A "nest" border of piped rum and mocha buttercream enclosed a clutch of pale blue marzipan eggs and a sugar-paste feather. The complicated yin and yang of rum and mocha, the "everybody loves" vanilla, Mr. Social white chocolate, tart and witty apricot, and artistic marzipan—all said "Gavin" to me.

"It looks too good to eat, Neely," he said as he carefully took the cake out of the box, slid it onto a little white plate, and looked at it from all sides.

"Let's get a casual shot of this quick," he told the photographer. And *click*, *click*, it was done.

Then Gavin brought the cake closer to him and inhaled the aroma once, twice, three times. "I have to taste this." He took a forkful, closed his eyes, and savored the tender cake, the smooth buttercream, the flavor energies I had animated just for him.

He breathed a sigh of pure pleasure. Then he looked at me, puzzled, as if I had seen into his deepest self. He ate a few more bites, nibbled each marzipan egg, and then breathed in, closing his eyes for a moment.

"I don't know what you put in this, Neely, but I find it weird and wrong that you knew how much I needed it," he said, eyes twinkling.

"I told you about the townhome rehab I'm doing for that cute Chicago couple, right?" He ate the last bit of the cake, plucking off the sugar-paste feather, which he put playfully behind his ear.

"Well, they want everything clean and spare and monochromatic. But it just doesn't fit them as people. They're quirky and relaxed—and they've hated every beige and winter-white scheme I've designed. Even though my gut keeps telling me to go another way, I've been fighting my instincts in favor of what the clients think they want. It's been driving me seriously nuts, if you want to know the truth."

Gavin licked a stray bit of apricot from his fork. "But after one taste of this cake, the whole direction of the project is suddenly clear to me. I'm thinking a streamlined version of homey—maybe a palette of mostly cream with some turquoise and chocolate-colored accents that pop. And a mix of comfortable modern seating with some carefully selected, not-too-crenellated, art nouveau pieces . . ."

"You had me at 'crenellated,'" I said, rolling my eyes.

He shot a wry look in my direction as his thoughts trailed off. "Hey, Neels, if this whole bakery thing doesn't work out, you could always be a cake therapist."

I smiled, and felt myself drifting off again. A cake therapist. Hmmmm.

"Uh-oh, earth to Neely. We need a latte over here stat!" Gavin snapped his fingers in front of my face. He put his arm around me and led me over to the other star of Rainbow Cake—my new La Marzocco espresso machine. Starbucks was as yet unheard of in Millcreek Valley, so if you wanted a real latte, Rainbow Cake was going to be your only source. All of us had had to learn to use the espresso machine.

"You need caffeine, honey, and you need it bad." Gavin ground the dark-roasted beans, tamped down the grounds into the holder, brewed the espresso, and steamed the milk. Then he handed me a latte, complete with a design in the froth.

My new leaf.

My smartphone began to *brrrrrrr* in the pocket of my jeans. I looked at the text message. The 212 number and *I Heart U* made my heart get back on that roller-coaster ride it had been trying to get off. "It's just the caffeine," I muttered to no one in particular, and walked back into the workroom to put March's cakes on trays.

MAY 1908

Ben Nash and Ethel Parsons stepped out of the hansom cab that had taken them to the Plum Street dock in Queen City. The *Aurora*, a blunt-nosed wooden canal boat sitting low to the water, awaited them.

It was a cool spring morning, and thank goodness for that, as the oily brown water showed the flotsam of all the breweries, tanneries, pork barreling works, and paper mills that lined the canal and dumped into it—including a dead mule that had yet to be hauled out.

Ethel was tempted to put her handkerchief to her nose, but decided against it.

The two young people stood quietly, their minds on what they were there to do. On the ride up the Miami and Erie Canal to the Simms & Taylor cotton mill and mattress factory in Lockton, they would show their drawings for brocade mattress covers that could be in the next Sears, Roebuck catalogue. The 1909 mail-order book would offer even more products to outfit the popular Sears homes that could be assembled from a kit.

Ben and Ethel had come by train from New York City, staying at the grandiose Alms & Doepke Hotel downtown, all expenses paid by Pearson & Associates, the forward-thinking design firm that had gone out on a limb to hire a woman. Ben had received strict instructions to do most of the talking, unless George Taylor asked Ethel a direct question. Nash was also to keep an eye on her, as a young woman staying unchaperoned at a hotel was not, of course, ideal.

Ethel, in a crisp Gibson Girl shirtwaist under a gray serge jacket and long skirt, her blond hair bundled up under a broad-brimmed black straw hat, thought about her older sister designing jewelry in Boston's Nob Hill. Like her sister, Ethel was determined to succeed. She tucked her flat black portfolio up under her left arm. Ethel hoped she could convince the men of Simms & Taylor that her designs would appeal to working-class women who, after all, dreamed of domestic beauty like their upper-class sisters, but lacked as much wherewithal to make that dream happen.

Ethel held out her right hand, unbuttoned and removed her gray glove—no true lady went about without gloves—and once more admired the ring her sister had made for her: a pretty sapphire surrounded by tiny gold leaves and seed pearls. Then she polished it against her skirt for good luck and put her glove back on.

Rounding the corner, three men in bowler hats and stiff-collared shirts strode toward the young people.

"Great morning for our little trip up to Lockton, Miss Parsons and Mr. Nash." The oldest-looking man nodded to them, tipping his hat to Ethel. He looked like a port-drinking gentleman, she assessed quickly, and she envisioned a well-run household with a potted palm in the front bay window of the parlor and maids in black dresses and white pinafores.

"George Taylor, at your service."

She extended her gloved hand to shake his, but he gallantly raised her hand to his lips and gave it a courtly peck. Ethel blushed as she withdrew her hand, then blushed at the thought that she had blushed to begin with.

Mr. Taylor smiled benignly at her, eyes twinkling, then informed the group, "We've asked the captain's wife to come along and make us coffee. She's also frying her famous crullers." The Simms & Taylor men's eyes widened in delight. Taylor turned back to Ethel. "You won't be able to wear your pretty gloves and eat one of Mrs. Skillman's crullers; I can vouch for that." She blushed yet again as all three men chuckled.

She stole a look at Ben, and he was smiling, too, not annoyed, so all was well.

The Simms & Taylor men led the way onto the short deck of the squat canal boat, then down the three steps into the hold, where a large enameled coffecpot sat on a small cast-iron stove. Mrs. Skillman, a rawboned woman in a long dark dress covered by a striped pinafore-style apron, smiled uncertainly. The little, low-ceilinged room smelled of coffee and frying, the welcome aroma of breakfast.

When everyone was seated, Captain Skillman roared the motor into life. It then quieted to a steady hum, and the boat slowly chugged upstream.

Taylor gave the two designers a bit of the company history, from their beginnings in the 1840s making special-order carriage uphol-stery in Queen City, to their expanded mill and factory fifteen miles north up the canal in Lockton. It was the modern Lockton mill that the boating party was now on the way to visit.

Ethel took out her sketches and arranged them on the gateleg table in the center of the small room.

Mrs. Skillman served the coffee in cups and saucers. She gave each person a starched and ironed napkin, then passed a basket of cinnamon sugar–dusted crullers, still warm from the lard in which she'd fried them.

For the next two hours, they sat around the table talking rose-buds, filigree, vines, and scrolls versus more classical acanthus leaves and urns. Ethel had brought several sepia wedding photos of working-class couples, borrowed from a photographer friend.

At first, the Simms & Taylor men saw only the unsmiling couples, looking straight into the camera, rigidly posed in their best clothing. But, as Ethel explained, this might be the only photo they would ever have taken of themselves, and they wanted it to be respectful, dignified. There was the requisite formal chair, with either the bride or the groom seated and the other standing. There was a suggestion of a Persian carpet on the floor. A bouquet of flowers. The bride's hand posed to show the ring, no matter how modest.

"They want better than what they've had," Ethel commented. "If you look closer at the dresses, you'll notice lace, satiny stripes, dressmaker details like bows and those tiny rosebuds sewn from ribbon." She pointed to several photos and the rosebuds just visible on the trim of a sleeve or a bodice. "These women may live in tenements, but they dream of gardens."

Ben sat quietly. Ethel had prepared well and the men seemed to respect that. Ben's job was matching the aesthetic to the technical—could these designs be woven, with an eye for the bottom line, on a factory loom? Would the design work for a mattress cover?

As Mrs. Skillman poured another round of coffee, Ethel boldly asked her, "Which design do you like best, ma'am?"

The men looked at one another. Why ask this poor woman?

"Oh, I'm sure I couldn't say," the captain's wife murmured as she noticed their puzzled frowns, backing away from the table.

And then it dawned on them. She was a working-class woman—their customer.

George Taylor motioned her back. "I'm going to give you twenty-five dollars." He reached into his pocket and pulled out bills secured with an engraved money clip.

Mrs. Skillman looked uneasy. "You're very generous, to be sure, sir." It was more than the Skillmans usually made in a week.

"I'm paying you for your opinion, Mrs. Skillman," George

explained. "If you were going to buy something for your home with that money," Taylor said, talking with his hands, "maybe it's wallpaper, curtains, a divan—"

"Or a mattress," one of the men joked.

"In one of these patterns," Taylor continued, "which one would you buy? It's important that we know. Very important. You would be helping us quite a bit."

"All right, sir, if you put it that way."

"Now, have a look at these," he said, motioning her to look over the drawings. Mrs. Skillman considered each one in her methodical way. She wiped her hands on her apron, then pointed with a blunt, work-roughened finger to the design with the most flowers— climbing roses on classical pillars against a background of scrollwork.

The men looked at one another, at Ethel, and they all nodded. Taylor gave the money to Mrs. Skillman, who didn't know whether to bow or curtsy, and so did a bit of each before nervously stuffing the bills in her apron pocket.

"Ben?" Taylor asked.

"The looms can handle it," he said. "Might take a week or so to set the pattern, but the design should work."

Now that one of the designs was settled, they looked over the other sketches to choose two more.

Mrs. Skillman was gathering up the last of the coffee cups when a sharp crack of thunder cleaved through the conversation. They all turned to look out the small eyebrow windows and saw an ominously darkened sky.

The boat seemed to shudder to a stop before the lock, which could gradually take a canal boat from a lower to a higher level of water before proceeding north to Lake Erie. But the *Aurora* would simply turn around and make its halfhearted trip back down to Plum Street.

Captain Skillman jumped down from the captain's berth onto the old towpath while his boy tied up the boat with a thick loop of rope.

"Let's finish this up at the factory," said Taylor, rising from the table.

They gathered up their belongings in a rush. Ethel's gloves fell on the floor, but she didn't notice.

This time, the captain handed Ethel up to the shelter of a large black umbrella, held by the factory foreman. She had just enough time to take a quick glance across the canal. The chimneys from the paper mill and the asphalt-shingle factory sent smoke up into the heavy air.

Rain began to fall like dirty net curtains.

The foreman walked to her left, nearest the canal, gripping her elbow. They hurried to the mattress factory, which was looming like a fortress.

When the foreman stopped suddenly on the towpath to navigate around a murky puddle, Ethel peered up again at the coal-darkened brick building. The factory's massive five stories rose like Sleeping Beauty's castle under the enchantment of a dark fairy, she mused. It was surrounded, not by a thorny thicket as in the fairy tale, but by a darker spell that Ethel sensed, but could not see: cotton dust, coal smoke, and tiny filaments of asbestos.

Close to the lock, the wind spun around, pelting them from the other side with cold rain. Her wet hands quickly reddened and numbed.

Ethel hoped her petticoat and skirt weren't ruined. But she couldn't ruck up her skirt and hold on to the foreman and her sketches all at the same time. As she tucked her portfolio higher up under her right arm, Ethel didn't feel the ring loosen, slip from her fingers, and disappear into the mud.

2

"Everything looks so beautiful," Mrs. Schumacher said, sitting demurely on the settee in my front parlor.

I hoped so. A lot was riding on this wedding cake tasting. The Schumachers were a Carriage Hill society family. If they booked their wedding cake with me, word-of-mouth alone would be just the start that Rainbow Cake needed.

The mother of the bride looked like a sixtysomething, well-to-do matron in her navy pantsuit, sensible shoes, and good jewelry, with those telltale vertical lines right above her upper lip. Her hair was expensively cut in a classic bob. Her face was reddened, with tiny capillaries visible on her nose. Not from drink, I decided, but from being outdoors. Like other Carriage Hill residents, the Schumachers probably had a stable on their property and rode their horses on the trails that meandered for miles in the wooded, hilly terrain.

Ellen Schumacher, the bride-to-be whose streaked blond hair

was pulled back in a charmingly loose knot, wore a fitted white shirt with a pale lavender cashmere sweater tied across her shoulders. Well-tailored charcoal gray trousers, good leather boots. Pearl earrings that caught the light. Understated makeup on a flawless complexion. Intelligent gray-blue eyes. Early thirties. She seemed sure of herself. Excited, but also composed.

They could certainly afford my services or they wouldn't be here.

My wedding and couture cakes were at the top tier, price-wise. Quality counted, but so did showmanship and ambience. Customers had to be convinced of that.

So, I took them out of the bakery and next door to my house, the front porch doorway now flanked by black iron urns filled with fresh evergreen boughs for winter. And, of course, I also had the dressed-up concrete goose that Roshonda had given me, just to keep things lighthearted. That wedding planning can get a little tense was an understatement, I was finding out.

My front parlor was simple yet sophisticated, with plaster walls painted a soft French gray, the woodwork a subtle ivory, and a few landscape paintings that I had brought with me from my Brooklyn brownstone. Here we could close the painted shutters halfway to block off the sights and sounds of Benson Street. I wanted my potential clients to feel that they were in another world.

A gas fire in the white marble Victorian hearth warmed the room against the chilly afternoon and cast the bookcases into shadow. The round table with its heavy cloth in nubby French linen was set with a coffee service and a French press coffeepot. A wooden tray shaped like an artist's palette—one I had specially made—held small clear cups of pastel-colored fillings and frostings. Miniature cupcakes in their paper frills filled a tiered stand.

Ellen sat next to her mother and reached across the table to take the thin china coffee cup that I offered. An antique ring was still a little loose on her finger.

"May I see your engagement ring?" I asked, mentally crossing off one of the questions during a wedding cake tasting, although in this case, I truly did want to see it up close.

With a shy smile, she let me take her French-manicured hand to have a good look. Old-fashioned. Yellow gold, fine craftsmanship, the patina of age. Tiny golden leaves inset with pearls held the oval sapphire. It was simply stunning.

"That is the most beautiful ring I've ever seen," I said, and meant it.

"It's been in my fiancé's family for quite some time," she replied. "Sam and I just got engaged."

We all sipped the coffee, and I took a moment to clear my mind so I could focus on this bride, this family. I closed my eyes for a second or two and let the flavor come to me.

What I got was a hint of spice.

When I lived in New York and went to Chinatown, I learned that these flavors and their meanings were actually a foundation of ancient Chinese medicine.

Salty translated to fear and the frantic energy that tries to compensate for or hide it.

Sweet was the first flavor we recognized from our mother's milk, and to which we turned when we were worried and unsure or depressed.

Sour usually meant anger and frustration.

Bitter signified matters of the heart, from simply feeling unloved to the almost overwhelming loss of a great love. Most spices, along with coffee and chocolate, had some bitterness in their flavor profile. Even sugar, when it cooked too long, turned bitter. But to me, spice was for grief, because it lingered longest.

The more intense the flavor, the more intense the feeling, I also knew. This taste of spice I was getting seemed a little dulled, but still apparent. Now I knew how to proceed.

I broached the subject gently. "Before we get started, I'd like to know a little more about your family."

Ellen looked at her mother, then answered. "I'm very lucky to have a great family. There's my mom," she said, and she smiled across the table. "She's helping me plan everything. My brother, Ted, who is also a good friend of Sam's, will be best man. My father passed away when I was in law school, so my uncle will walk me down the aisle. My cousin," she continued, but I was not really listening.

So there it was. The loss of her father softened by the passing of time but brought back by this family milestone.

A little girl sits high up on her horse, gripping the reins tightly in pudgy little hands. The strap on her velveteen riding helmet fits firmly under her chin. A tall, good-looking man with dark, wavy hair leads the horse by the bridle, but lets her think she's doing it all herself. He gives her a tender, wry smile. "Keep your heels down in the stirrups, Ellie. And loosen that stranglehold you have on poor Snowflake. She's never going to let you ride her again." Ellie angles the heels of her short paddock boots downward, loosens her grip on the reins, and finds that she sits better on her mount. The delight of her discovery shows on her face, and her dad beams. "That's my girl."

". . . and my other cousin, Alicia, will be taking care of the gift table."

I smiled and nodded. "You've obviously got everything well planned. Now, for the cake!" I said brightly, getting down to business. "Your wedding cake should reflect not only the look of your wedding, but the flavor of your partnership, your unique blending of two lives."

Ellen and her mother were both nodding, taking in what I was saying.

"We're tasting today so we can create a signature cake for Ellen and Sam. This cake will be your love story translated into cake, filling, and frosting. So we want to make sure we get it right."

"Just like a perfumer who would create the perfect scent for you with top, middle, and base notes, we'll build the perfect cake that really captures the two of you."

"But," Mrs. Schumacher interrupted, "shouldn't we be choosing a cake that our guests will like? What if Ellen wants banana or Sam's favorite flavor is chocolate? I know her grandmother hates banana, and a chocolate wedding cake . . . I just don't think . . .'"

Ellen smiled. "Don't worry. I won't choose banana, Mom. And Sam doesn't like chocolate all that much."

I poured more coffee for them both. "We're talking about subtle flavor here, Mrs. Schumacher," I reassured her. "We can even make an all white cake with white buttercream frosting taste different for each bride and groom." She looked back at me, perplexed.

"I thought all white cake tasted like white cake."

"Not if we add subtle flavorings. Let's just begin tasting, then, and you'll know what I mean."

I took two of the unfrosted, miniature cupcakes and placed them on a small tray in front of me. "Now, this is our pound cake that has been infused with vanilla bean. Let's try this first with a blood-orange mousse. It's made with one of our French syrups added to the mousse. This also has a slight hint of spice—China cassia cinnamon and star anise. I find that the spice gives a little lift, but you hardly know it's there." I'd used a palette knife to smooth the filling on top of each cupcake.

"I love the color," said Ellen. "That pale coral would be beautiful with the cobalt blue and ivory—they're our wedding colors."

"Yes, that *would* be lovely," I continued. "Now, let's also smooth on the classic buttercream and see if you like the combination."

Ellen and her mother took one bite, then another. They looked at each other and smiled. I knew that the cake made them think of the husband and father not with them anymore. They remembered him smiling, happy, young, as I had seen him, too.

Ellen looked away, and I felt her sadness for a member of Sam's family who also had passed. I wouldn't ask who it was, as I didn't really need to know. The subtle spice flavor would recognize Sam's family's yearning to see that loved one again, too, then feed it.

We sampled other cakes—the white cake that tasted faintly of almond, the chocolate with its hint of coffee. And the other mousses—the raspberry with a drop of rose syrup to bring out its fruitiness. Lemon, almond, lavender, pistachio—but I knew this was it.

My laptop with its PowerPoint presentation of cake designs was ready to cast its magic on the smooth wall between the two long front windows. Seeing the cake bigger rather than on the small laptop screen always made it seem more real.

After the tasting, we chose a cake design. Ellen had brought photos of her wedding dress and bridesmaids' dresses. The Schumachers also wanted sugar cookies decorated to look like the bridesmaids' dresses and wedding cakes—wrapped in cellophane and tied with ribbon in the couple's wedding colors—for the bridesmaids' luncheon and as wedding favors for guests.

After an hour, we went over the contract. I sensed a slight hesitation from Mrs. Schumacher. That was understandable. Rainbow Cake was new, and this was the first wedding cake the bakery would craft. I emphasized my experience with wedding cake artist Sylvia Weinstock in Manhattan, how I had assisted with many cakes for many notable weddings, cakes Mrs. Schumacher had seen on my laptop and tasted in my parlor. She finally gave me her credit card for the deposit. In my office on the second floor, I made copies of everything for them and put all their materials in Rainbow Cake's signature robin's-egg-blue-and-chocolate-brown folder.

I gave them each a business card, as well as the rest of the cakes, fillings, and frostings to take home in a Rainbow Cake box, along with a few cellophane-wrapped sugar cookies. If Mrs. Schumacher told the other ladies who lunch about Rainbow Cake, maybe I would get more special occasion commissions. A debutante ball, a fund-raising gala, a patron's party.

"I'm so glad we caught you right when you were opening," said Ellen, as I walked them out to their car parked at the curb. "With our wedding coming up so quickly in April, we'd never have been able to book with you otherwise. I know you'll do a fabulous job."

"And we can cross this off our list," added Mrs. Schumacher. "I'm just glad I didn't want to try on any mother-of-the-bride dresses today," she joked, patting her stomach. "On second thought, maybe we shouldn't be taking all of this cake home, as delicious as it was," she said to Ellen, who was holding the cake box. "I'm not certain I have that kind of willpower!"

Barney, who was making his daily rounds with Mrs. Amici, took Mrs. Schumacher's words to heart and immediately jumped up on Ellen, trying to sniff the box. "Cake!" his big eyes and wagging tail seemed to say.

"Barney! Get down!" Mrs. Amici practically growled.

But he kept jumping up, barking excitedly.

Laughing, Ellen held the cake box up higher with her right hand, and bent down to pet Barney with the left. Her ring sparkled in the cold winter light. "You've got good taste in cake, don't you, boy?"

She held out the cake box to Mrs. Amici. "Would you like to have these little cupcakes? They're absolutely delicious."

I expected Mrs. Amici to snarl a reply, but for once she seemed speechless and a little shaky. "Where did you . . . ?" she stammered, looking at Ellen's ring.

Ellen held out her hand. "It has been in my husband's family for a long time," she said. "I just love it."

"Some families have all the luck." Mrs. Amici pulled Barney away. He stopped and howled before trotting down the street again to check out the enigmatic scent of yet another streetlight.

"I'm sorry about that," I said to my new clients. "I had hoped the spell of cake and frosting would have protected you a little longer. Mrs. Amici is our resident snark."

"No problem," Ellen said, still smiling. "It's that poor puppy's loss. I'm sure he's never had anything as tasty as what's in this box." She opened the car doors and put the cake box in the backseat. The mother and daughter drove off just as the postman handed me my mail.

Too bad the spell didn't last for me, either, I thought as I shuffled through the bills and the junk mail.

A card with handwriting all too familiar to me would go straight in the trash when I went back inside.

Next, I pulled a plain postcard out of the stack, postmarked Kansas City. I didn't think I knew anyone there.

I turned it over and immediately recognized the spiky handwriting.

Dad.

When I tried to picture my father, what I got was the snapshot from my fourteenth birthday—Dad looking away from the camera, his long arm looped around my bony shoulders as if I were the stake to which he was tethered.

When I imagined Dad's voice, all that usually came to me was a Ray LaMontagne song, strummed on a guitar, about how his hometown was bringin' him down, and how he was going to finally stay gone. If Dad had a theme song, that would be it.

From my sixteenth birthday onward, I'd gotten a postcard or two every year, from all over the country. They were always mailed to Gran's old house in some misguided way, I surmised as I got older, to avoid my mother. But they eventually reached me. As far as I knew, he had never sent money, even after Mom and I lost our house on the hilltop.

His greetings were always brief. Just a "Happy birthday" or "I love you." Never anything about how or what he was doing or where he really was. Or asking about me, either.

He didn't know I had graduated from college and pastry school, worked in small-batch bakeries and high-style patisseries, gotten married, and become a professional baker. He didn't know his absence had been both an unlikely gift and an ongoing curse; I'd had to stand on my own two feet, but maybe I had taken that a little

35

too far. He didn't know that I now owned a business, and had recently bought Gran's old house. He didn't know his own mother was slowly losing her memory. What he didn't know took up more than half of my life.

As I held the card, I felt a conflicting mix of emotions—sadness, irritation, yearning, and, I was almost embarrassed to admit, still a little girl wanting her daddy.

I debated whether to just pitch the postcard, but instead I started reading. And it took my breath away.

It wasn't the message: "Sorry for all this. Miss you. Love you. Dad."

It was the return address printed in the upper left corner.

Project Uplift, a homeless outreach program.

Homeless?

MARCH 1932

Two little girls in short-sleeved cotton dresses, ankle socks that just wouldn't stay up, and scuffed saddle shoes held hands as they crossed the brick street—just as they promised their mama they'd do.

The older sister, Olive, held the market basket and the money. As they walked into Amici's on the corner of Pearl and Benson streets, the familiar glass case along the left side of the store displayed a meager selection of meats and cheeses. Along the right, tins of Worthmore's and Stegner's chili, Dinty Moore beef stew, and several varieties of Campbell's soup lined the shelves. And in the middle, boxes of cereal and crackers, jars of Pond's cold cream, and tubes of Ipana toothpaste all jumbled together.

Young Frankie Amici looked up from his faded red wagon in the back of the store, two grocery bags packed up for delivery.

A booming voice greeted the girls. "Well, if it isn't Pickle and Olive, my two favorite young ladies," Mr. Amici teased from behind the meat case.

"My sister's name isn't Pickle," Olive reminded him. "It's Edie." But he just chuckled. Olive, the short, pudgy, older sister. "Pickle," the tall, gangly, younger one.

"What is it going to be today, ladies?" he asked.

"The Fairview lady paid Mama for her true show, so we get to have city chicken," Edie piped up. Olive narrowed her eyes at her sister.

"It's not 'true show'; it's 'trousseau,' dummy," she said.

"So how much city chicken does your mother want?" Mr. Amici asked.

"Two pieces for Daddy and one for the rest of us," Edie said.

"You mean you ladies have to share one piece of city chicken?" he teased again.

"No," said Olive, the literal one. "Edie means that Mama, Edie, and me each get a piece."

Mr. Amici grabbed five wooden skewers threaded with cubes of boneless pork and veal, and placed them on a sheet of white butcher paper, then on the scale. He wrapped up the package and tied it with red-and-white-striped twine. "That will be fifty-seven cents," he said, and Olive pinched open the old red coin purse.

Olive licked her lips, thinking about how her mother would soak the skewered meats in milk and egg, then roll them in cracker crumbs and fry it all in lard until crispy and tender as a real chicken leg. Then Mama would make gravy to go with the mashed potatoes and green beans.

Edie drifted over to the middle aisle. While Mr. Amici gave Frankie his instructions, she turned the red, yellow, and green Rice Krispies box to see the back. "Snow White and Rose Red" was the Singing Lady's new story. Edie hadn't heard that one yet on the radio, and she had never tasted Rice Krispies—it was always oatmeal at home. She thought maybe she could read this one quickly before it was time to leave. "Once upon a time . . ."

Mr. Amici watched Olive and wondered whether the girls were getting good food, not just something to fill them up. They were both pale. Although he had plenty of customers who still owed him money and he couldn't afford to just give food away, he wrapped up a couple of hot dogs. "For my two favorite customers," he said, and pushed the bundle over the top of the glass case. Olive had to stand on tiptoes to reach it.

Olive licked her lips. "Oh, Edie!"

Edie turned the cereal box not quite all the way around and ran to her sister, who showed her the package. "Hot dogs!" Olive told her.

"Thank you, Mr. Amici," they piped up in unison.

They held the door open for Frankie and his wagon. They all walked together until he headed toward the arched concrete bridge over the creek to Lockton. The girls went the other way to Goldberg's Department Store on the corner. Olive remembered to hold Edie's hand.

Notions were in the back of the store. So was the formidable Miss Goldberg.

She wore her long dark hair, with its wings of silver, in an old-fashioned style—high up on her head—and her eyeglasses on a chain. She patted her plum-colored wool gabardine dress, which was in the new drop-waisted style. Last week, she had made the long trip downtown specifically to purchase the chic new design. The ready-made clothing she and her father sold in the store was fine for their factory-worker customers, but Miss Goldberg required better.

She raised her pince-nez to peer at the girls in their hand-me-down dresses, old shoes, and droopy socks, marching toward her counter, the chubby one holding tightly to the younger one.

"Don't you children touch anything. Your hands are probably dirty," she said in her chilly voice.

Edie shrank behind her sister. Olive ignored the slight. "Our mama needs . . ." Olive fished in the basket for the list, written on the back of a torn envelope.

Miss Goldberg rolled her eyes. "We cannot put any more items on Mrs. Habig's account," she stage-whispered, but there were no other shoppers in the store to hear. "I thought I explained that to her last week."

Olive plunked the coin purse down and passed the list across to Miss Goldberg's reluctant grasp. "We can pay for it all," Olive said staunchly.

Miss Goldberg sniffed as she removed a lined note card from the accounts box, then rang up the sale. Olive stopped to look at the costume jewelry in carnival glass colors, but Miss Goldberg glared and Edie nudged her away.

The girls crossed Jefferson and walked toward the library, saving the best for last, Edie thought.

Olive looked longingly at Oster's bakery window and could almost taste the cream horns and cherry coffee cake with that crunchy topping, but there was no money for that.

As they walked on, they muttered to each other—"Oh no." Old Jimmy McCray limped toward them, but Mama said they mustn't call him Jimmy, just Mr. McCray. Papa said he came back from the Great War and was "never the same," but Edie was not quite sure what that meant because Papa came back all right and then married Mama.

Jimmy McCray couldn't even see straight, thought Olive, with one eye looking up and the other looking down, and that raised purple scar down the side of his face.

"You 'fraid of me?" He asked the same question of every child he saw on the street, in the dime store, at mass.

"No, Mr. McCray, we're not afraid of you," Olive said yet again, but hurried by him, shielding Edie, just the same.

They escaped into the library, where it was dim and cool, smelling of dust and old paper. The low children's bookshelves were near the front, while the adult section was up a few steps in the back of the long, narrow building. Edie skipped over to the fairy tales and sat cross-legged on the floor while she looked for a book. Olive, impatient already, walked around to see whether anyone they knew was here.

Miss Phillips, the librarian, wished they would look through her new display of Newbery Award winners—books that no child had yet checked out. You'd think with times still so hard, parents would take advantage of things that were free, she mused. But many children had to help out at home, she reminded herself, as the ragman and his young son passed by the window in their horse-drawn cart. *Even the horse looks down on its luck today*, she thought.

Just this morning as she brought the milk bottles in from the back porch, she saw a young man jump on top of a coal car as the train slowed to the station on Market Street. He knocked over as much coal as he could onto the grassy verge of the track, then jumped down again, gathered it all into in a burlap bag, and ran off.

She pictured the coal bin in her cellar at home, three-fourths full, and the way the flames lit up her father's craggy face when he opened the metal furnace door to shovel in another load. How she took her comfortable life for granted sometimes . . .

Olive was too old, but Edie might like this one—Miss Phillips took *Downright Dencey* from her display. Hard times in Nantucket. Plucky little Quaker girl with a father away on a whaling ship, and a mother who finds it hard to cope. Dencey befriends the town outcast, Samuel Jetsam. Good story. Wonderful writing.

Olive checked out yet another Nancy Drew—*The Secret Staircase*, which she probably would not finish, thought Miss Phillips. Olive just can't concentrate. It must get her into trouble at school.

It began to rain.

"Why don't you girls stay in here for a while, till it lets up?" suggested Miss Phillips. "Olive, would you help me put these books away? Edie, you can get started on your new book."

Edie plopped down like a rag doll behind the bookshelves where Miss Phillips couldn't see her. The new book could wait. From her torn dress pocket, she took out her battered copy of *The Princess and the Goblin* that her father found by the towpath of the old canal. He was always finding things. He found Mama's ring by the canal, too.

The pages had browned with age and the type was small, but Edie didn't care. As she started to read, the library faded away and she was once again in the wild mountains, with a little girl her own age—eight-year-old Princess Irene—and goblins who lived underground. Were goblins scarier than Jimmy McCray? wondered Edie.

Edie loved the parts where the princess followed an invisible thread to find her beautiful great-great-grandmother in the tallest tower of the castle, the lady with blue eyes that seemed to have melted stars in them. Edie could just imagine how the lady looked with her black velvet dress and the long white hair that reached past her silvery lace collar.

But she was not to that part yet. She was still at the place where the princess first gets lost. Ohhhhh, shivered Edie, thinking of the goblins and then, suddenly, of Jimmy McCray. What if Edie got lost and Jimmy McCray was chasing her?

She snapped the book shut and quickly ran to find Olive.

3

When I got back to the bakery from the Schumachers' wedding cake tasting, Maggie was in the middle of packing little boxes, each with a different kind of small cake: January's mocha truffle plus our everyday cream cheese–frosted carrot cake, red velvet, almond-flavored blue suede, and, of course, rainbow cake.

"I just couldn't decide," explained the customer, breathily.

"Well, then you shouldn't have to," I told her, tucking a cellophane-wrapped snowflake sugar cookie into a bag as a little gift. "My treat." Such a little thing—a sugar cookie—can be an unexpected kindness, if the expression on her face was any indication.

As soon as she had gone and the bakery was quiet again, Maggie looked at me expectantly.

"Well? How did it go?"

I beamed.

"I knew you could do it! I knew it!"

"This calls for a celebration latte," I said, and revved up the ol' Marzocco. When I guided the froth with a long spoon, I tried to make a wedding cake shape, but it turned into a mountain.

"Yep, that's about right," I muttered.

"What's right?" Maggie asked as she clinked her cup with mine. "Cheers!"

"We've still got an uphill battle," I said, pointing at my artwork.

"That's not all we've got," Maggie said in a conspiratorial whisper. "We're gonna be slammed for Valentine's Day. I've charted our foot traffic and our orders for the past two weeks, and they've more than doubled each week. We're still not where we want to be, but we're getting there. The upshot is that you better get some more help, unless you think Vampira back there is up to waiting on customers." She gave me her skeptical look.

Well, now, that's a thought.

I found Jett in the workroom, a scowl on her face and a chain from her nose ring to some nether region beneath her black T-shirt. She was fashioning delicate sugar-paste roses and leaves. Her hands looked clean, though it was hard to tell with her fingernails painted black.

"How's it going?" I asked.

"Things are pretty fucked."

My eyes widened, but I collected myself. I saw beautifully rendered rosebuds, fully opened roses, and rose leaves in the pale colors of our next black-tie event, a charity ball for the Rose Family Foundation.

My puzzled look prompted, "It's not the work," from Jett.

"Well, that's something."

I couldn't even tell what her natural hair color was. Jett told me she dyed it "Deadly Nightshade." On rainy days when she walked down the Benson Street hill from Millcreek Valley High on the crest of the hilltop—and she never seemed to have an umbrella—her hair dripped purplish black. I kept some old towels on hand now.

I was convinced that somewhere behind all that Queen of the Dark was a fresh young girl. Last year, when I had gone to visit my old high school art teacher, Jett was the one I saw doing the most exquisite work—her clay modeling, charcoal drawing, and her sense of color all pointed to real talent. I was hoping she'd stay here after graduation and go on to art school in the area. But it wasn't easy for anybody to get past her scary, hard-ass exterior. I couldn't imagine her interviewing for another job and getting the notice she deserved.

"You know we're glad to have you with us, don't you? And at least you'll never go hungry working here," I said.

"Yeah. Everything else sucks, but I like it here."

"Good." What else could I say? But Maggie was right. Jett wasn't ready for prime time.

I was going to have to get more help. But I didn't want to hire anyone else full-time unless I knew the business could sustain an additional employee.

My mom would come in if I were desperate. And maybe Norb's wife. Poor Norb.

My phone rang and I grabbed it from the pocket of my trousers.

"Come over for dinner tonight," Mom wheedled. "Before you tell me you don't have time, think about this: We're having cottage ham and green beans."

"Are you making dinner or is Aunt Helen?"

"I am."

"Sure, Mom. And I'll bring dessert. What time?"

"Whenever you're finished. I'll just keep everything warm until you get here."

I tapped my phone off and felt as if I had just been enveloped in a warm, familiar sweater. My mom's home cooking.

If it were Aunt Helen's turn for dinner, I would have found some excuse, not that I didn't love her, of course. But she was too fond of taking cooking shortcuts that didn't work out most of the time. Her exploding cottage ham that covered the kitchen in dark pink shreds was a disaster we still talked about.

Cottage ham, that cured and hickory-smoked pork shoulder that Millcreek Valleyites loved, needed long, slow cooking with green beans and onions. To go with it, Mom would make real mashed potatoes, while Aunt Helen would have grabbed a box of instant flakes and turned them into a gluey mess.

When I finally finished up about seven p.m., the parking lot was dark and cold. I didn't feel like walking over to Mom's small house on Church Street, so I drove the short distance.

As I passed Mrs. Elmlinger's dark brick bungalow where I used to take piano lessons, I saw her concrete goose dressed up like Lady Gaga, safe from snow and sleet on her front porch. Her students must still think she was really cool. Mrs. Elmlinger always chose a musical theme for her goose outfits—Mozart, John Philip Sousa, even Elton John—so she had to sew many of them herself.

If you wanted your goose dressed up like a high school graduate, a nurse, a pirate, or a football player, you could find ready-made outfits at any gift shop. But the whole point to this yard art was to have a little fun and make your own statement. If you didn't sew, you could always buy a wackier goose outfit at the craft and antique mall farther down on Millcreek Valley Road.

Mom's goose nested under the overhang of the front stoop of the small brick workman's cottage that she shared with Aunt Helen, Dad's sister. Mom always stuck to the tried and true; her goose was dressed like Cupid, complete with a bow and arrow slung over its wing. She must have just changed its snowman outfit in the past few days. If Aunt Helen had been in charge, the goose would have morphed regularly into Indiana Jones and Han Solo—like her other sixtysomething friends, she still had the hots for Harrison Ford.

Inside, Mom puttered in the kitchen while Helen watched *Jeopardy!* I gave them both a peck on the cheek, then slung my coat over the back of the sofa.

"Want a whiskey ssshhour?" Helen asked. "I'm ready for one." She sounded like she really meant "another one."

One of Helen's cocktails actually sounded good. She did know how to mix a drink. But as I took a sip, I grimaced. "I think you put a little too much lemon in it this time."

"Here, I'll just shhtir in a little shhugar and it will be fine."

"Mmm." I sipped again. "Perfect, Helen. A toast to my first big wedding!" We clinked our glasses together.

"Who? When?" Mom and Aunt Helen asked at the same time, then laughed.

"Well, it will be at Carriage Hill Country Club. Ellen Schumacher is the bride and Samuel Whyte the groom."

"Society people?" Mom asked.

"How would we know if they were or not?" asked Helen.

Mom gave her a look.

"The Schumachers were lovely and gracious people," I said, hoping to nip the quarrel in the bud, "society" or not.

"What are their colors for the wedding?" Mom continued.

"Cobalt blue and pale coral."

"Ahhh," Mom sighed. "That will be beautiful."

"I think I'll be pretty busy this April," I added.

"You're pretty busy now!" Mom said, looking at me with motherly concern. "You've worked so hard, maybe too hard, honey." I guess she couldn't help that her eyes darted to the ring finger of my left hand, newly bare. "Is everything . . ."

It wasn't like I hadn't thought the same thing, over and over again. Maybe if I hadn't been so set on making my own way, maybe if I had been home more, maybe . . .

I shook my head and flicked my hands to deflect that question. I hadn't allowed myself to think much about Luke. I didn't *want* to think about Luke. And I left my rings locked up in my jewelry box because I didn't want to lose them when I washed my hands for the umpteenth time.

I had other things to occupy my thoughts. Like the troubling message from Dad that I was not about to share, either.

I couldn't do anything about Luke or Dad, but I could do something about Rainbow Cake. I wanted to focus on what was going well.

"I've had a very good day and that's all I care about right now," I said in a tone designed to quash the mini-inquisition.

Mom and Aunt Helen looked at each other knowingly. "Another drink, anyone?" Helen offered.

When we sat down at the table, Mom made the sign of the cross. "Bless us, oh Lord, and these thy gifts. . . ."

Then we all began talking about our days—Mom as the elementary school secretary at Saints Peter and Paul a block away, Aunt Helen as the power-behind-the-pump at a water sprinkler company.

"Sister Mary Alphonse has been sick with the flu all week and her sixth-graders were almost uncontrollable," Mom began. "You could hear the ruckus all the way down the hall."

"You mean Brenda Jean Overbeck, don't you?" Aunt Helen commented, adding a dab of horseradish to her cottage ham.

"That's ancient history, Helen, and you know that. Brenda Jean has been Sister Mary Alphonse for over thirty years!"

"That long." Aunt Helen looked at me and winked. "I guess I keep expecting her to cut and run. She never seemed like nun material to me, anyway. In high school, she used to have that hard orange line of makeup around her face, and she always wore fluorescent blue eye shadow. Remember when she was caught with Joey Ashbrock behind the bleachers and—"

"Helen," Mom warned. "We've all heard that story at least fifty times."

I laughed because we really had heard that story fifty times.

"By the way, I'll have extra cupcakes that I can take up to the nursing home and maybe to the convent tomorrow," I said, changing the subject. That was sure to smooth things over. My mom was Catholic to the core and the one person in the Rosary Altar Society who never, ever missed a meeting. She also never missed seven a.m. mass before she walked on to work. Mom would have made a great nun. Maybe my dad had come to that conclusion, too. . . .

"Speaking of goodies, Doreen at work gave me a new recipe for a 'quickie,'" Helen said with a knowing smile. I looked at my mom—did she even know what a quickie was?

No.

Nun material. Poor Mom.

Helen, however, sure did. "A quickie is a pie that only takes three minutes to make. Can you believe that? You use a graham cracker pie shell, instant vanilla pudding, a little milk, a can of cherry pie filling, and some frozen whipped topping. I might make one tomorrow."

Note to self: Have other dinner plans.

I kissed Mom and Helen good night and went back out in the cold. As I stopped for a red light, I caught a glimpse of something just behind me in the rearview mirror. For a moment, it seemed as if the warm exhaust from my tailpipe had morphed into a gaggle of wispy white geese, waddling behind me in the frigid air.

That was what I wished I had seen.

Otherwise, how could I explain the figure in the white hoodie and dark jeans that tumbled out the door of a pickup truck as it turned left from the alley onto the street? The ghostly figure got up on hands and knees and crab-walked to the sidewalk. The hood fell back and I could see that it was a young woman. A scared young woman.

"Leave me alone!" I heard her yell.

When my light turned green, I didn't go forward. Still looking in the rearview mirror, I fished around in my purse for my cell phone, just in case I needed to call 911. I locked my doors.

The truck fishtailed to a stop. The driver got out, stomped around the front of the truck, then walked around to slam the passenger door shut.

The girl staggered up from the pavement into the dark shadows just out of the streetlight's weak glow.

The driver, a stocky young man in jeans and work boots, lumbered back to her, yelling, "Shit. Shit. Shit!"

But she had a head start. And then a light came on in the second-story window above Bliss Honeymoon Travel, right above her. The curtains parted. The angry man looked up, then seemed to change his mind, coming to a swaying halt.

"You asked for it, bitch," he bellowed, raising his fist. "You asked for it."

He wheeled around, still unsteady on his feet. He kicked the tire a few times. "Bitch! Bitch! Bitch!" he yelled, almost falling over with the third kick. Then he threw himself in the truck and slammed his dented door shut. He gunned the engine and peeled off down the street, laying a zigzag patch of rubber across the two-lane bridge to Lockton.

The light had gone red, then green again, but I still waited. Luckily, every sane person was home and warm on this cold and dreary night in January.

I could see the girl, holding her stomach with one arm, limping toward my car.

Her face was turned away from me, but I saw the dark stain blooming on the front of her white sweatshirt. There was also something in the way she held her head up, as if wounded pride was even more painful than any physical harm. I knew that girl.

I rolled down my window.

"Get in, Jett. I'll take you to my house."

Later, as she sat with a bag of frozen baby peas on her swollen eye and tissues stuffed in the nostril where her nose ring had been, I poured her a cup of creamy hot cocoa, stirred with a stick of cinnamon. The tiny marshmallows that bobbed on the top almost made her smile.

Although I bundled her up with blankets and pillows in front of my parlor fireplace, she still shivered. I had cleaned her up as best I could, offered to take her to the emergency room and call her mother. I tried to get her to talk.

"Did you know that guy?" I asked.

"Stupid Sean. The peas are starting to thaw," she said, handing me the semi-frozen bag.

I went back to the kitchen, threw the peas back in the freezer, and rummaged around for something else. Mixed vegetables. How I hated those except in a spicy chicken chili I had yet to make this winter. But they would do.

"So you do know him," I said, handing her the mixed vegetables.

We stared into the fire.

"Maybe we should report this to the police. He could try it again, you know."

But she was adamant.

"It's just a black eye, Neely. No big deal. I don't want to talk about it anymore."

I was tempted to pry, to center myself and let the flavors lead me to the tale of what had happened. It would, after all, have been for her own good. Wouldn't it?

But how did I really know what her own good was? Jett wasn't a client. She wasn't a family member or a good friend who invited such intimacy. She was my young, scared, confused, and angry employee.

So I soothed her as best I could.

I didn't ask any more.

I couldn't judge.

I wouldn't leave her.

I startled awake before dawn from a dream in which I was chased by a man with a jagged scar down the side of his face.

Jett's blanket was folded neatly.

She was gone.

AUGUST 1932

The little brick house seemed to exhale in resignation, its sharp sighs starting in the stone cellar where Gustaf Habig had first fermented vinegar in the 1840s when Millcreek Valley was still known as Gansdorf—Goosetown. The oak barrels were long gone, but the residual tang moved languidly up the wooden stairs, through the middle room, and out the back screen door when anyone came inside.

Grace Habig, in her faded blue housedress, had drawn the shutters to help keep the interior as dark and cool as possible. Edward napped on the bed in the middle room.

In the kitchen, she took the enamelware colander down from the shelf and sat down with a paper bag of green beans and a paring knife. She had the radio on low to her favorite program, *Ma Perkins*.

She started to top and tail, then string each bean as the vibrato of the organ music swelled. She listened through several minutes of "deep cleaning, *deep* cleaning, *deep cleaning*" Oxydol detergent extolled by the announcer.

Grace already bought Oxydol, so she wished they'd just hurry up with it.

Finally.

"Now for *Ma Perkins* . . ." and this week's story began. Trouble with Cousin Sylvester again. At least Ma Perkins, too, had her troubles. Grace plunked another bean in the colander.

Most of the Fairview society ladies—at least those with still-employed husbands—had traveled north to their cottages in northern Michigan, resulting in scant seamstress work. But it was only a few weeks more until Labor Day. Then they would be back and Grace could count on back-to-school and cotillion dresses.

Edward's former boss dropped by yesterday to leave a twenty-dollar bill. That loosened, a bit, the tight clenching that Grace felt from the right side of her temple, down her spine, and into her hip. The tension also seemed to ease up a little, she realized, when she was listening to *Ma*.

Later on in the morning, the ice man came around in his cart, using the large metal tongs to hoist a big block onto his burlap-covered shoulder. He hummed the bouncy tune "Whistling in the Dark."

At least the ice business must be good, thought Grace.

He brought it into the little kitchen and placed it in the top compartment of the metal icebox. He held out a few chips in his gloved hand for Grace—a treat on this hot day. She gave him a nickel and he tipped his hat as he left.

Now that the icebox would be good and cold, Grace got out the rotary beater with the jade green handle. She whipped a can of sweetened condensed milk with lemon juice and a little grated lemon peel, and poured it into a graham cracker crust to make a lemon bisque dessert that would firm up as it chilled.

A few minutes after the bisque was in the icebox, the insurance man came around to the back screen door, and Grace had another nickel for him—the weekly life insurance payment for her husband. Mr. Kellerman sat down on the painted kitchen chair, tired in this heat. He took out his limp handkerchief and mopped his brow. The few strands of hair he had left were plastered to the top of his head. Grace asked if he'd like a glass of water, but he declined. She recorded the payment in her narrow brown ledger, and Mr. Kellerman did the same in his. She hoped he left before Edward woke up and started coughing again.

She didn't want any questions about mill fever. A lot of men got mill fever during the first months of breathing in the tiny cotton fibers that floated in the air. But then their lungs got used to it. Men like Edward, who had been gassed in the trenches of the Great War, however, didn't always get used to it. Coughing led to not sleeping, which led to lethargy and weakness.

She'd also heard from a neighbor that if Mr. Kellerman thought someone was sick, he conveniently "forgot" to come to their house for the payment. If it looked like they'd skipped a payment, the life insurance company would drop them, and then they'd get nothing when they needed it most.

Mr. Kellerman stood up to leave just as Olive and Edie came in with stacks of old newspapers under their arms.

"Frankie let me pull the wagon," Edie told her mother. Her face was flushed with the heat.

"Shhhh, Edie. Papa's sleeping," Grace said to her with a smile. And for Mr. Kellerman's benefit as he tipped his hat on the back porch, she nodded toward the front of the house and lied: "He's on the night shift now."

When he was out of sight, Olive fumed. "You always say we have to tell the truth."

"Just put the newspapers over here, Olive. Little pitchers have big ears." Grace draped a length of oilcloth on the kitchen table. She placed some of the stacked newspapers down the length of the fabric, folded the fabric over, and started to whipstitch the open sides together with a thick needle meant for leatherwork.

Just before noon, she heard the ragman's cart. His little son ran to the back and knocked on the screen door.

Olive let him in. "It's that boy again, Mama."

"That little boy has a name, Olive." She looked at him. "Come in, please, Shemuel."

"Do you have anything for us today, Mrs. Habig?"

"Yes, I do, so please sit down for a moment while I get things together."

The ragman's son sat down at the little table, eyeing the beans in the colander.

Grace cut a slice of bread, then opened the peanut butter tin and gave it a good stir to blend in the oil that had floated to the top. She spread the peanut butter on the bread and took a raisin cookie from the cookie jar.

"Here, Shemuel, eat this while Edie gets your bundle." She placed the bread and the cookie on a plate at the table. She pointed to Edie, and Edie knew to get the unusable fabric scraps that Shemuel and his father would take to the paper mill.

"Olive, please get our guest a glass of milk."

"But, Mama," Olive started to complain.

"Olive, do as you're told."

Olive poured the last of the bottled milk into a glass.

The girls had milk for breakfast, Grace told herself, and she couldn't let this hollow-cheeked boy go hungry. She just couldn't.

Shemuel wolfed down the peanut butter bread and ate the cookie in two bites. He gulped down the milk, then jumped up from the table.

"Thank you, Mrs. Habig."

Grace looked at him sadly. *What a life he must live.*

Shyly, Edie handed him the bundle.

"See you next week, Mrs. Habig?"

Grace smiled. He bolted out the screen door and back to the cart, where his father was probably fuming, thought Grace. *Serves the old bastard right.*

"He smells poor," blurted Olive.

"He can't help it," Grace gently replied.

That night, when the upstairs still held the heat of the day, the little family settled in for the night in the back room of the cellar, away from the empty coal bin, but right near the wringer washer and the laundry tubs, the packets of starch and bluing. It smelled clean and fresh down there, and it was certainly cooler.

Grace spread an old tarp on the packed-earth floor and then arranged the oilcloth pallets she had made earlier in the day for the family to sleep on. She lit a kerosene lamp that cast a shadow on the whitewashed stone walls.

"Guess what this is," Olive said to Edie, making shadow puppets on the wall.

"A rabbit," Edie guessed.

"That was too easy. How about this one?"

"It looks like a snake."

"That's because it *is* a snake. But what *kind* of a snake?" Olive tried to stump her sister.

They soon tired of shadow puppets, and Grace began reading

to them, by the glow of the lamp, from their favorite book—their only book.

"Let me tell a story, Mama," begged Edie.

"Oh, Edie," Olive fumed. "You don't tell good stories."

"I do so."

"You do not."

"Girls," Grace Habig said in a short but emphatic reprimand. "Edie, you can tell a very quick story. So why don't you start?"

"Once upon a time, there was a princess and a goblin and a boy named Curdie," Edie began.

"That's the same story that Mama was reading. You really are a pickle," Olive complained to her sister. "You're as dumb as a pickle."

"Olive, we don't talk like that in this house," Grace wearily chastised. "That was a good little story, Edie, and thank you. Now both of you close your eyes and I'll keep reading."

The princess got lost again. Ohhhhh, shivered Edie, thinking of Jimmy McCray.

Olive fell asleep easily as her mother read, but it always took Edie longer.

The book was too long to read in one night, so when Edie's breathing became slow and measured, Grace closed the book and blew out the kerosene lamp.

She lay down next to, but not touching, her husband. Edward, propped up against the cool wall with two pillows, held his blood-ied handkerchief in his fist. His head lolled to one side, and Grace thought, *That can't be comfortable*, but lying down brought on the coughing again.

"It has gone into brown lung," the doctor had told her this afternoon, taking her aside and talking quietly, shaking his head sadly.

"Well, it's better to know than not know," Grace had replied. She didn't think she'd ever wish mill fever back, but brown lung was much worse. Thankfully, the doctor had finally given Edward something to help him sleep.

After Grace nodded off, Edie stirred.

She opened her eyes wide, startled. How did she get underground? Had the goblins taken her? She lay still, afraid to move.

With the cellar windows open, Edie listened to Olive's quiet breathing, the summer sound of cicadas, and the lap of the creek at the end of their yard. A light sleeper, Edie also heard the familiar sounds of the eleven o'clock factory whistle, a car shifting into a higher gear, a midnight train rumbling by in the distance. Slowly, she sank into dark oblivion, as soft and cool as the bridal silk her mother kept in a bolt wrapped in blue paper.

Sometime during the night, Olive pulled up the chenille spread to cover them both. They slept on, tangled together like puppies.

4

FEBRUARY

Raspberry and Blood Orange

Dawn was still hours away. The only building with lights on was Rainbow Cake, a sweet beacon in the night.

Norb was taking a batch of breakfast pastries out of the oven. He was not surprised to see me so early. The bakery was where I went to push "play" instead of that mental rewind button that always looped back in the same order: Luke and our marriage . . . Dad . . . Where my life was going . . . or not going.

And now, Jett.

When I woke up this morning to find her gone, I felt a mix of emotions I was still sorting out. I was sad that she didn't really trust me or feel comfortable staying where it was safe. Yet I admired her for being so tough and independent. I was angry at the asshole who'd hurt her and still stunned that I had seen it happen, literally in my rearview mirror, on our main street. Added to that was the confusion as to what I should do about it all. I lurched toward the coffee bar. Maybe caffeine would help.

I ground the dark-roasted coffee beans, tamped down the grounds, and fired up the La Marzocco. I made myself a large latte, foaming the milk. When I tried to guide the froth into a plucky new leaf pattern, it drifted into a lopsided heart instead. "Perfect," I muttered.

I took a sip. Was the milk starting to curdle? The froth had the faint suggestion of sour. I stirred in a teaspoon of sugar. I leaned down to check the sell-by date on the carton in the under-counter refrigerator. Okay. I sniffed the carton. The milk didn't smell like anything, which was what you wanted milk to do.

I snatched a miniature croissant stuffed with ham and cheese and downed it in two bites, wiping the buttery flakes from my fingers on my work apron. I was starting to feel human again.

It was too early to call Jett at home or on her cell. I needed her to come in today, but at the same time, I hated to ask. She had been beaten up last night, emotionally and physically. And who knew what her home life was like? Could she tell her mother? I didn't want to make things worse by her boss—that was me—adding even more stress by pressuring her. But she was a young girl in trouble and I wanted to help. So what to do? I sighed.

I wasn't getting any flavor, any story, that took shape in my mind. But that was no surprise, really, so I was annoyed at myself for even wandering in that direction. I limited my ability to "read" people to those I barely knew rather than those I did. It would mean an unfair advantage in personal relationships. In business, an advantage was a good thing. But in private life, my insider info could lead to a host of happiness busters, such as an "I know best" attitude and being privy to things I was better off not knowing about friends or relatives. We were all entitled to our privacy.

Sigh.

I would have to fall back on simply doing the right thing. I texted her: *Hope you're ok. I will help you in any way I can.* I'd wait for her reply. If I didn't hear from her by midmorning, I'd go to her house. I felt better now that I had a plan.

A watched phone never beeps, so I got back to work.

If Jett couldn't come in today, I would have to do the cake-top decoration myself. Which meant that I first needed to tackle the six dome cakes—from our couture line—for a special catering order that had to go out in the afternoon.

While I warmed the eggs in a bowl of hot water (which would help them hold more air when beaten), I gathered the rest of the ingredients from the pantry—sugar, a little baking powder, flour, and blood oranges. As I cracked each egg into the bowl and added the sugar while the mixer did its work, I wondered whether I was the only person who found the whir of a stand mixer oddly comforting. For me, it was the sound of something good about to happen.

And right now, I needed that.

After the egg-and-sugar mixture thickened, turned a pale yellow, and ribboned off the whisk attachment when I flipped it up to check—yes!—I folded in the dry ingredients and the blood-orange zest by hand. That was when the classic genoise batter bloomed into the most beautiful, aromatic coral. I loved blood orange.

When each jelly-roll-style genoise had baked, I rolled it up in a confectioner's sugar–dusted towel to let it cool into a coiled shape.

After cooling, I carefully unrolled each one to spread on the seedless raspberry jam, then rolled it up again tightly. Then I cut each sweet cylinder into thin, spiraled slices with an inner stripe of dark pink.

Assembling the dome cake was the easiest part. I arranged the spiraled slices flat on the bottom and against the sides of small stainless steel bowls lined with plastic wrap. Then I filled the center with blood-orange mousse and arranged the rest of the slices on top. I had leftover cake spirals and mousse, so I created a tiny cake, too.

Nothing went to waste here.

Into the refrigerator went the cakes for an hour or so of chilling until each had set.

Meanwhile, Rainbow Cake's e-mail held no surprises, only that Mr. Wa-chen of Hong Kong, who was somehow stuck in Kenya—no, that was yesterday—had found me here as well as on my personal e-mail. He must be desperate. But the good news was that if I needed a penis enlargement, help was on the way. Spam, spam. Delete, delete.

Several late-night e-mails from Luke, which I also deleted. In simply thinking his name, an iceberg of frozen emotions loomed on my horizon. Everything I knew about icebergs I learned from the *Titanic*. You saw the tip of the iceberg floating in the water, but what you didn't see was all that lurked beneath the surface. I didn't want—and I couldn't afford—another shipwreck in my life. Avoiding my husband was a good thing, I told myself.

When the hour was up, I retrieved the dome cakes from the refrigerator, turned each one out, peeled off the plastic wrap, and smoothed on the palest pink, raspberry-flavored glaze so the spiraled design could still be seen.

Their topping would be clusters of raspberries, miniature blood oranges cut in half, and a few tiny pale green leaves, all made out of sugar paste and marzipan.

Just thinking about today's to-do list propelled me back to my good buddy, the La Marzocco. Another latte. I didn't even bother with a pattern on the foam. And it still needed a little sugar.

When I looked up again, it was seven thirty, dark was turning to dawn, and Maggie was coming in the back entrance. I always checked her face because it showed everything. Whether she'd had an easy morning before her mother took Emily to preschool. Whether she'd had yet another fight with her ex-husband, usually about the late or nonexistent child support. Or having Emily rate so low on his priority list. This morning, Maggie looked a little frazzled.

"What is it?" I asked.

"Well, it's the shoemaker's children all over again," she said. "Not having shoes themselves even though their parent works in a shoe shop . . ."

"You mean Emily was supposed to bring a treat to school today and everybody forgot and you're feeling guilty because you work in a bakery." I speak "Maggie" quite well.

"Got it in one."

"I could use a break before we open, so why don't I run some cupcakes up to the preschool and then we can cross that off our list?"

"Would you?"

"I'll be there when preschool starts."

I quickly lined up three dozen miniature cupcakes on a tray, got out my piping bag, and filled it with pink raspberry buttercream. I piped a rosette on each cupcake, then dusted each with those colored sprinkles that all kids—even big ones—love.

As I put the package in the passenger's seat of my car, Mrs. Amici growled something at me, raising her hands and Barney's leash in the air. Barney didn't like that one bit. But as she walked by the car, I realized she was just talking to herself. Uh-oh. Something that sounded like "abandon." Was she planning to dance with wild abandon on the rickety tables at the American Legion this weekend? I'd love to see her do that, the cranky old bat.

I drove up the hill and turned left where the old Civil War–era convent used to be. A newer, more modern building now housed the nursing care facility, a residence for older nuns, and Ladybug Preschool. Mount Saint Mary High School, built in the early 1960s, sat closer to Benson Street at the southern end of the convent grounds.

I tried to sneak into the back of the class of four-year-olds, taught by another high school friend, Mary Ann Brown. But blond and blue-eyed Emily came running over and hugged me at my knees. "Your mommy sent these," I whispered, showing her the cupcakes through the clear top of the bakery box.

"Neely, Neely, Neely!" she shouted, overjoyed. It was not entirely about me—it was the power of cupcakes.

But she had started a rampage of four-year-olds not yet corralled for the start of their morning. They hopped and skipped and twirled around me. Mary Ann just laughed.

"You brought us treats!" A calm, quiet voice somehow could be heard over the din.

An elderly woman in a pale blue warm-up suit smiled at me. She glided her walker into the room.

She looked so familiar to me. And then a flashback to my own childhood made me smile. "Good to see you again, Sister Agnes. I took your story-writing day-camp session at Mount Saint Mary the summer before sixth grade." I still had the stories I'd written in cursive pencil, illustrated by crayon, somewhere in a box I hadn't unpacked yet.

"Neely just opened the new bakery, Rainbow Cake, Sister," Mary Ann explained.

"So now you tell stories with cake," Sister said, smiling.

"I do, in a way," I replied, delighted.

"We're in for a sweet treat today."

"I think the children need a story treat, too, Sister Agnes," Mary Ann said. "Maybe something scary." She made her eyes wide as she looked at the kids. "Oooohhhhh. Something scarrrrryyyyy." The children giggled and squirmed.

The nun smiled. "I have just the scary story," she said, and carefully sat down in an armchair, keeping her walker close by. "Come, children, and sit by me. This is one you have to act out. I'll say something and then you do it."

The kids pirouetted, windmilled, and finally plopped down on the carpet.

"They're full of beans again today," the old woman said, bemused. She held her long, elegant finger up to her lips and waited until the last fidgety child was still.

"It was a winter day like today," she began dramatically, "and the wind was blowing, blowing, blowing through the trees. Whooooooooooo . . ."

"Can you do this?" She began to sway in her chair like she was a tree blown by the wind. One little boy swayed so far to the left that he knocked over another boy, and they both wrestled until Mary Ann stepped in. One little girl swayed as if she might be doing it wrong. Emily and another little girl swayed with everything they had.

Sister continued. "A little goat wanted to cross a bridge and go over to the other side where there was more grass to eat. So he goes clip-clop, clip-clop, over the bridge." Sister made the sound like the little goat walking on the bridge, and the kids did likewise.

"'Who goes clip-clopping over my bridge?' said the mean man who lived under it, and he shook his fist at the little goat. . . .'"

The children shook their fists as I backed away from little goats, mean men, nuns, and storytime. All in a day's work.

Well, almost all.

The late-morning text message from Jett was brief: *OK for work. Don't say anything.*

And then a second one: *Thanks.*

Without spilling any secrets, I warned everyone that Jett didn't feel good and needed her space today. And when Jett finally stomped her way into the bakery just after lunch, Maggie didn't look at her twice.

Good job.

Jett had on a nose ring with a wider band, probably a clip-on to hide the wound. Her eye shadow in stormy blues, purples, and greens masked the bruising around her eye. She pounded a straight, silent line back to the workroom, seeming to be her old Goth self.

I could feel the stiffness in my shoulders relax a little bit.

I let her get settled, then casually walked back to the workroom.

"How are you?" I asked quietly.

"Those peas were killer. My mom didn't even notice."

Jett had done a pretty good job of camouflaging the exterior, but it was the interior that worried me.

"I don't want to think that this guy is still running around and could hurt you again."

"He won't."

"How do you know that?"

"I won't be alone. And then he can't get me." Her face showed a steely resolve. I wasn't getting anywhere.

"We'll talk more about this when you've had some time to think about it."

Late that afternoon, with the bakery bustling up front, a corporate event planner came in to pick up her catering order. If she liked what I did and brought us some of her business, Rainbow Cake might meet its financial goals for the next few months.

Might.

"Do you have time for a coffee?" I asked her. "I'd love to show you where I do the wedding cake tastings."

"This was the last thing I had to do today so, yeah, sitting down for a little bit actually sounds good," she said with a tired smile.

I put the tiny dome cake in our signature pale turquoise box, and we walked next door and into the warmth of my parlor. I bent down to light the gas fireplace and settled Val on the settee, where Jett's folded blanket still rested from the night before.

When I brought in the tray with the French press coffeepot, the thin china cups, and the dome cake on a small glass cake pedestal, she visibly relaxed.

"It's so nice just to be waited on a little bit, you know?"

I knew.

I passed her a slice of the tiny dome cake, an ombre of dark coral mousse, lighter coral cake, and pale pink glaze.

I poured her coffee and waited while she ate every bite.

She put her plate and coffee back on the tea table in front of us and leaned back into the cushions. "This is perfect," she sighed.

Maybe everything was going to be all right.

That night Gavin, Roshonda, Mary Ann, and I were all crammed in a booth at the House of Chili. Everyone who lived in the Queen City area had to get a chili fix at least once a week, and this was our local parlor. But I knew, from serving this tangy, fine-textured, cinnamon-spiced concoction at football parties in New York, that Queen City chili was an acquired taste.

"Here's to the institution of marriage, God bless it," Roshonda said. The other two looked at me, then back at her as if she had said something off-color. "Nah, you got that all wrong. I'm proposing a toast." She raised her glass of diet cola. "Here's to the bridal district that keeps us in business. Here's to my clients who want me to plan their extravagant weddings. Here's to Neely's wedding cake customers. And if those newlyweds figure it all out," said Roshonda with a throaty chuckle, "Mary Ann eventually gets a new crop of preschoolers."

"And what do I get?" Gavin asked, faking a pouty expression.

"More design business from the rest of us," I said.

"Hear, hear." We all clinked glasses.

"And another toast to Neely's big day," Mary Ann added and we clinked again.

"What have I missed?" Gavin asked from across the table, tearing open a small bag of oyster crackers. "Hey, I designed your bakery and do your marketing. I'm supposed to know this stuff."

"It just happened late this afternoon," I explained. "Matters of Taste catering has decided to put Rainbow Cake on retainer for all their society functions."

"Woo-hoo!" Gavin raised his glass of iced tea and we clinked yet again. I noticed his gaze stray to the door. "And look who's here," he said quietly, and looked meaningfully at me.

The old wooden booth was high-sided, so I couldn't see who it was until he was standing in front of our table and practically blocking all the light.

"Big Ben." Gavin started to get out of the booth and offered a handshake.

"Nichols," Ben said, shaking Gavin's hand and firmly putting his other on Gavin's shoulder. "Don't get up. Good to see everybody." Ben nodded to us all, his eyes lingering on me.

Ben Tranter. Everyone called him Big Ben for obvious reasons.

The two of us had known each other since grade school. We had been in college prep classes together, but had hung out with friends who liked to have fun rather than study on weekends. Shortly before high school graduation, our constant good-natured sparring had turned flirtatious. We were both planning to attend Queen City University in the fall, so it seemed only natural—like banking a healthy fire—when my feelings for Ben suddenly felt like romance. But I hardly ever got to see him. Ben was always at football practice or meetings or labs or drills. And I had a job as a waitress in the evenings. He had to be up early. I needed to stay up late. He dated around and I just worked, studied, went to class, and collapsed at the end of each long day.

Ben had won a football scholarship to QCU, and it was there that he became Luke's go-to receiver, quarterback to tight end. We'd heard about Luke before college, of course—he was already famous to us for being a superstar athlete at neighboring Fairview High, first scouted by the NFL when he was only sixteen. But both of us got a lot closer to Luke in college than we'd ever expected.

By our sophomore year, I had managed a combination of student loans and a scholarship, so I didn't have to waitress anymore. Once again, Ben and I were on the verge of romance. We were on our first date at a keg party when Luke finally noticed "that girl from the bakery" and I was starstruck. When Ben took me home that night, we hugged a little awkwardly, and he said, "Our timing sucks, Neely. You know that?"

I knew that now, thirteen years later.

"I heard you were back," Ben said, giving me a look I couldn't quite read.

"Bakery start-ups cost too much in New York," I replied. This was true, but of course, it was not the whole truth.

"You must be busy," he said.

I took in his crisp blue shirt and khaki pants under a down parka. Fleece-lined leather gloves stuck out of his pocket. The parka made him look even more imposing. A Bluetooth hovered over his ear.

"You're working this evening?" I asked.

"Yeah. We've got a private fund-raiser in Fairview. I'm just here picking up dinner for the guys working on the grounds." After

Ben's shoulder surgery ended his NFL career, he started his own private security business.

"If they want people to pony up the big bucks, they should be serving some of Neely's cakes," said Roshonda. "I know I've put on ten pounds since she opened that damn bakery."

Ben chuckled. He and Roshonda always did get along. "You always look good, Ro," he said gallantly.

The cashier put Ben's order up on the counter, and Ben went back to get it. On the way out, he stopped at our booth again.

"Stop in some time," I said, all of a sudden. "It's not quite coffee and doughnuts, but we'll see what we can rustle up. We're right across from Finnegan's Pub."

"I'd like that," he said. "We've all missed you." Again, he gave me that look.

For a moment, I wondered what my life would have been like if I had been with Ben. He was smart, a little shy, funny in a dry-wit sort of way. Surprisingly kind and so, well, solid. When my mom and I lost our house, he helped us move in to Gran's. He just showed up with his dad's pickup truck, and a good thing, too, as Mom hadn't coped very well.

When Ben kissed me, I remember it being more of a warm glow that started in my heart and spread everywhere else. When Luke kissed me, it was like an electric current that ran from somewhere I won't mention to all points beyond. Why couldn't I have been happy with a glow instead of a jolt?

When Ben left, the chili parlor suddenly felt much emptier.

Then my chili spaghetti arrived. The first bite was tangier than usual. A trainee cook, perhaps.

I piled on soft tangles of shredded cheese and tasted to see if that mellowed it. Nope. I piled on even more cheese.

"Does this chili taste the same to you?" I asked around the table, stirring my four-way chili with a fork.

"Mine's fine," said Gavin. They all nodded in agreement.

"Well, I think they went a little heavy on the sour this time."

"You'd think everything would taste sweeter to you at this particular moment," Gavin said slyly, slurping up the dregs of his iced tea through a straw.

Roshonda didn't miss a beat. "Yeah, especially since you just got you some big sugar, Sugar."

DECEMBER 1932

Edie sat cross-legged, rapt with attention, in front of the bulky RCA Victor console radio-phonograph with its central, drop-down door that hid the big turntable.

"Do we have to listen to this again?" Olive complained to her mother, who looked up from her sewing and frowned. "This show is for babies!" she said, and Edie saw that narrow-eyed look Olive got when she didn't get her way.

Edie looked pleadingly at her mother, and Grace gave her a quick smile. "You can listen to your show, Edie. And, Olive, you shush, or you'll upset your father and get him coughing again."

Olive crossed her arms, fuming, and dramatically stomped to the kitchen at the back of the house. "I'm going to make Ovaltine."

"You'll have to make it with water," Edie reminded her. "We don't have any milk."

Olive flounced out of the little front room as the WGN radio show came on.

Edie heard, "And now, children, Kellogg's of Battle Creek, Michigan, brings you the Singing Lady, with the best-loved stories and songs from all over the world."

Once, on the back of a Rice Krispies box, Edie had seen a black-and-white photo of the Singing Lady instead of a story. Ireene Wicker looked like a movie star with her dark hair parted on the side, curling softly around her face and neck. She had long fingernails, probably painted shiny red, and a diamond-shaped pearl pin at the neck of her dark dress. In a big city like Chicago, Ireene Wicker probably had to dress up like that all the time, just like some of Mama's Fairview ladies.

"Remember to check the back of your Rice Krispies box for a new Singing Lady story this month . . ." the announcer continued.

"What story do you have to tell all the children tonight, Singing Lady?" the announcer read from the script.

"'The Little Match Girl' by Hans Christian Andersen," the Singing Lady said.

"It was late on a bitterly cold New Year's Eve. The snow was falling. A poor little girl was wandering in the dark, cold streets. . . ."

Ireene changed her voice to that of a little girl. "'I'm so cold, sooooo cold.'" Her teeth chattered. "'I've lost my mother's old shoes. They were too big, anyway, but now my bare feet have turned blue.'"

Edie heard the cold winter wind blow over the airwaves. She felt the snow on her own bare feet.

"'Here's a man who might help me. Mister, will you buy some matches?' the little match girl asked. 'If I go home without selling these matches, my stepfather will beat me,' cried the little girl.

"'Go away!' the man's voice thundered."

Edie heard the padding of a child's feet against the snowy cobblestones and the child gasping for breath as she ran away.

"'I'm still so cold.' The little match girl shivered, blowing on her hands. 'Maybe if I light just one match, against the brick wall of this house, I can get warm.'"

Edie heard the match rasp against the brick.

A small *whoosh*. "'Oh, the flame is so bright. It's like I'm sitting in front of a big stove with polished brass feet and handles.' The little match girl's voice brightened. 'It's so warm. Maybe if I stretch my feet out, close to the fire, they'll get warm, too.'"

Edie stretched her feet out toward the radio.

A hissing sound faded away. "'Oh no!' cried the little match girl. 'The match has gone out. The stove has disappeared. And I'm colder than before,' she sobbed."

Tears sprang to Edie's eyes.

"'I'll strike another match,' the little match girl said urgently."

Whoooooosh. The match made a bigger sound.

"Now she was back in front of the same lovely stove, only this time there was also a table set for dinner with a large roasted goose on a platter in the center. But the fragrant meal vanished just before the match went out. When the little girl struck another, she saw a family seated around the table and behind them, a Christmas tree all aglow. And then, of course, the match burned out again.

"The wind whistled and shrieked even louder.

"'I see a shooting star travel across the night sky. That means someone is dying,' the little girl said in a sad whisper.

"'My old grandmother, the only person who has ever loved me, used to say that when a star falls, a soul is going up to God. I wish

I could see her one more time. Maybe if I light the rest of the matches . . .'"

Edie heard one, two, three rasps and then a large burst of flame.

"'Oh, Grandmother!' cried the little girl with a voice full of wonder. 'You look so beautiful. And the light around you has so many colors.'

"'Come here, my little one.'"

The old and tired grandmother's voice, full of sorrow and love, despair and hope, startled Edie.

"'There, there, my sweet girl. Everything will be all right now. I will take you in my arms and we will go where there is no more cold, no more hunger, and no more pain. Only love.'"

Edie wrapped her arms around her knees and crushed them to her chest. How could this be happily ever after?

5

Rainbow Cake smelled exceptionally wonderful. In the back of the bakery, Norb was infusing our browned butter with vanilla bean.

He slit several vanilla beans lengthwise and scraped the tiny black seeds into a large saucepan, which already held a quantity of unsalted butter. The scraped-out vanilla bean pods went in, too. Over medium heat, he let the butter cook until brown bits rose to the surface and the liquid butter had turned a deep golden color. He always attached a metal thermometer with a large round face to the side, so he could check the temperature even across the room.

When the butter reached 250°F, he took it off the heat and let it cool. After we took the used vanilla bean pods out, we'd use it just like regular butter, cream it with sugar until it was light and fluffy, add the flour and eggs, and make our popular yellow cake. It also made delicious browned-butter cookies. We kept a tub of it in the refrigerator that we replenished every week.

In a little while, Norb would pour the cake batter into large sheet pans to bake. Then he'd cut three-inch circles from the cooled cake and cover them with plastic wrap until later on this morning, when I would assemble twenty-four individual three-layer cakes, with both lime and tangerine mousse fillings, then spray them with an orange-scented white-chocolate ganache. As a final touch, I would add a sprig of sugar-paste orange blossoms on top—all as the sweet finale to a private anniversary party for a couple who had met and married in Florida. The wife was supposed to pick them up early in the afternoon.

"The gods on Mount Olympus didn't breathe air any more ambrosial than this," intoned John Staufregan, a regular customer whom Maggie had unfortunately dubbed "the Professor." He taught in the biology department at Queen City University, but was now on sabbatical. During his time off from teaching, he was working on a project involving flies and zebrafish at the Genome Research Institute on Millcreek Valley Road. The institute's high-tech building had replaced a sixties-era complex that once housed a big pharmaceutical firm. He had told us about this project several times, but we still couldn't understand what fly and zebrafish genes have to do with real life.

The Professor was usually the first person in the door every morning when Rainbow Cake opened. He always ordered the same thing: a grande latte, skinny, with a double shot and a lemon blueberry muffin, which I was trying to get everyone to call a breakfast cupcake, with mixed results.

"A muffin's a muffin," Maggie kept telling me. "What in the hell is a breakfast cupcake, anyway?"

"A muffin. It's got a cupcake paper around it."

"So what? It's still a muffin. Just call it a muffin. At least fifty percent of the people who come in here are literal-minded, and they think a muffin is a muffin and a cupcake is a cupcake. They won't order either one if you confuse them."

So the debate raged on.

"I'll have one of those glorious muffin, er, breakfast cupcakes again," the Professor told Maggie. She took a small sheet of waxed bakery paper and plucked one out from the case. Turning her head so only I could see, she glowered at me.

"They're still warm," I told him brightly as I gave him back his change.

"Well, my compliments to you ladies," he said, taking the muffin and latte over to his table.

"Just our luck he's picked here to hang out," Maggie muttered.

"He's here, what, maybe thirty minutes?" I reminded her.

"Well, it seems like thirty hours."

Our morning business had become so intense that I'd had to hire a barista, a graduate student who was working on his thesis and needed a part-time job. Part of his job description was suffering through the Professor's early-morning lectures.

"As Immanuel Kant once said"—the Professor's baritone reverberated as our barista frothed the milk for his second latte—"'All our knowledge begins with the senses, proceeds then to understanding, and ends with reason.'"

"Who cares?" sniped Maggie, under her breath. "*Kant* he mutate on over to White Castle and spare us, just one morning?" She bent down to retrieve a half dozen breakfast cupcakes from the case for another customer.

The Professor ambled across the bakery—with his latte and

breakfast cupcake in hand—to check out our February display. Framed against the sunset-colored curtain, he looked pale and drab, the combination of his comb-over, sallow skin, wrinkled gray shirt, and old-man pants not doing him any favors. I wouldn't be surprised, however, if he was only in his early forties, maybe ten years or so older than Maggie and me.

"You know, he could be much better looking if he'd shave his head, wear a little color, and knock the cobwebs off his ironing board," I whispered back to Maggie, who shot me an "Are you nuts?" look. Not that I was in the market for a fortyish professor—that was for sure.

Neither was Maggie. She had enough trouble as it was with Mark, who seemed to think he was still in his glory days as our high school basketball hero. He wasn't even that good back then. If he didn't show up to take Emily on his scheduled weekends or pay his child support on time, it was because he had more pressing things to do. Like play golf with his buddies or bed a barmaid.

With straight blond hair cut in a bob, blue eyes, and a smooth complexion, Maggie could pass for a Swiss milkmaid. She wore little makeup, although her raspberry T-shirt made her eyes look really blue today. She had put on a little weight since the divorce and looked worried sometimes, but was holding up well, considering she was raising a child by herself and living with her mother.

She nodded over at our Professor. "He needs more than just an Extreme Makeover. Even if you spiffed up his looks, there's still the fact that his personality is beyond dead boring," she said quietly out of the corner of her mouth. "Why can't he just stuff that muffin and get out of here?"

"Breakfast cupcake," I reminded her.

"Whatever."

The cold wind cut through the warm coziness in the bakery as more customers came in, wafting a fresh current of vanilla-infused brown butter around.

"Well, ladies, you're certainly using all of your olfactory enticements today," the Professor said in an attempt at humor. "You know—"

"We don't have 'factory' anything here," Maggie replied, cutting him off. "Everything we do is made from scratch. You want factory, you'll have to go to the Wonder Bread outlet." And then she stomped off to the back of the store.

"I, uh, I said 'olfactory,'" he sputtered. "I know I said 'olfactory.'"

I held up my hand to let him know he didn't have to explain, but he still looked pained.

"I was going to comment on the mystery of how scent triggers a memory, then a feeling."

Oh no, another lecture. And that was not quite how it worked with me, but I wasn't going to get into that.

He carried on in full Professor mode, undeterred. "The aroma travels up the nostrils about seven centimeters."

At this I began to cringe and hoped I didn't show it.

"It then dissolves in mucus . . ."

Oh no, not mucus, I thought. I tried to draw him farther away from where people were trying to eat their breakfast cupcakes.

". . . within a membrane called the olfactory epithelium . . ." he droned on.

I saw one lady grab her purchases, shoot him a dirty look, and hurry out. 'Mucus' is never a good word to hear when you're eating.

". . . areas of the brain that are part of the limbic system—the oldest instinctual, primitive portion of the brain. So, scent, and the flavor/scent combo, really hit us where it counts," he finished, rocking back and forth on his heels.

He paused and got a faraway look in his eye. Suddenly he looked vulnerable to me, like a lost little boy. What had our bakery scent touched in him?

I knew if I focused on him, I'd begin to get the answer, but I didn't have time for that today. And while I was dimly aware of his potential, I had too much going on right now to embrace a fixer-upper side project.

The moment passed and he returned to full Professor mode. "No one knows what actually causes the olfactory receptors to react to a scent—is it the size, shape, or electrical charge of the scent molecule? Maybe one day we'll find out." He looked at his watch and made for the door. "Please tell that pretty girl I'm sorry for the misunderstanding."

The bell on the door jangled again as he left. I could see the skimpy strands of his comb-over stand straight up in the cold wind. Yes, Maggie was right. Extreme Makeover.

She popped her head out again from the back of the store.

"I'm sorry," she said, looking abashed.

"Don't tell me; tell him the next time he comes in. You knew the Professor meant 'olfactory,' didn't you?"

Maggie laughed. "I just couldn't take him anymore."

"Interesting. You think he's insufferable and he thinks you're pretty," I said, and left her to digest that little tidbit.

The morning progressed, and soon I came out from behind the counter to greet Roshonda, who had become another regular.

When no one else was in the bakery, she told me wedding planner horror stories. Like the bride who wanted her wedding party dressed in traditional German lederhosen or the bride who gained fifty pounds before her wedding, then blamed Ro when the gown didn't fit and refused to go three sizes larger. They ended up having a seamstress make a panel in the back of her dress and squeezing the bride into a corset.

"Hey, girl," she said, her smile always bright, as she took her complimentary Americano with a sweet lick of caramel syrup.

"Who's jumping the broom today?" I inquired.

She leaned forward to whisper. "You can't tell anybody, but I know you'll love this. Tyrone Spencer, the rapper who calls himself Dime."

I was shocked. "Your first celebrity wedding, Ro! That's amazing. Even if it is for Dime. I have to wonder, though, who on earth would have him?"

"His baby mama, apparently."

"Isn't there more than one?"

Ro had a wicked laugh. "Yes! But the bride-to-be is the most recent. And let me tell you, that woman is pretty damn impressed with herself for getting Dime to commit. She kept telling me that the theme of her wedding is the theme of her life: 'Go Big or Go Home.' How gross is that?"

"Pretty gross," I agreed.

"Yeah. And I know I said I needed a super-high-profile gig to launch myself to the next level, but I now fear I may live to regret those words. Dime's girlfriend threw an honest-to-goodness fit when her driver refused to park in the handicapped spot next to my door. Poor thing was forced to walk a full twenty feet in her Louboutins."

"How horrible for her. That chauffeur is monster," I said, and we both laughed. "And you clearly need that coffee."

"Actually, I have to drink and run. My next client is a corporate attorney coming in for her second consultation. She's a lovely person, so I hope she cancels out the memory of Nickel."

"Nickel?"

Roshonda laughed. "Dime's fiancée, although that's not her real name. I've decided to call them Nickel and Dime. Makes me feel better."

"Fun with customers." I winked.

"By the way." Roshonda came up close and whispered in my ear. "I got a call from Mariah Fleetwood earlier. Luke asked her to book two first-class airline tickets from New York down to the Super Bowl this Sunday. She said she wasn't planning on gossiping to anyone else, but if it were her husband, she'd want to know." Ro gave me a sympathetic squeeze and a rueful smile. "So now you know." Mariah was a buddy of Ro's from college who now ran a luxury travel agency out of Queen City. It was part of Luke's image to remain loyal to hometown businesses when possible, so of course he'd contacted Mariah to manage his itinerary. Either that or he was trying to get a message to me through a friend of a friend.

The whole story made Luke's phone message from earlier this morning all the more puzzling. All I heard was a man singing that it was not your fault but mine, and a banjo thrumming. Oh, yeah, Mumford & Sons. As if that explained anything.

OCTOBER 1941

Mrs. Ellison was a Fairview lady who paid well and paid on the spot, and Lord knew, Edie and Olive needed the money. Since their mother died, they'd been on their own. What nineteen-year-old Olive earned at the bakery and Edie made from sewing after she got home from high school barely put food on the table. But Mrs. Ellison was a good customer, and Edie kept concentrating on that. Edie couldn't afford to show Mrs. Ellison how she really felt.

Jean Ellison, that spoiled brat, didn't know how lucky she was.

Instead, Jean complained because another girl in her class was having McCall's pattern 4054 made into a dress for the autumn dance.

"We've already bought the pattern and the fabric and we've had Edie make up the dress, Jean," Mrs. Ellison explained to her daughter. She played with the pearls at the neck of her burgundy gabardine dress. "It won't be the same as Betty's, unless she bought the same fabric and had Edie make it, too," she reasoned. She turned to Edie. "You didn't make a dress for a Betty Simms, did you?"

"No, ma'am."

Then Jean wanted the neckline lower on the already off-the-shoulder dress.

"Don't be ridiculous, Jean," replied Mrs. Ellison, losing patience. "You're only sixteen. Do you want the dress to fall right off in front of all the boys?"

Jean smiled a dreamy smile into the long mirror. She preened and turned in the pale blue gown, raising a shoulder in a pinup girl pose, flipping her long honey-colored hair back with one hand.

"The bertha collar won't lay right with a lower neckline," Edie blurted out as she took a straight pin out of her mouth, then wished she hadn't said anything. "Plus," she said more meekly, looking over at Mrs. Ellison and then back at Jean, "your brassiere would show."

Jean's soft smile turned to a furious frown. "Who cares?"

Pouting into the long mirror, Jean did a quick turnaround on the step stool to face Mrs. Ellison. "You're just such a fuddy-duddy, Mother. You still want me to look like a little girl!" She stomped down, almost knocking Edie backward, and ran to her room, tripping on the still-unpinned part of the hemline. She slammed the door shut and then, with even more drama, locked the door.

Mrs. Ellison rolled her eyes heavenward.

Edie sighed, but tried to hide it. She'd never be home in time to listen to *The Aldrich Family* at nine o'clock if she didn't get this hem finished. And she still had to press the gown once the hem was done.

"El, dear." Mrs. Ellison walked to the top of the stairs and called down to the living room. "Please do something with your daughter."

"I'm trying to listen to Edward R. Murrow," he called up to his wife. "There's a war on in Europe, you know."

"Well, there seems to be a war on up here, too, dear."

In his own good time, Mr. Ellison came upstairs in his reasonable, measured way, his cardigan sweater buttoned over office shirt and tie, pipe in hand.

He gently rapped on Jean's bedroom door. "Princess," he cajoled.

No answer. "Sweetheart," he tried again. The door stayed shut. He looked at his wife, whose mouth was set in a firm line.

Come on, come on, Edie thought. *At this rate, I'll be here all night.*

Then he looked back at the door, as if the wood held the answer to his problem. He took several thoughtful puffs on his pipe.

"Here's what we'll do," he announced to them all. He turned his face back to the door. "When you make your debut next year, Princess, we'll talk about a different style of dress. But not before. And that's that. Let's not waste any more time. You've got homework to do. So open the door right now, Jean Ann."

"Oh, Daddy," Jean sighed dramatically, swinging the door open. She flung herself in his arms. "I'm glad you understand." He gave her a hug and absently patted her on the head.

"Now, let's not have any more foolishness." He gestured toward Edie with his pipe. "Miss Habig was good enough to come this evening at short notice, and we shouldn't keep her any longer."

"All right, Daddy." Jean fluttered her eyes down toward the big-patterned carpet, seemingly contrite. Her father, his duty done, went back downstairs to the big console radio.

Jean's head snapped back up. She flounced past her mother and got up on the step stool again so Edie could finally finish hemming the long gown.

And now it was time to get home, Edie thought, as she briskly walked, almost at a run. Although Mrs. Ellison had suggested that Mr. Ellison drive her home, Edie declined and Mrs. Ellison didn't press the matter.

Under a streetlamp, she bent down and removed a piece of gravel from her red shoe and hoped it didn't put a hole in her anklet sock.

By the time Edie reached the old canal in Lockton, a smoky yellow fog had rolled in, blanketing the stone slab sidewalks and brick streets. She could hardly make out any of the familiar landmarks. Except for the pitifully weak circles of coal-dusted light that the streetlamps beamed out, everything was murky.

The smoky air seemed to muffle sound as well. No cars, no streetcars, no one out walking. Even the *clack-clack-clack* of the machines making cotton batting and mattress covers was muted.

Edie walked past the warm light of the Friendly Café. It was after dinner hours, so only one couple sat in a booth at the window, drinking coffee and eating pie. Pie sounded good, thought Edie, and almost stopped in. But home sounded better.

She quick-stepped through a puddle of darkness between the streetlamp and the pedestrian walkway on the side of the two-lane bridge. Almost home.

The tall man startled her, staggering up from the creek, reeking of whiskey and stagnant water.

He came right up to her, blocking her path, and whistled low.

Edie's heart pounded. There was something familiar about him, but she was too frightened to think what. She stood absolutely still, as if that way she'd be invisible and he'd move on.

He leaned so close to her that his chin almost touched her forehead.

That was when Edie tried to scream, but nothing came out.

He wove back and forth, unsteady on his feet.

He grabbed her face with his big hands, leaning in to kiss her. She twisted away and tried to run past him, but he was suddenly alert and fast.

He grabbed a sleeve of her coat, yanked her toward him, then gripped both of her arms. The sudden movement threw them both off balance. He fell backward, pulling her down the steep bank, and they rolled to a stop.

Edie felt cold stones against her back, the weight of him. Her right arm went numb, pinned under her at an awkward angle.

He put his hand over her nose and mouth, and she couldn't breathe. She heard the water trickle past, a car shift gears as it rolled over the bridge, several sirens in the distance.

She tossed her head back and forth, moving the big hand a little, and gulped in air. She tried to scream again, but still nothing came out.

She blacked out for a while, but came to with the pain.

It hurt so bad, she thought she was on fire and she wondered if she was. She could hear a fire truck's siren getting closer, then fading away. *I'm going to die.*

It seemed to go on forever. She blacked out, woke up to the searing pain, and drifted off again to nothingness. When she surfaced again, she kept her eyes closed. The pain was still there, but not as bad. He grunted, then rolled off Edie and onto his back, spread-eagled. He didn't move.

Edie turned her head slightly and saw that his mouth had fallen open, but she was still too scared to move. Everything was black again for a while.

And then Edie opened her eyes. She heard something, but it stopped. The cold, muddy creek water had seeped into her clothes. Her body hurt all over. She shivered. If she just let go, she could drift down, down, down to another place.

Her eyelids flickered shut for a few moments, but the sound woke her again. A sound like the whirring of wings.

She felt the lap of small waves from the direction of the oxbow bend, where the wild geese still flocked in cold weather. The vibration hummed just above the water and echoed back under the bridge.

"Get up, Edie."

Wings beating on water.

Somewhere inside that sound, she heard her mother's voice carrying down the creek.

"Get up, Edie. Get up. Go on home."

But that can't be, Edie thought dully. Mama was dead.

Edie closed her eyes again. She must be dreaming. But her mother's voice grew louder.

"Get up, Edie. Go home."

A fearful thought slashed through Edie's cloudy brain. What if the man heard and woke up?

Her eyes flew open. She felt the small, choppy waves lapping at her feet. The factory whistle shrieked. There was a humming in her ears. "Hooooooooommmmmmme."

She eased up so she could feel her arm again, and the pain made her wince as she moved it from under her body to her side. The effort made her lightheaded.

But still the hum like the steady drone of bees carried the word she clung to: "Hoooooooommmmmmme."

She knew that once she moved, she would have to keep going or the man could wake up and hurt her again. She rolled over on her hands and knees and got her bearings for a few seconds.

He was still passed out.

She felt the gravel in the creek bed bite into her palms. She had lost a shoe somewhere. But she moved.

Lurching forward, she slipped in the mud, then twisted to stiffly pull off the torn panties down at her ankles and the other shoe. She shoved them both in her coat pocket. Edie crawled on hands and knees up the steep and slippery bank, grabbing at the scrub trees and clumps of tall weeds. She made it to the pole of the streetlight on the other side of the bridge and dragged herself upright. She stood under its dim circle and caught her breath.

"Better go home and sleep it off, doll," a man muttered as he walked past, clutching his metal lunch box under his arm. He didn't tip his cap. "Hate to see a woman drunk," he said, shaking his head as he walked by and then was lost in the smoky haze.

Mr. Schramm, she thought. She called out to her friend's father, but her voice still didn't work. *How could Mr. Schramm not know me? How can he not see I need help?*

She heard more men, talking quietly, walking home from the three-to-eleven shift.

She had to get home.

Edie steadied herself, then hobbled from the support of the streetlamp and turned the corner.

Home. Home. Home.

She lurched toward anything to hold on to—wrought-iron gateposts, a parked car, the broad girth of trees—until she reached the little house and let herself in the front door. With her last bit of strength, she threw the bolt on the old lock they never used and slid down against the door, onto the floor.

She heard Olive snoring softly upstairs.

Edie lost consciousness again, her head lolling on her shoulders as she slumped against the door, legs splayed out.

The violent trembling brought her back to the surface again.

Where am I? she wondered. In the dark, she saw the familiar outline of the hallway, the light of the streetlamp coming in the window.

I'm home. I must have fallen. I'm cold.

And then it all came back, and Edie started to cry. She wrapped her arms around herself, trying to stifle the sobs. She didn't want Olive to hear. And she couldn't stay on the floor where Olive might see her.

Edie crawled to the bathroom, dragged herself up on her knees, and filled the claw-foot tub with hot water until the bathroom was steaming. While the water was running, she tore off her clothing, stained with blood and mud. She gathered it all up in a ball and limped naked through the dark house to toss it on the back porch. In the morning, she would get rid of it. Maybe she would give the clothing to Shemuel, the ragman's son. Shemuel could keep a secret. And the paper mill didn't care whether rags were clean or soiled.

She locked the back door and wedged a chair beneath the handle.

Edie climbed in the tub and submerged herself in the water. When she pushed back her wet hair and wiped her eyes, she almost screamed. The water had turned a brownish pink. She drained the tub and filled it up again. She soaked until she was not cold anymore. She scrubbed herself clean until her skin turned pink and the hot water ran out.

She wrapped herself in a towel and tiptoed upstairs. She took a clean nightgown from the dresser drawer, pulled it over her head, and climbed into bed beside her sister.

"You're late," mumbled Olive.

6

Sunday was my day off. I hadn't been to see Gran in two weeks, so I agreed to go with Aunt Helen up to Mount Saint Mary's.

The convent grounds on the crest of the hill had been overlooking Millcreek Valley since the 1860s. Long gone were the mansard-roofed school buildings and the basilica-style church. The newer complex—Mount Saint Mary High School, a residence for older nuns, a preschool, and a nursing home—had a modern, functional look. Even the iron scrollwork gate, at the end of the old circular drive that wound down the hill to the town, had been padlocked. Everyone used the hilltop entrance now.

My mother and Helen were Mount Saint Mary Academy alums, but had been in different grades. After eighth grade, they'd gone to Millcreek Valley High School. They didn't hang out together back then, and that was really no surprise. My mother got her sense of duty, deportment—and a nervous tic, I always teased her—from her years in convent school. Helen went the other way—she drank, smoked, fooled around with boys, and generally had a good time. "I knew I was going to burn in hell anyway," Helen always joked.

When Mom married my dad, Helen's brother, the two women gradually got to know each other. After we lost our house when Dad left, Mom stayed on at Gran's only long enough to see me off to college. Mom still somehow blamed Gran for Dad's defection, but Helen was determinedly neutral. Still, nobody thought Mom and Helen's living arrangement would last as long as it had.

Mom needed routine, stability, and neatness. Helen thrived on chaos and was an unrepentant slob. But they were both hardworking and practical. And they both liked rules—Mom to follow them, Helen to break them. Maybe that was what made it work.

When Helen and I pulled up outside the covered entry of the nursing care facility, a goose and a gander dressed up like George and Martha Washington offered a silent but lighthearted greeting. Although this was a warm and caring place, it was still hard to see those you loved in decline.

Helen punched in the security code to the memory care wing. Sister Agnes, the nun from Emily's preschool, was talking calmly to Gran, who looked like a bewildered doll sitting in a chair that was too big. I knew that the nuns who still lived at Mount Saint Mary's went back and forth between the nursing home and the preschool, so I wasn't surprised.

Sister smiled at us. "She has been a little agitated this morning," she said. She smiled at Gran. "But I kept telling Dorothy that her two favorite people were coming to visit." She reached over and patted Gran's hand. "And here they are."

"Thank you, Sister," Helen said gently. "Mom, let's walk a little bit. You were always the best walker around."

"Walk," Gran repeated weakly, as if she wasn't quite sure what that meant.

We both helped Gran up from the chair and held on to her until she became steadier on her feet. Gran seemed to think more clearly when she was moving.

We meandered down the hall, while Helen chattered on.

Gran shuffled to a stop and turned to me. "It's an orange day, isn't it?" she asked.

An orange day?

Helen shook her head sadly. "Mom, let's keep walking." Helen gestured to me to take Gran's elbow to get her moving again.

But I was starting to taste it, too. Orange. I squeezed Gran's hand and we both smiled.

Suddenly she was younger. I was younger, maybe eight years old.

We were in her kitchen at the back of her house that was now mine.

It was a snowy day. She stood at the big enameled sink in the corner, washing dishes and putting them on the draining board to dry.

"Go into the pantry, Claire, and get the box grater for me, will you, sweetie?"

The tiny pantry smelled of spices and danced with color from the small stained glass window high up in the wall. I had to climb onto a stool to reach up into the cabinet where Gran kept her baking utensils.

When I swung the pantry door back open, it was like I had stepped into a good dream. My father was sitting at the kitchen table, smiling into his coffee mug.

Smiling.

Gran wiped her hands on her apron, then took a blue bowl of pillowy dough and turned it out onto a floured pastry board in the center of the table.

"Remember these sweet rolls, Jack? The ones with the cinnamon filling and the orange icing?"

My father looked up at Gran, and his eyes twinkled.

When he saw me hesitate, he reached out to pull me close and nuzzled my ear. I could feel his scratchy whiskers. "Are you going to help Gran make Daddy's favorite rolls, Punkin?"

I put my arms around his neck and held on tight.

"It's not every day your daddy starts a new job," Gran said. "That's an orange day."

Gran rolled out the dough, spread it with softened butter, and sprinkled on the cinnamon and sugar. She rolled it up into a cylinder and Daddy cut the rolls with a bread knife, sawing through the dough so gently that each roll was a perfect spiral.

While the rolls baked, he helped me grate the orange rind and squeeze the juice into a bowl of powdered sugar to make the icing.

We frosted the warm rolls, the aroma wafting through the kitchen like a bright orange scarf that loosely bound us together.

An orange day, a happy day, a brand-new day in the secret language that only the three of us seemed to understand.

"Mmmmm," Daddy said, taking a bite of his roll. "Orange wakes you up, but cinnamon makes you remember. I guess you can't have a future without a past." The brightness started to dim.

"The past is past, and nobody can change it. It's what you do with your new day, Jack." Gran looked at him seriously.

"I know it will work out this time, Ma. I'm putting all the other stuff behind me. Right, Punkin?" he'd said.

"Right, Claire?"

Helen was almost shouting.

"I heard you, I heard you," I said.

The orange band faded and then vanished. Gran had a vacant look about her again.

But I felt calmer. Although I had a million other things to do, just being with Gran, slowing down, and sharing our special bond had helped. I hoped it had helped her, too.

In the hallway outside the nursing care wing, we passed Sister Josepha, Helen's teacher from grade school who was now retired. Sister was decked out in a mint-green blouse and a skirt that looked like a patchwork quilt. She had short, silver pixie hair and a medal of Saint Joseph around her neck. In fact, she looked better than Helen, who wore her mom jeans and Fighting Irish sweatshirt, neither of which did her lumpy figure any good.

"We're looking for the *Infant of Prague*," Helen said, out of the blue.

Sister Josepha rolled her eyes in my direction and laughed. "You may not know this, Claire, but Helen was always the one who wanted to change the outfits on that little statue." I must have looked blank again because she added, "The *Infant of Prague* is Jesus depicted as a toddler. We have that little statue perched on a marble stand somewhere." Josepha looked up and down the hallway. "The cleaners must have moved it for some reason. Anyway, the colors of the Infant's robes reflect the seasons of the Church. You know, red for Pentecost, white for Easter and Christmas, rose for Laetare Sunday, purple for Advent and Lent, and so on. Helen was always lobbying hard to change those little outfits."

"Aunt Helen lobbied to dress the *Infant of Prague*?"

"Better than cleaning erasers from the chalkboard," Helen said. "Unless you could clap them together and get chalk dust all over some kid you didn't like."

"Oh, Helen." Sister Josepha laughed. "You never change."

Helen grinned.

Sister Josepha left us to our rambles.

"I know it's here somewhere," Helen said as we slowly walked by the preschool rooms. "You can't have a bunch of old convent nuns living together without that statue somewhere."

We didn't find it, but it was so like Helen to try to turn our stroll with Gran into an adventure.

On the way home, Helen said, "Mom seemed all right until she started talking about that orange stuff. What was that about, anyway?"

"I remember Gran always made those orange cinnamon rolls that were so good."

Helen agreed. "They were good."

"Maybe she just imagined a happy time and that's how she was trying to explain it."

Helen seemed to accept that explanation. "Mom always did have a vivid imagination."

Imagination and vision. I was beginning to appreciate those qualities more and more now that I was back home. Sometimes you had to look past what was and imagine what could be.

At one time, you could head west from where we had been up on the convent hill to the Miami and Erie Canal. I imagine that in the early days of the canal in the 1820s, when boats were towed by mules and the pace of life was just as slow, Lockton had looked picturesque and bucolic. The lockkeeper's cottage and a few farms on either side of the canal. But after the Civil War, the Machine Age finally arrived, mules were replaced by motors, and factories displaced the farms, taking advantage of the available waterpower.

In the 1980s, the Machine Age went. It took the rosiest of rose-colored glasses to look past the vacant paper, shingle, and mattress factory sites now. These "brownfields" awaited federal cleanup money for asbestos and petroleum contamination. The huge Simms & Taylor complex was being demolished, brick by brick. The canal had become part of I-75.

In comparison, blue-collar Millcreek Valley had given itself a much-needed makeover. It had always had a mom-and-pop, cottage-industry sort of downtown. Now it had a theme, one that would not go out of style—weddings. As we drove in companionable silence, we passed boutiques, florists, and travel offices. Luckily for all of us, here came the brides.

The front of my bakery even looked like a wedding cake, or a massive old Victorian headboard painted white.

"I won't ask what your plans are tonight because I know you won't tell me," Helen said as she got out of the car. "Just don't sit home by yourself and think about your old life in New York and what might have been. You can always come with your mother and me to the Legion."

I tried to edit my horrified expression, but I wasn't quick enough.

Helen grinned. "Gotcha!" she said, then got serious again. "She worries about you, you know."

I was going to respond, "When doesn't Mom worry?" but that was childish. I smiled and shrugged. "I know. I'm okay. Really."

But really, I wasn't. My showing up to watch the Super Bowl

at Finnegan's was going to be a game-time decision. Was I strong enough to brave the "Why is she here and not there?" stares from people I knew, but not well? Or even worse, was I strong enough to see Luke with someone else on national television? Was I strong enough to go to Finnegan's and pretend my life was just fine, thank you very much?

Yes, I was. I'd had years of practice already.

By the time I was sixteen and Mom and I were living with Gran, we didn't have a car anymore. My mother had to get a job and walked to work. I hiked up Benson Street hill to high school or got a ride from Gavin. But then I got my dream job at the Fairview Pastry Shop two towns away.

After school, I would run down the hill, grab my bike, then pedal to work from Millcreek Valley through Lockton and on to Fairview.

It was a mile and a half, but two worlds, away. Blue-collar Millcreek Valley to no-collar Lockton to white-collar Fairview.

Fairview was all broad, treelined streets with gracious Queen Anne–style homes, many of them with carriage houses. Long ago, factory and mill workers may have lived in Millcreek Valley and Lockton, but the owners built their mansions in Fairview.

Fairview households had maids and housekeepers, whom they often sent to pick up their bakery orders—miniature Danish, crinkle-top spice cookies, and rococo birthday cakes in a fantasy of roses, leaves, and borders piped with a frosting that tasted faintly of coconut.

Early one Saturday morning in the pastry shop, right before Mother's Day my senior year, people were standing in line and we were already on number sixty-two.

"Claire, do you think you can wait on customers now?" owner Mrs. Merz had asked me in her typically passive-aggressive way. Hadn't I just carried in trays of Danish and replenished the stack of bakery boxes? Wasn't that me scrubbing out the icing that had stuck to the interior of the inwardly slanting glass display case? And before that, who took the phone order when she was busy with a customer? Didn't I always do as she asked?

I heaved an internal sigh and pulled the chain that changed the number on the old-fashioned sign, calling out, "Sixty-three!"

I knew I looked flustered. My hair was pulled into a topknot and a few strands escaped over my ears and down my neck. I had on jeans and a T-shirt with a limp bakery apron in a washed-out brown and yellow sunflower print. I stuck out my lower lip to blow air upward and get the bangs out of my eyes. If I touched my hair with my hands, I'd have to leave the customer to go wash them and get another snide comment from Mrs. Merz.

But I was in luck. A tall, muscular guy stepped up to the counter. "Well, it must be my lucky day," he said in a deep voice.

Startled, I looked into his green eyes, noticed the smirky grin, watched the way his sun-streaked light brown hair fell over his forehead.

I kept staring, wide-eyed. I couldn't speak.

"Uh, I think I have an order to pick up. Davis."

I nodded and turned to look at the orders lined up on the shelves behind me. Davis. Davis. Davis. DAVIS!

The Davis who threw six touchdowns to beat Millcreek Valley in last November's game. Luke Davis. Preacher's kid. The one all the guys talked about. Mr. Football himself.

"Found it," I said, trying to act normal, as if this kind of thing happened to me every day. "Let's see, here. A loaf of buttercrust. Cinnamon-apple streusel coffee cake. A dozen Parker House rolls. Anything else?"

He kept watching me as he paid and I gave him his change.

"Will you be here next Saturday?" he asked.

"I'm here every Saturday."

He winked at me and was gone.

The next Saturday, the bakery wasn't as busy.

"If you want to sit down for a while, I can tidy up here and wait on customers, too," I suggested to Mrs. Merz. She gave me a narrowed-eye look, as if she were searching for something to criticize but couldn't find anything, took her coffee mug, and trudged back to her cluttered office.

And just in time.

"Don't tell me. . . . Davis." I smiled as he came up to the counter. I retrieved the order, along with a little white bakery box I had filled at home.

"You just happen to be our ten thousandth customer," I lied, "and this is our special thank-you." I slid the bakery box across the counter to him.

"Hmmmmm. Usually, I prefer to be number one, but I guess I can make an exception this time." He grinned. "What's in here?" He snapped the red-and-white-striped string on the white bakery box and opened the lid.

A little greedy, too, I thought. Wanted to enjoy life *now*.

He downed the cupcake in two bites—all moist devil's food with a dark truffle center, spread with a white-chocolate-and-coffee frosting I made with confectioner's sugar, the easy kind of buttercream. He grabbed a napkin to wipe the crumbs from his lips.

"That was some cupcake, Cupcake." And I knew I had gotten him right. Strong, dark, and handsome chocolate truffle—that masculine "shoulder to lean on" fix that women loved. Risk-taking devil's food. Gregarious white chocolate, because it's boring alone, but good with almost any other ingredient. And take-charge coffee.

Yet in baking, as in life, proportion was everything. I may have gotten him right, but he had turned out to be Mr. Wrong.

That night at Finnegan's, I didn't have to pretend alone. I had Roshonda, Mary Ann, Gavin, and Ben. Flat-screen televisions on every wall helped deflect any possible interest in Mrs. Luke Davis, runaway wife of a popular NFL quarterback who was a spectator at this year's Super Bowl.

Pitchers of beer foaming on every table also helped.

I was getting a little peeved at myself for thinking this night was going to be all about *me*. So narcissistic.

And then, all of a sudden, it *was* all about me. Luke's famous grin flashed on the screen during the pregame show.

"Luke Davis, you had a Pro Bowl year as a quarterback, but somehow that didn't lead to a Super Bowl appearance," the tall blond reporter began.

He leaned down to the microphone. "I'd trade the Pro Bowl for the Super Bowl any day, you know," he said, and flashed his trademark grin. Then he seemed to get serious. "We had some adversity this year, as many teams do, and we just couldn't seem to rebound from it. Personal and otherwise."

My heart stopped.

The reporter smiled. One crook of a pretty finger, one smile or a wink, and Luke's brain shut down. If the NFL let good-looking women play football, he would never throw an accurate pass.

The reporter ramped up the sexy charm. "A lot of personal, it seems," she purred, and touched his arm, faking an intimacy that he always fell for. "Besides the injuries to players, Jay Jacobs' father died, Jamarcus Robbins and his wife lost a baby, and there are also rumors your wife has left you."

For Luke, that verbal jab seemed to come out of nowhere. I could see his eyes widen in surprise, but he recovered quickly. "It's no secret that professional football can take a toll on family. But not on mine. Football has been my dream come true. That's why it was important that my wife have the time to make her own dream happen. She's happy; I'm happy. That's all that matters." He pulled back from the reporter and gave a big smile and a thumbs-up to the camera. "Next year, man, next year." And then: "Keep the light on for me, honey."

He was good. I had to give him that.

But what a liar.

LATE OCTOBER 1941

Shemuel hated to leave the warmth and comfort of Mrs. Handorf's farm kitchen, but the autumn sky had darkened and there was still the horse to feed, water, and bed down for the night. He scraped his plate clean with a slice of bread, capturing every last bit of the tangy gravy. He downed his third glass of cold milk.

"I've got sauerbraten for you to take to your poor mother, too, Shemuel," Mrs. Handorf said, indicating the small bowl covered with a round of waxed paper secured with string. A few slices of bread rested on top. "You bring the bowl back, I give you some more."

He could eat that bowl and all the bread, too. The taller he got, the hungrier he became.

If it weren't for the kindness of the women he visited on his after-school rounds, they wouldn't eat, Shemuel knew.

Ever since his father dropped dead and was brought home doubled up in the small cart, his mother faded more every day.

Shemuel didn't understand. His father had cursed at her, demanding hot food or drink at any hour. She had spent her days almost tethered to the stove.

Now that Shemuel was seventeen, and a man, his mother didn't have to worry about that. He knew he could make a better life for them. Shemuel brought *her* food.

But day after day, his mother sat near the stove in the one-window lean-to, feeding the fire with chunks of coal that Shemuel collected every morning. She left the room only to use the outhouse or dump the coal clinkers that could burn no more.

She forgot to eat. She forgot to bathe. And when she was too tired to sit anymore, she took to her pallet bed in the corner of the dim room. But always, she kept the little stove going.

Maybe Mrs. Handorf's stew would cheer her up.

Mishka, the horse, nibbled on the scant grass around Mrs. Handorf's elegant old iron fence that had once fronted the towpath of the canal. The path was just wide enough now for the horse and cart. The canal bed was full of weeds and stagnant water. Shemuel scanned the shallow depths for anything to salvage, but he could see nothing in the gloom.

He secured the old copper boiler, the roll of chicken wire, and the tin vents from the roof of Mrs. Handorf's old barn in the bed of the cart. When he finally snapped the reins to move Mishka forward, his thoughts were on the money he would get from the copper. Even the snips of pipe in his pocket. If there was one thing he had learned from his father, it was that nothing goes to waste.

Soon the dirt road joined the brick street leading past the mattress factory. The massive old brick buildings on either side created a wind tunnel, and Shemuel had to take one hand off the reins to keep his cap from flying off.

Suddenly, he smelled something burning.

Lockton was not the place to go for fresh air, he well knew, as there was always something carried by the wind—coal smoke, paper mill exhaust, horse droppings, the fetid aroma of the canal. On a good day, the breeze would blow the clean smell of freshly cut wood from the lumber mill.

But this was different. When he guided Mishka onto the main street, he saw a reddish-orange glow in the sky a few blocks away. Sparks flew high in the air above a billowing cloud of smoke.

Just as he and Mishka plodded past the fire station, the siren sounded. The horse, startled, reared up, and it was all Shemuel could do to get him back under control. The fire truck roared by, bells clanging.

Toward the salvage yard.

And his mother.

With furious snaps of the reins, Shemuel whipped Mishka to life again and the cart careened down the street.

Shemuel brought Mishka to a hard stop near the salvage yard. Between the houses, he could see that the yard was filled with people in a bucket brigade trying to put out the fire. He dropped the reins, jumped down from the cart, and started to run.

Later, when he tried to piece together the events of the night, this part was a blank.

The next thing he knew, he was sitting on an overturned bucket with a horse blanket draped over his shoulders. He raised a tin cup to his face and it smelled like bourbon. *He* smelled like bourbon and the odorous canal water they had pumped to fight the blaze.

From the blackened, steaming ruins, he watched the firemen bring out a stretcher and what he assumed was his mother. They looked over at him grimly, shaking their heads. Doc Cunningham quickly examined what was left of the body, then covered it with a blanket.

"She should not have been left alone like that," Shemuel heard the doctor pronounce. "She was not in her right mind."

Shemuel's cup clattered to the pavement.

"That's a hebe for you," a firefighter muttered. "They only think about money."

Money . . . money . . . money . . . The word landed repeated blows where Shemuel least expected them.

When the yard finally emptied at dawn, Shemuel ached all over. He had mud on his boots. How had that gotten there? The smell of wet ash clung to his damp clothes. He shivered.

He made himself get up, shake off the filthy blanket, and walk to the burned-out ruins. He picked his way around the blackened debris.

There was nothing and no one to save here.

But there was Mishka. He had forgotten all about Mishka.

As he turned to leave, Shemuel saw something in the corner of the room on a metal stool his father once found by the side of the road. The tiny mother-of-pearl button glowed softly, like a pale moon in a troubled sky. As he picked it up, a scorched tatter from a woman's dress floated away.

Shemuel put the button in his pocket.

Nothing goes to waste.

7

※※※

VALENTINE'S DAY

Instead of romance at the bakery, the mood was more "keep calm and carry on."

While other people—especially our brides-to-be—probably had bubble baths, romantic dinners, and champagne sipping on their to-do lists today, everyone at Rainbow Cake was just trying to get through the afternoon.

Norb had his usual long-suffering air about him. He told me he would stop on the way home to pick up a heart-shaped box of chocolates and grocery-store flowers for Bonnie and be rewarded with a frozen dinner zapped in the microwave.

True love.

But the rest of us weren't faring too well, either.

Jett had come in early, deep circles under her eyes. Judging from what she was wearing, she chose her mismatched and wrinkled outfit from clothes scattered all over her bedroom floor. Good thing nobody would see her working in the back.

"Do you want a latte or some tea or something?" I asked her, trying to keep the worry out of my voice.

She closed her eyes tight, pressed her lips together, and exhaled heavily through her nose, as if I was getting on her last nerve. Then she collected herself. "I'm kinda off caffeine right now. I'll stick to water," she said, and then mumbled, "Thank you."

I handed her the little cellophane bag with a heart-shaped sugar cookie in pink icing. "Edible valentine."

She gave me a weak smile and trudged to the workroom.

As for me, I was just glad to be busy. Saturdays had been generally crazy for us, with lots of brides-to-be and their friends or moms dropping in. But this one literally took the cake.

We had fifty-seven special orders that customers were picking up throughout the day. Most of those were already packaged, but I had four more rainbow cakes to assemble.

With an assembly-line strategy, I could have them ready before we opened in an hour.

Norb was busy baking the breakfast cupcakes. I had made extra tubs of various buttercream flavors and baked plenty of heart-shaped cookies, but it turned out that our signature Rainbow Cake was the number-one seller this weekend.

After a double shot from the old Marzocco and an extra spoonful of sugar in my latte—the milk tasted nasty again, although Norb said it was fine—I put my earbuds in and cranked up my iPod to get in the mood.

I chuckled to myself as the IZ ukulele version of "Somewhere Over the Rainbow" played. How appropriate.

I hoisted one plastic tub of the robin's-egg blue buttercream up on the counter and set my cake-decorating turntable right in front of me. When doing cakes, even small ones, it was all about making the most of every movement. I shingled rounds of each flavored and colored cake layer down the stainless steel counter to the left of me and an empty tray to my immediate left.

In their turn, I spread each cake layer with the buttercream—lavender cake on the bottom, then coral, lime green, lemon yellow, and raspberry pink—and stacked one on top of another. Then I frosted the top and sides. I still wasn't sure why rainbow cake with sky-blue frosting made me happy just to look at it, but it did. Judging from our orders, a lot of other people felt the same way.

Maybe rainbow cake signified our yearning for a pot of gold in deficient parts of our lives. Physical? Yes. Financial? Yes. Emotional? Hell, yes. And I was just getting started. Maybe my own personal rainbow cake needed a few extra layers.

I was making great time, so I refueled with another latte, triple sugar this time, and then went back to the rainbow rhythm.

Maggie came in at seven thirty. My mom had volunteered to keep Emily for the day, so it was all working out.

We hardly had time to talk until the Professor came in with a bouquet of red carnations. Not anybody's favorite flower, exactly, but the thought was nice.

Before he ordered his latte and breakfast cupcake, he held the bouquet out to Maggie. I wished I had a photo of the look on her face.

"You are always so sweet to me when I come in here every morning," he said shyly.

Sweet? I wouldn't exactly say that.

Maggie found her manners just in time. "Well, you're sweet to give me these. They smell so good. Sort of spicy. Thank you."

He cleared his throat and stammered out his order. We all knew it by heart.

"Why don't you try something new this morning? Our treat," Maggie coaxed. "These orange-glazed cinnamon rolls are to die for, and I mean that sincerely. Want to try one?"

Maggie sweet-talking the Professor? I wondered whether there was a full moon tonight, too.

By late morning, most of the special orders had been picked up. And I refueled for the umpteenth time at the trusty Marzocco.

A florist's truck double-parked in front of the bakery, and out from the back of the truck came a huge box for somebody. I sighed. Gone were the days.

"Claire Davis?" the delivery guy called out.

"I'll take it," said Maggie, coming from behind the counter to grab the box and shoo him out. "And I'll see that she gets them."

It was a good try, but I was right behind her. With a wry and understanding smile, she handed me the long white box tied with red ribbon, and I retreated to the workroom, where Jett had her back turned to me at the stainless steel worktable, oblivious. She wasn't swaying and humming to her usual dark, creepy music, but rather sat quietly on a stool, sculpting sugar jonquils in a pale yellow and green. It looked like a mini spring meadow around her. I could swear I heard a little Pachelbel's *Canon* escaping through her earbuds. Jett continued to surprise me.

Her black eye, fading this past week to a yellowish green, had almost disappeared—and was expertly concealed by her usual Goth garishness. She still refused to go into any detail about the night she was attacked; I would try to talk with her later this afternoon.

But I had to get through the day myself.

I put the box on the marble-topped area where we do our chocolate work. It must have been the lattes making my fingers shake a little bit.

The long-stemmed roses in the pale pink I loved best brought tears to my eyes. The card said, "I'm still yours if you'll have me. Be mine again."

That old feeling came rushing back, even though I tried to fight it. I felt myself flush with pleasure. It was almost as if Luke were standing right here, willing me, in that intense way he had, to surrender and let myself be carried back to him on a wave of longing. It had happened before.

We had always had some distance built in to our relationship. In college, we would break up, get back together. Break up, get back together. He was the risk taker; I wanted a surer thing. When Luke left for an uncertain career in the NFL, I went to pastry school and then worked in artisanal bakeries and high-style patisseries, honing my craft.

During the times we could be together, he focused on me, learning my playbook with the same intensity he applied to studying for a game. Luke understood I was determined to further my own career, on my own steam, even though he was soon making enough money to fund a small Third World country. I guessed my mother's helplessness had affected me more than I was willing to admit at the time.

And so, when Luke finally proposed, he bought me the simple

diamond solitaire I had admired in a shop window weeks before. "The jeweler assured me that buttercream will rinse right out," he had joked.

He knew me so well.

· He was the only one who could make me feel as if the world were right once again, and I was loved and cherished and known and he would never, ever leave. Maybe all girls whose fathers had left them needed that. If my dad had not disappeared, would I have married someone like Luke? I didn't know.

Even at a distance, Luke could read me. He could find that vulnerable spot and say the right words, do the right things, that brought me back time after time.

Time after time.

I gave the roses one last glance, then snapped the lid back on the box and quickly replaced the ribbon. Luke could read a lot of women well, I reminded myself. He was so good at this because he was so practiced. Charm came natural to him. Courtship was what he did best.

He almost had me there for a minute. And in that short span of time, my joy turned to anger once again.

Maybe Luke should have used his free time more wisely. Maybe he should have thought with his brain instead of . . . Maybe he should have loved me enough to stop.

I didn't want the roses in my bakery or in my life. They were just a reminder of what could not be. I grabbed my coat.

"I'm taking these to Mom and Aunt Helen," I called out to Maggie.

"Good plan." She handed me three Valentine cookies in their little bags and opened the door for me.

When I got to Mom's, she was snuggled up with Emily on the couch, reading a story. As I put the flowers in a vase on the dining room table, Mom told me about their day so far.

"We just got back from the antique mall, Claire, and I found an old reader we used at Mount Saint Mary's. It's pretty bad when your schoolbooks are considered antique," she sniffed. "But it was only two dollars. So I bought it to read to Emily. We didn't really have anything here, since I had to get rid of a lot of your childhood things when we lost the house."

Yet another person wasn't having a good Valentine's Day. Best not to go there.

"Well, I hope the roses and the cookies tell you that I love you and Aunt Helen and little Emily."

Emily beamed at me, but zeroed in on the cookies.

"Can we have one now, Mrs. O'Neil?" Emily asked.

"Let's read another story first—how about it?" Mom said, picking up the book again. "I loved this one, Emily, when I was a girl," she added as she patted Emily on her chubby knee. "'The Dimity Dress.'"

I was about to ask, "What's dimity?" but they settled back in, so I dashed out again before Mom could ask me any questions I'd rather not answer.

Back at the bakery, I put on my apron and looked in the mirror. I had a wedding cake tasting in a little while. I didn't look too bad for such a hectic morning. I tamed my hair and swiped a little lipstick on. And good thing, too, because when I walked out to the front, Ben was making his way to the counter.

"So you finally decided to take me up on the coffee and doughnuts?" I teased him.

"Actually, I was wondering, at this late date, if you have dinner plans tonight?"

I was shocked. We'd seen each other socially a few times in the last month or so, always in the company of other friends. And while Ben was unfailingly polite in a group setting, he wasn't exactly comfortable, either. It was clear he still hadn't forgiven me for choosing Luke. I wasn't past hoping the chill between us would someday thaw, but, under the circumstances, the last thing I was expecting from Ben was a date. Especially on the biggest date night of the year.

He held his hands up, palms toward me. "It's just dinner, Neely, not a proposal of marriage." He laughed in that deep, quiet voice that settled you right down. "I figure if we're going to live on top of each other and work the same events, we'll need to learn how to be easy with each other again. One of my restaurant clients owes me a favor and I don't have plans. So, if you also don't have plans, then let's go."

"Well, when you put it like that, how could I refuse?" I smiled wryly at him. *What a way to sweep a girl off her feet.* But then, instantly, I was ashamed to have thought it. He was just trying to be friends again. And I knew how that sweeping thing worked. When you got swept off your feet, you eventually fell.

After Ben left and the after-school crowd had thinned, I went back to the workroom to talk to Jett.

"Are you doing okay?" I asked her.

"I've got all the jonquils done for that special order, and I was debating whether to do some rosebuds because we always need those," she said.

"That's not what I meant," I said gently.

She looked at me with a matter-of-fact expression and a flat, smart-ass voice. "Everything's just peachy. My mom has an asshole boyfriend that she just dumped and she's crying at night when she doesn't think we can hear her. My little brother is useless. And I have a stalker."

My eyes widened and I gasped.

"Nothing I can't handle," she said. "It's Sean, my ex-boyfriend. The guy who gave me the black eye. He just drives around and follows me when I'm out with my friends. I tell him to get lost, he gives me the finger, and then he drives off. And does it again a few days later. Just brilliant."

"Okay, Jett. I'm giving you a deadline. If he doesn't stop this by the end of the week, you tell me. And we tell your mom and go to the police. This kind of thing only gets worse if nobody intervenes."

"It's just stupid Sean being stupid."

"It's stupid Sean being stupid, *plus*. Assaulting you, stalking you, and basically threatening to hit you again. It's got to stop."

Jett sighed. "It is pretty ass-backwards, huh. . . . Okay. We'll give it till the end of the week."

By the time we closed up at five thirty, I had been working for twelve hours. At home, I soaked in the tub until I felt somewhat human again, and scrubbed the buttercream out of my fingernails.

I also realized that I was starving.

I put on a good pair of black pants, a crisp white fitted shirt, and a ballet-style black cashmere sweater that tied in the front. I wore my hair down and put on my good diamond earrings. A little spritz of Chanel No. 5 and I was downstairs when Ben rang the doorbell.

"I hope you like this place," he said as we drove across the bridge, through the blighted areas of Lockton, over the railroad tracks, and into the gentrified air of Fairview. "The restaurant's in an old mansion. The chef trained at the French Laundry in Napa," he explained as he opened my door of the car.

"If you took me to the House of Chili right now, I'd be happy. I was so busy today I forgot to eat."

"I don't think I've ever forgotten to eat," he said, and we both laughed.

Maybe it was the Prosecco we drank to start or maybe it was that I was tired, but the evening passed in a warm and wonderful blur. It occurred to me that it was quite a novelty having the undivided attention of a good-looking man, not only for a few moments at a time, in between his noticing the other women in his orbit, but for an entire evening. Okay, make that a good-looking man with a squashed nose, a scar over his eyebrow, a few knuckles that had seen better days, and who knew what else from playing the violent sport of football. Well, none of us had gone through life without a few nicks and dents. His were just more visible.

It was certainly different from being with Luke, whose neck sometimes swiveled like a bobblehead doll, not wanting to miss anything or anybody when we were out in public.

This was just what I needed, and when I told Ben that, he looked pleased.

On the way home in the car, I fell asleep.

Ben put his arm around me to help me up the steps and in the door. I was so tired, I fell against his chest and just leaned into him, resting my head under his chin. I could hear the steady beating of his heart. His big, big heart. He held me for I didn't know how long.

"I've got to go, Neely," he said, clearing his throat, "and you need some sleep. Do you want me to help you upstairs?"

The thought of that was strangely tempting. But I waved him toward the door.

"I'm fine," I said with the last bit of energy I had left.

It was a lie. I wasn't fine yet. But an evening in Ben's company had given me hope that I might soon be.

EARLY DECEMBER 1941

It was just getting dark when Olive let herself in the front door, bringing a box of day-old cloverleaf rolls and chocolate éclairs from her workday at Oster's. She could smell the turkey vegetable soup simmering for the fourth night in a row, and it didn't make her mouth water. The sweetness of the vegetables had long been gone from the broth, leaving the strong, lingering taste of old turkey bones, which had given all that they had to give.

At least we'll have something halfway decent, she thought. Even day old bakery goods were better than tired soup.

She set the white box and her crocodile-patterned pocketbook on the little hall table before she hung up her coat in the closet. From the hook on the back of the door, she carefully removed her mother's old gray sweater, hand knit so many years ago, now lumpy and boxy. One of the buttons was missing and the sleeves were hopelessly pilled. There were spots where moth holes had been repaired, some more expertly than others. Olive put the sweater on and hugged it to her, shivering. She was glad to be home, but it was not as warm here as it was in the bakery. With their father and their mother both gone now, the sisters' budget didn't stretch to coal fires on a regular basis.

Edie had the radio on again, turned up loud so she could hear it back in the kitchen. It was that stupid Singing Lady show. Edie was too old to listen to fairy tales, even this creepy one about the girl who couldn't stop dancing in her red shoes.

Ah yes, the shoe.

Olive took a folded-up rag from the cleaning bucket in the closet. She spread the rag on the floor, then opened the front door again to retrieve the muddy shoe that had been left on their front stoop.

Then Olive turned the radio off and waited.

In the sudden quiet, Olive heard Edie's footsteps patter from the kitchen, through the middle room, and into the entry hall.

Olive looked her sister up and down. She gestured to Edie, then to herself. Olive snorted. "Look at us. Just look at us."

Edie had their mother's faded yellow gingham apron tied around her thin waist. The leaf-patterned dress with the big shoulder pads and their father's old cardigan hung on her, Olive suddenly noticed. Edie wore a pair of their father's old brown trousers underneath the dress, the cuffs rolled up.

Without a word, Edie shuffled past Olive and bolted the front door.

"We're beginning to *look* like orphans," Olive said. "And I guess we're not expecting company this evening, since you've got us padlocked in again."

Edie stared blankly at her sister.

"What is it with you lately?" Olive grumbled, grabbing her things from the hall table. "Ever since you got home late the night of the fire at the ragman's, you haven't been the same. It's a terrible thing, and nobody knows better than us what it's like to lose your mother, but you didn't even know her."

Edie looked at her blankly.

"Shemuel's *mother.*"

Edie shook her head and turned back to the kitchen.

"Wait a minute," commanded Olive. "Your boyfriend left you a present."

Edie stopped and pivoted toward her sister again, her face expressionless.

"Shemuel is not my boyfriend, Olive, and you know that."

Olive sighed. "I don't know that. But what I do know is that it's going to be a long, boring evening again if you keep acting like this. I can't take much more of this crap, Edie. I can't do everything. All you do is sit at home here and wring your hands. I miss Mama, too, but we have to get on with it."

Edie looked so forlorn that Olive felt an unaccustomed stab of guilt.

"Are you sick? Do you need to see the doctor?"

Edie shook her head no.

"Is something else wrong?"

No again.

"Well, I can't do anything about it if I don't know what in hell it is," Olive said, her temper rising.

Edie turned to go back to the kitchen.

"Wait a minute. You haven't seen what your boyfriend left for you. Maybe that will cheer you up." Olive pointed her toe at the muddy shoe.

Edie's eyes widened and she stepped away.

"Well, isn't it yours? It sure looks like yours."

Edie didn't answer. She stared at the shoe.

"Well, it's not like we've got a closetful of shoes and we can't keep track of them all. Doesn't the red shoe belong to you? Edie?"

Edie nodded weakly, still backing away. "How did it get here?" Edie whispered.

"Somebody left it, I guess," replied Olive. "Maybe you were like that girl in the Singing Lady story. You danced your shoe right off."

Edie didn't smile.

"He found my shoe."

"Shemuel did?" Olive asked.

"No, not Shemuel."

"Well, who, then?"

"I don't know," Edie said.

"Well, if you don't know him, how does he know you live here?"

Edie looked alarmed.

Olive sighed and picked up the shoe. "Maybe we can clean this up," she said, turning the shoe to inspect it more closely. Bits of caked mud fell to the floor.

A faint stink of creek water rose in the air. Edie clutched her midsection as if her stomach hurt.

"Get rid of that," Edie groaned. She put her hand to her mouth, ran into the bathroom, and shut the door. Olive heard her sister retching.

8

"We have to do something." I overheard Mrs. Amici talking to her daughter as they pushed a cart with one errant wheel through Valu-Save.

Normally, I didn't like to shop here, but Valu-Save had my nighttime herbal tea on sale this week. My plan was to get what I needed and hurry back to the bakery before we had another busy stretch. I tried to stay well to the right of the Amici women in the coffee and tea aisle, but their loud complaints carried.

"Here we go again," muttered Diane, as she grabbed a plastic container of Brand-Nu coffee. "Why does everything in this damn store have a dumb-ass name?"

Grocery shopping with Mrs. Amici wasn't likely to bring out the best in anyone. Diane looked exasperated, and they were only halfway through the store.

I hadn't seen Diane Amici in quite a while. Her frizzy hair had now gone almost completely gray. The ends were a metallic purple-red, like you get from cheap hair dye. Her tired lavender sweatshirt was the wrong color for her sallow complexion, and it looked like she had spilled oatmeal or something on the front and didn't realize—or didn't care—that it was there. The sweatpants bagged at the knees. She and Aunt Helen were about the same age. Helen was no fashionista, but at least she didn't go out in public like that.

"We have to do what, Mom?"

"Don't you ever listen to me, Diane? Get it back. It's about the only thing you and Bobby can expect, besides my old, fallin'-down house."

"What are you talking about?"

"Oh, for hell's sake, Diane." Mrs. Amici glared at me as I tried to maneuver past them.

I turned the corner and cruised the canned soups and vegetables and then the peanut butter and jelly aisles; nothing I needed there. On to the pharmacy section.

As luck would have it, they stopped there, too.

"Wait here for a minute, Diane. I've got to sit down." Mrs. Amici sank into a chair next to the pharmacy pickup window at the back of the store. She closed her eyes and breathed deeply.

"You all right, Mom?"

"It's just upsetting to an old woman like me," Mrs. Amici whimpered, doing one of her lightning-fast turnarounds, from junkyard dog to teacup poodle. "Especially since I don't really have anyone."

Oh no, I thought. I looked around for a way to avoid their drama, but the "digestion" aisle was next to them, and I really needed those acid reflux tablets.

"What do you mean, Mom?" Diane asked with an edge to her voice, and then caught herself. I could tell she had immediately regretted being drawn in like that. Besides practiced surliness, button-pushing seemed to be Mrs. Amici's other special talent.

"You and Bobby together couldn't pour piss out of a boot," Mrs. Amici said, shaking her head. "Neither one of you can hold down a job. Who's going to take care of me when I get old?"

Get old? I thought uncharitably. Mrs. Amici had to be well into her eighties.

"Well, Mom, you can sell the house," Diane said, trying to placate, "or we would move in with you."

Mrs. Amici snorted. "We've already tried that a few times. Didn't work out too good, if you recall."

The old woman stood up again with the aid of the cart and they wheeled down the canned-goods aisle. "They owe us, Diane. It could make all the difference."

I ran my cart up to and then across the front of the store, quickly scanning my list to see whether there was anything else I needed to get.

Were the saltine crackers with the other snack crackers and cookies or with the soup? I could never figure out grocery store logic.

At the self-checkout, the "pomegranate" button wasn't working on the produce screen. I waited for the manager to come over with his key and cancel my transaction. Meanwhile, Mrs. Amici and Diane carted their groceries to the next checkout. Their cashier looked like a bored high school dropout in a dead-end job. From what Helen had told me, Diane could relate.

Mrs. Amici fumbled in her wallet for the money. She handed the girl a dollar bill.

The cashier rolled her eyes at the old woman. "The total comes to fifty-two dollars, ma'am."

"So?"

"You gave me a dollar." The cashier popped her gum and waved the dollar bill in front of Mrs. Amici's face. "I can't bag these up if you don't pay for them."

"Keep your shirt on," Diane said. "We're gonna pay for this stuff."

Mrs. Amici looked through her wallet again for several moments, but her eyes looked blank.

"Here, Mom, I'll do it." Diane took the wallet and handed the cashier a wad of cash. As her mother stared off in another direction, Diane pocketed the change.

They wheeled out to the parking lot as I finished bagging my groceries.

As I got into my SUV, I saw Diane settle her mother in the front seat of an old beat-up Pontiac. She put the grocery bags in the trunk and slammed it shut.

Diane got in and gripped the steering wheel, looking like she was ready to scream, and roared off.

I thought I'd drop a few things off at Mom and Aunt Helen's, hoping that I wouldn't run into Mrs. Amici and Diane once again on my way over there.

I knew where Mrs. Amici lived, but I hadn't really noticed her place for years.

The old redbrick house was a few blocks away from my mom's. It had a door to the right with a plain transom window above it and one window to the left. Three rooms down, two rooms up. Just like the other houses on her street, one of the oldest in Millcreek Valley.

There was no driveway, and the small backyard stopped at a fringe of scrub trees and tall weeds, then dropped off a few feet to the Mill Creek.

It looked run-down and deflated.

Just how I felt after listening to the two of them.

I drove past, then turned left to go to Mom's. I hung the plastic grocery bag of stick pretzels and paper towels on her front doorknob.

At the bakery, Maggie had everything ready for my afternoon wedding cake tasting. I so looked forward to these moments when I could focus on people and not on tasks.

Every bride-to-be had a story. It was like picking up a novel that you could read in an hour or so. There were the stories they told me: how they met, fell in love, how he proposed, their future plans. And then there were the stories I sensed: the fear of getting marriage wrong because their parents had, the joy of finding love after heartbreak, the yearning for a family of their own.

Love made them brave.

Maybe some of that would rub off on me eventually. As angry as I still was at Luke, I wasn't quite ready to end that chapter in my own story—or begin another one—but someday I hoped I would figure out more of the plot.

It was the pure sensory pleasure of these cake-tasting moments that could lift me and make me forget I had any troubles at all. I loved seeing the colors of the bridesmaids' dresses, the bead or embroidery details of wedding gowns. I loved the crackle of the fire in my hearth, the soft cushions to lean against, the muted sparkle of the silver coffee set.

I smiled as I gathered up the boxes of miniature cupcakes and clear cups filled with the different mousses. I already had buttercreams in my refrigerator at home. I had thirty minutes to get set up.

On the porch, I looked over the privacy fence to my plastic garbage bins. The lids were off and the bins were empty. It was not trash day.

I stood there a moment, puzzled. It didn't look like someone had gone through the trash searching for something and making a mess. It was all gone.

And then a jolt of electric worry zipped across my midsection, a feeling I usually woke up with in the middle of the night when I had dreamed about Luke or my dad.

Now I could dream about a mysterious identity thief. All that junk mail and bills and my personal info. I tried to remember what I had thrown away that week. Why didn't I have a shredder?

And there, propped up at the front door, was a large FedEx box. I got bakery deliveries at the bakery, not here. But I hadn't ordered anything. The sender's address was in New Jersey.

I would think about all of that later. I had work to do now.

I sighed as I walked into the house, and let its calming atmosphere do its work. I took the FedEx box back to the kitchen, preferring to keep it out of sight.

I placed the miniature unfrosted cupcakes on the tiered stand in the parlor, spooned dollops of the different flavored mousses on my artist's palette, brewed coffee, and made tea. I scooped a few different buttercream frostings into small china bowls.

When the doorbell rang, I was ready. I took a quick look at my mobile device again: Thomas Edgerton and Roberta Canfield. A December wedding.

They both seemed to be in their early forties.

Thomas was pleasant and plain, with sandy hair and a receding hairline, a freckled complexion, and clear frames on his glasses. Slightly plump, he was dressed in a brown sport coat, plaid shirt, and khaki pants. According to my notes, he was a self-employed accountant.

Roberta, on the other hand, was a stunning brunette, taller than her fiancé, with mahogany skin that looked like dark chocolate mousse. Were those Manolo Blahniks she was wearing? She was a marketing specialist for a Fortune 500 company.

We sat down, and I explained the tasting procedure.

Roberta looked over the little cupcakes on the tiered stand. "Don't you have carrot cake, too? I read a review online that your carrot cake was good." She was the most well-groomed person I'd ever seen, but something seemed a little off about her.

"Well, carrot cake would be great for a groom's cake, but it doesn't slice cleanly—all those little carrot and raisin pieces in it. That's why it's not usually done as a formal wedding cake," I explained. "But we can certainly include a groom's cake if you'd like."

Thomas took Roberta's hand. "Whatever makes you happy, sweetheart."

Sweet. Just sweet. My mind formed the word before it registered that I actually tasted just that. Sweet.

Okay.

That was what had made Thomas happy over the years. Anything sweet.

Now, if I could just get a taste of what Roberta was all about.

I turned to her and smiled. As I spread a little raspberry filling on two chocolate cupcakes and dabbed them with a little chocolate buttercream, I let my mind relax, hoping it would all come to me.

"We can do a really stunning chocolate cake, if you like bigger flavors," I told the couple as they sampled. "The raspberry has a little drop of rosewater in it to bring out the berryness of the fruit. Raspberry and chocolate is a classic combination."

"No, I don't want chocolate for a wedding cake," she decided, putting her half-eaten cupcake on the service plate. Thomas just nodded as he finished his.

"All right. How about this, then?" I dabbed both apricot and almond fillings on browned-butter vanilla cupcakes and smoothed on just a bit of vanilla buttercream.

She took a bite, patting her lips with her napkin. "Too much going on."

This half-eaten cupcake joined the other one. Thomas looked at the discards yearningly.

"Maybe a more seasonal touch, perhaps? Pomegranate and pistachio will be our signature flavors for December."

"Ooh, that sounds interesting. Let's taste that combination."

"If you'll excuse me for a moment, I'll be right back." I went to the kitchen and poured a little salt into a ramekin.

Roberta had a secret. A big secret. What it was, I didn't know yet.

The salty flavor I was getting from her was all about her fear of being discovered. Carrot cake had a saltier flavor from both the batter and the cream cheese frosting. I should have guessed that right away.

"I'm not sure I've got enough salt in this pistachio buttercream, so I'll just sprinkle some extra on," I said as I chose a white cupcake, spread on a rosy pomegranate mousse filling, dabbed it with the palest of pistachio-green buttercream, then sprinkled on a little salt. Of course, the buttercream didn't actually need salt. Thomas could taste that, and tried to suppress a grimace. For once, he left something on his plate.

But Roberta wolfed hers down. "I think we might have a winner," she said.

"Let's just taste a few more to be sure," I said. I hope this worked.

I offered her cupcake after cupcake, filling after filling, all kinds of buttercream, and a sprinkle of salt on each. Thomas had called it quits after the pomegranate, but she ate on.

Her voice seemed to get lower, and lower, and lower with each sample. She had had enough salt to feed her fear, and now she was letting go a little bit, getting careless.

Thomas looked at her with the beginnings of alarm.

And I got a glimpse.

Black men at a neighborhood barbershop, one getting a shave, others sitting and joking with one another in the shabby waiting area, the linoleum floor worn through in spots. A handsome teenager in the second barber chair—Roberta's brother, maybe?—kept saying, "No, I want to keep it longer on the top." He fluttered his hands to indicate volume. "I need volume."

"You're as damn fussy as a girl," one of his friends cackled.

"You don't mess with his 'do," another friend joined in.

"Can I use your bathroom?" Roberta suddenly asked, her voice gruff, and I pointed the way. She got up from the table with her handbag over her arm. "Just one more bite. I can't stop." She reached over to pluck another salty cupcake from the stand, then click-clacked her stilettos across the wood floor to the hallway bathroom.

"They've all been delicious," Thomas said. "But I think planning this wedding is making her a little nervous."

"Weddings can be stressful," I said, pouring him another cup of coffee. I smoothed filling and frosting over another chocolate cupcake, left off the salt, and passed it to him. He smiled gratefully.

I made him three more cupcakes before Roberta finally returned.

Her shoulders drooped. Her makeup was smeary. It looked as if she had been crying. She sank into the chair.

"Sweetheart, are you all right?" Thomas asked her, taking a folded handkerchief from his coat pocket and offering it to her.

I looked at Roberta, and she knew that I knew something was up. I didn't need to know her secret, but I wasn't the one who mattered.

She slumped back down in her chair. "I don't know what's come over me."

I did. The salty pistachio buttercream had fed her fear to the point that there was no hiding it anymore. But fear of what?

Thomas took her hand in his. "What's the trouble, honey? You can tell me."

"Why don't I leave you two alone for a bit," I said and stood up, but Roberta grabbed my arm and pulled me back to my seat. That woman didn't know her own strength.

"No, please stay with us for a moment," she said.

Thomas looked from her to me, concerned.

No one knew what to say next.

She reached for another salted cupcake, closed her eyes as she ate, and then sighed. She turned toward her fiancé. "You deserve the truth, Thomas. Whatever happens next, I want you to know that I love you. I love you and I want to spend the rest of my life with you, but you may not feel the same way."

"Nothing you can tell me will change the way I feel about you," he reassured her.

She looked at me, woman to woman, as if she'd heard that all before.

This was making me very uncomfortable. "Why don't I give you two some privacy?" I tried again, and started to back out of the room again.

"No, please stay." Roberta grasped my hand this time and gave it another hard squeeze. Yet she looked softer and sadder. "Please. I realize we barely know each other, Mrs. Davis. I understand we're not friends. But you seem kind, and I could use a woman here with me when I do this."

I nodded.

She turned to Thomas, who looked bewildered.

"I have become the woman I always knew I could be," she began, "the woman I have dreamed of being since I was a teenager. But it hasn't been easy. . . ." She delicately wiped away a tear with his handkerchief.

"And then I met you, and I was so happy," she sniffed. "I am happy."

Thomas squeezed her knee.

That made her cry more.

"You are the best man I have ever known, and I'm so sorry I have to do this." She opened her handbag and lined up several pill bottles. "I want to show you something, Thomas." The first brown plastic pharmacy bottle looked plain against her perfectly manicured fingers as she held it up for Thomas to see. "This is the estrogen hormone that I have to take with a progestogen," she said, then pointed to the second bottle. "And an antiandrogen," she added, pointing to the third one. "These drugs help my skin stay soft, my voice stay sweet, my figure stay rounded. And this"—she indicated the fourth bottle on the table—"helps me be less anxious about the changes I've made."

"You've already told me about your hormone therapy and your infertility," said Thomas, shaking his head. "And if you need anti-anxiety medication every once in a while, so what? You have a high-stress job. And we're planning a wedding."

"That's not what I mean," Roberta said. She took a deep breath and closed her eyes, gathering her resolve. "The reason it hasn't been easy, the reason I take all those pills, the reason that I haven't been able to be completely honest with you is . . . I started out as a man."

Whoa. The teenage boy I had thought was Roberta's brother was actually Roberta?

The color had drained from Thomas' ruddy face. His breathing became shallow, as if he were starting to panic.

"Are you sure . . ." I started to ask again, half rising from the table.

"No. Please." Roberta placed her shaking hand on my arm. I sat back down and took her hand in both of mine, giving her what I hoped was a silent message: *Be brave.*

Where Thomas had looked freckle-faced and robust, he now seemed pale and weak. He stared off into space.

I closed my eyes and felt the colors flash. The unpleasantly briny flavor was gone, much like the relief of spitting and rinsing after a saltwater gargle.

Roberta sat with her hands folded in her lap. She had faced her fear.

Now it was up to Thomas.

I cleared my mind again. Almost at once, I sensed a warm cocoon of feathery pink cotton candy. The first wisp melted on my tongue as cotton candy does. Sweet. This was Thomas.

But each successive taste became a little abrasive, more burnt and bitter, as if the sugar had cooked too long past a pleasing caramel to a dark and inedible sludge. All things sweet fed his optimism and kept bitter disappointment at bay, but this wasn't working for him anymore. Roberta had seen through the brown sport coat and plaid shirt to the kind, loving, and faithful person he was inside. She was the sweet he craved now.

But could Thomas accept that he had been intimate with a man who had become a woman?

"But you're not a man," he finally sputtered, as if he had heard my thoughts. "We've been together. I've seen your body. You are a woman. You're a beautiful woman."

She looked at him hopefully.

"How long has it been?" he asked, his voice barely a whisper.

"I should have told you in the beginning," Roberta confessed.

"No, I mean how long has it been since . . ."

"Since I became a woman? I started at one university as a male and got my degree at another as a female. Twenty years or so."

Distractedly, he reached for the sugar bowl, spooned some in his coffee, and took a sip. He scowled and placed his cup back on the saucer with a clatter.

"Damn it, Roberta." He looked at her, at all of her, with a fierce expression. "I can't do this." He rose, threw his napkin on the tea table, and walked out. We heard the door slam.

I turned to face Roberta.

"I should have told him sooner," she admitted. "I should have told him before he even kissed me—that took forever. So, if he waited a month before he kissed me, I thought I had plenty of time before, you know. And then we got serious so fast," she said dully. "And I didn't want to lose him."

I squeezed her hand.

I let myself drift for a moment and we were back at the barbershop.

Robert was sitting in the barber chair. His eyes followed another young man, who paced the waiting area, talking on a cell phone that looked as big as a space station. The young man carried a backpack heavy with books. His prominent black eyeglasses were taped in one corner. "What is this, Ranelle?" he yelled into the phone. "You don't want help with chemistry, like you said at school? You have something else going tonight?"

"I need help with chemistry," the boy who became Roberta called to him. "Forget Ranelle."

The boy gestured for everyone to be quiet so he could hear above the noise, but he lost the call. "She hung up. Damn," he muttered. He pressed several buttons, pulled up the antenna, listened in again, then shook his head in disbelief. He unzipped his backpack and jammed the cell phone in, opened the barbershop door, and stormed out.

This time, with Thomas, Roberta had come so close to letting a person she loved see her true self—but not close enough. I sat with Roberta until our coffee got cold.

"I shouldn't take up any more of your time. I know you have a business to run, and it's not psychotherapy," she said with a wry, watery smile.

"Sometimes it is." I took Roberta's card and gave her mine. I urged her to stay in touch. I genuinely wanted to know she was going to be all right.

Back at the bakery, Maggie's shock registered in her raised eyebrows. "They didn't book their wedding cake? That's a first."

"There were issues," I said vaguely.

"Here's another issue. Somebody has taken the bakery trash," she said. "Whyte's doesn't come until tomorrow. Who would want our garbage?"

"I wish someone would take mine," Jett said as she came in the door, swathed in multiple scarves over a bulky jacket. In one ear, she sported a hot-pink feather earring, in the other a silvery disco ball that swayed like a metronome when she removed her earbud. We could hear the tinny, thumping sound of the Lumineers' "Ho Hey." Surprisingly upbeat for a Goth girl.

"Ever since my mom finally kicked her drunken boyfriend out, my lazy-ass brother forgets to put out the garbage or puts it out so that the dogs get in it. White trash. That's us. But—news flash— at least we're white trash without stalker ex-boyfriends anymore. Thought you'd like to know." She filled up her coffee mug, saluted Maggie and me, and clomped back to the workroom.

"I'm on those little puffy thingies you wanted," Jett yelled from the back. We could hear her opening plastic tubs and clattering metal cake-decorating tools on the stainless steel counter.

Maggie looked at me for a translation.

"Remember that girl who brought in a vintage chenille bedspread as inspiration?" Maggie nodded. I tapped my phone and showed her the photo I had taken of a tufted white spread with a central flower outlined in a wrapped yarn stitch. "Those are the 'puffy thingies,'" I said, and I pointed to the raised designs. "Jett is making them out of royal icing. The cake will look great; you'll see."

It would all be great. Jett's problem was resolving itself. Maybe mine would, too. I just had to keep thinking that.

Otherwise I would be freaking out about that FedEx box from Barney's full of high-end perfumes, creams, and body scrubs, along with a brochure about a spa weekend in Sedona. Luke must have had the team secretary send it. No way was I going on a spa weekend with him. No way was I going anywhere with him.

I was beginning to realize that I had been under the spell of my own magical thinking. When I told myself that Luke would have been faithful if I had stayed at home, or focused on his career and not mine, I was deluding myself. Just like Thomas, Luke had made his own choice, despite what the woman in his life wanted.

It was my choice, now, to stay right where I was.

DECEMBER 8, 1941

Bundled in her father's old cardigan, Edie shivered as she pumped the treadle of the sewing machine, forcing the needle faster and faster through the thin, striped cotton of her mother's dimity petticoat. The fine embroidered muslin gown that Grace Habig had worn over it—captured forever in the wedding photo—had long ago been used to make a christening robe for a good customer's grandchild. Mama could not afford to be sentimental.

And neither, really, could Edie. When they buried their mother, she and Olive had had to grow up fast. They were still paying off their mother's funeral, a dollar a week.

Mr. Amici was kind and sometimes tucked something extra into their bag of groceries—a jar of Ovaltine, a sleeve of crackers, a can of Vienna sausages. Edie sometimes wondered whether Frankie Amici liked Olive, but he was so shy, it was hard to tell.

Edie stopped to tie off a seam with fingers stiff from the cold, and absently stroked the glass of her parents' wedding photograph propped up on the little shelf above the sewing machine. She knew every detail by heart. The damask drapery in the background. How her father was seated in an ornate wooden armchair and her mother was standing behind him, a pose to better show the simple lines of her tea-length white dress. They were not smiling. In her left hand, Mama held a tiny bouquet of lilies of the valley—"the return of happiness," Mama said they signified—picked the morning of the wedding from neighbor Mrs. Seebohm's shady front yard. Edie could just see the outline of the beautiful ring that Papa had been lucky enough to find glinting in the muck by the banks of the canal. Her father liked to tease that the universe had delivered the fiery sapphire right into his rough fingers at precisely the right moment. The ring was meant for Mama, he'd said, because she was a jewel herself.

Edie had her mother's pale coloring and lithe figure, her creativity with the needle, her love of reading. But none of this paid the bulk of the bills. It was Olive who had Mama's blunt practicality. And Olive who worked two jobs—days at Oster's and some nights at Hinky's waiting tables. If Olive didn't sass the customers, she made good tips. But that was rare.

"Why do they think they can pull that crap with me?" Olive usually complained when she got home late, slamming the door for good effect. "I tell those bozos I'll pour the next beer in their laps."

The attack that miserable night could never have happened to Olive.

Sometimes, Edie wondered whether it really did happen at all. But even Edie couldn't imagine it away.

She had been so close to home.

Since that night, she relived the attack when she fell asleep, exhausted, long after Olive had drifted off. But the man didn't wait for the dark before he frightened her anymore. She had only to shut her eyes and he appeared again in her mind. Tall. Faceless. Smelling of whiskey and creek water. Cruel. Coming out of nowhere.

Every day had become a waking nightmare. Edie startled at every sudden noise, every shadow.

She had been walking home so happy to have the money from Mrs. Ellison. The money more than made up for how long she'd had to stay at their house, how late she would get home. She remembered crossing the street from the café and walking under the aureole of lamplight, dim in the fog.

He had gotten a good look at her. He had chosen her. He could choose her again. It was only a matter of time before he saw her and followed her home.

But when Edie tried to visualize him, she couldn't. He had been hidden in the shadows, and it had all happened so fast. Edie didn't want to remember the attack, but she had flashbacks more and more often. . . . After these incidents, she combed her memory for a detail that might reveal something. She knew how tall he was, a head taller than her. He was strong. She could still smell the stink of him. She heard the rasp of his zipper, the grunting noise he made. But she didn't remember what he looked like. The color of his hair or his eyes, the shape of his face. Whether he was slender or stocky. She didn't know.

And that terrified her. He could be almost any man.

Every night, Edie startled awake, her heart pounding so loudly she thought it would surely wake Olive. Her mind played back that night like a black-and-white newsreel, with the same story over and over and over again. And each time, Edie thought she had to pay even closer attention. Maybe this time, she could slow it down. Maybe she would really see him.

Edie didn't have much to tell anybody. Olive would want facts, and Edie had very few.

Olive would be mad—and ashamed of her. Olive would say it was all Edie's fault for being so stupid, for not accepting a ride home from Mr. Ellison. For always having her head in the clouds and not paying attention. Olive would tell her to stop being a baby. To stop being scared.

"You don't look right, Edie," Olive kept saying after the night they found the red shoe on their front stoop. "You've got big circles under your eyes, and you're throwing up all the time. You should go see Doc Cunningham. You could have a stomach ulcer. There's a guy at Hinky's who says he has one, but he still gulps down that boilermaker every night when he gets off work. And then he doubles over, acts like he's dying. Stupid." Olive shook her head.

But they could afford Doc Cunningham just as much as they could afford a full load of coal. Edie shivered again.

She quickly folded the dimity she had fashioned into a nightgown and placed it in the bottom of the needlepoint sewing bag she would use for a suitcase. Her mother's wedding ring, wrapped in a twist of a fine lawn handkerchief, was safe in the side pocket that snapped closed. She didn't really want to take the ring. It belonged to her and Olive both. But she didn't have much money in the red coin purse. She should have thought of that when she paid the milkman yesterday. Olive would be okay. Olive always was.

Edie knew she had to go where he couldn't find her. One day, maybe, she could come back. One day.

One day when she remembered. Or was stronger. One day after she had slept and dreamed undisturbed. One day when she felt better.

In the kitchen, Edie stacked the dishes from the draining board on the open shelves. She swept the worn green linoleum floor. She folded and hung the embroidered towel on the handle of the gas oven.

In the middle room, she paused, memorizing the details: the tailor's dummy, the long coatrack hung with finished garments clothespinned to hangers, and the small plum-colored armchair where her father used to sit before he got sick.

That reminded her. She picked up her favorite childhood book from the little table and slipped it into her bag. The childish penciled handwriting of the girl who owned it first—Caroline Edwards—was barely legible on the yellowed front page. Olive would never miss it because she never read, if she could help it.

Maybe, like Princess Irene, Edie would someday follow the magic thread to the top of the castle and escape the goblin below.

The clock ticked each second in the silent house.

If she waited any longer, she would have to run.

Reluctantly, she changed into a dress. But it was too cold for the dress, so she put on the old cardigan, then her spring coat, and buttoned it up. It still hung loosely, even with the extra bulk. She pinned the hat with its pastel flowers to the back of her head. It was too cold for a spring coat and too late in the year for pink flowers. But her winter coat was gone.

How the man had hurt her, how she ruined her coat, how she ruined her life—it all threatened to play again. He had hurt her so bad that Edie had not had her period yet. Nobody talked about things like that, and Edie was too timid to ask. Maybe she could see a doctor somewhere else.

Edie locked the front door behind her, started to run, and almost slipped on the stone slab sidewalk in the freezing drizzle. She slowed down, careful on the wet pavement, almost skating in her shoes to Market Street, then turned for the station, looking wildly around her. She didn't see the man, but he could jump out from anywhere like he did before.

She waved her arm at the ragman's son, parked with the horse and cart at the side of the brick-paved street, taking meager shelter under the few dried leaves still left on a big sycamore.

Edie climbed into the cart next to Shemuel, and the horse began to make its way down Market Street to the train station.

Shemuel's plan was to sell the horse and cart to Mr. Steingarten. Edie stepped down from the rig and stood outside at the ticket counter. She could see over to the Steingartens' house right on the railroad tracks, a short walk from the station. Shemuel walked toward the old carriage barn in the back, waving his arms at the stout woman in her blue housedress and sturdy shoes. A gust of cold wind blew the woman's skirt and Edie saw her stockings secured in knots above fat knees.

"Young man," she heard Mrs. Steingarten reprimand. "You can't leave that horse and cart here. You'll have to come back later. Mr. Steingarten isn't home yet."

But Shemuel kept arguing with her.

It was no use. Edie knew from dealing with her Fairview ladies that Shemuel would not be paid today. He wouldn't be paid at all because he wouldn't be back.

Something else to go wrong.

She'd have to buy his ticket, too.

She reached in her purse.

"How much is two tickets for as far as this train goes?"

"Well, miss, this train goes all the way to Chattanooga with one stop at Queen City Terminal."

Edie remembered the last movie she and Olive went to see together at the Vogue. *Sun Valley Serenade*, with the Glenn Miller Orchestra playing "Chattanooga Choo Choo." That was all she knew of Chattanooga.

"Miss. Miss! One-way or round trip?" the ticket master asked impatiently, peering at her through his wire spectacles.

"One-way."

"Pullman berth for overnight? That's two-fifty extra. Each."

"No, just the tickets."

He squinted, licked his pencil, and did the math. "That will be sixteen dollars and twenty-four cents."

Edie reached into her purse. Her hands were so cold, they didn't seem to work. She pawed out the small roll of bills from the inside pocket of her bag. She should have remembered gloves.

She looked down the tracks. Mrs. Steingarten was pointing a shaming finger at Shemuel as he stomped around in her front yard.

The ticket master rolled his eyes as he separated and smoothed out each folded bill before giving her the change. "You should go inside where it's warmer," he chastised.

She blew on her reddened hands, but it helped for only a moment. She put the two tickets in the pocket of her bag.

Inside, she sat on a worn bench by the potbelly stove.

Edie closed her eyes, tried to relax her tense shoulders, willing it all away. She shook her head as if to loosen and turn the page stuck in her own story.

She kept her eye on the only door, through which that man could walk at any moment. The small room started to close in on her.

She got up, suddenly, and ran outside onto the wooden plat-form. She felt the snow beginning to fall in heavy white tufts. Edie turned her face up to the sky and let the gentle snow drift, whisper-soft, on her skin. She fought the urge to run home, get under the covers, and never leave her bed again.

She noticed the quiet, as if the whole world had stopped spin-ning and was still for a moment. Maybe Shemuel and Mrs. Stein-garten had reached some agreement.

Tufts of falling snow covered everything—the tracks, the scrubby trees up the hill on the other side, the rooftops—like a thick chenille bedspread.

But something was coming.

Edie saw the rumbling dark shape of the approaching train plowing through the snow. Its shrill whistle made her jump.

And there was Shemuel still stomping around Mrs. Steingar-ten's yard, insisting on being paid.

"I'll call the police if you don't leave this minute," Mrs. Stein-garten shouted.

But Shemuel was caught up in his own rage.

He won't make it.

Edie walked back to the ticket master. "Can I have an envelope, please?"

Rolling his eyes, he passed her a large, much-used manila envelope. "This is the only one we have. Will this do, miss?" Edie didn't catch his snide tone.

The train pulled to a stop.

With numb hands, and looking worriedly down the tracks to the Steingarten house, she put the ticket into the envelope. "This is for Shemuel Weiss. He'll be here in a moment."

On shaky legs and with hands that didn't seem to work, Edie wrapped an arm around the frozen iron railing and pulled herself up the steps of the last passenger car. She would be able to see him from there.

"The ragman's son?" the ticket master called after her. Edie heard the scorn in his tone. "Are you sure about that?"

Edie nodded yes through the train window.

She sank into the last seat. The conductor, trying to keep warm in a woolen scarf and fingerless gloves, punched her ticket. Holding on to each seat, he stiffly made his way to the front of the car, then opened and slammed the door behind him as he walked forward across the coupling to the next car. Edie felt the rush of cold air and again wondered whether she was doing the right thing.

And where was Shemuel? Could she do this by herself?

She couldn't see out. The windows started to fog up. It was eerily quiet, the snow muffling all sound. Edie felt cut off once again, so close to home, yet so alone in a place where danger could come out of nowhere. Something was about to happen; Edie just knew it.

What would Olive do? Well, for one thing, Olive wouldn't run away. Olive would stick to the facts. She would take stock.

Edie tried to calm herself by turning her bag out onto the seat and bending over to look more closely at everything she had packed. One item at a time, she tallied the two changes of undergarments, dimity nightdress, half-used jar of cold cream, comb, sweater, the old storybook, some rolled bills and loose change in her coin purse. The ring in a twist of handkerchief. Quickly, she did it all again. And again.

Why wasn't Shemuel there yet?

She looked to the front of the car and saw a man's silhouette through the grimy, fogged-up door window. It was not the short, squat conductor, but someone else. Someone tall. His profile was somehow familiar to her, and Edie gasped, her eyes wide. He turned the metal handle on the door, but it was stuck. He banged on the window, tried the handle again.

The train whistled its departure. She had only a few seconds.

She stuffed her things back into her bag and stumbled down the aisle. The door to the caboose was not locked. She let herself in, slamming the door shut behind her. She raced through the car to the very end of the train with just enough time to jump out the back as the locomotive lurched forward. She went down hard on the gravel between the tracks, but picked herself up and started to run.

The snow was coming down so hard that she could barely see a foot in front of her. She crossed to the other side of the tracks, like a ghost drifting through a dream.

She steadied herself and looked up as a vee of wild geese flying low in the heavy air pointed the way forward, up the convent hill.

Edie wove through the brush after them, toward flickering colors she could just make out—blue, then rose, then gold. She almost tripped over a downed sapling, but finally reached the circular brick driveway. She veered to the left, toward the light.

Edie's footprints disappeared in the snow almost as fast as she made them.

As she got closer, she saw that the glimmering lights came from an arched stained glass window.

Edie felt around the rough stone walls until she found the door.

In the dim interior, Edie recognized the statue of Bernadette kneeling below Our Lady of Lourdes set in a high stone alcove. Light haloed from votive candles in each deep windowsill.

Edie could see her breath. She put her carpetbag down and sat beside it on the thin padding of the long kneeler. She pulled her knees up and gathered her coat around her, trying to bury her numb hands in its folds. Maybe if she just rested a little bit . . .

There was a stillness and a quiet that came from more than the snow. Her thoughts slowed down. Her breathing became deeper, calmer. For the first time in a long time, Edie felt that maybe here she could be safe for a while. She leaned her head against the side of the kneeler, exhausted.

When Edie woke up, it was dark outside. One of the votives had gone out, but she was warmer.

More light, more warmth, her instincts told her. She took a long match from a cup and lit a pillar candle on the tiered iron stand next to her.

As the flame burst into yellow light, pulsing off the plaster

walls, she saw her father, coming home from the cotton mill, twirl-
ing her mother around, and giving her a kiss. Olive clapped her
hands and laughed. A young Edie looked up from her book. And
then the image was gone.

Edie touched another match to a candle, and this time, the
expanding light turned golden. In her pale blue housedress and
the yellow checked apron, Edie's mother rolled out pie dough in the
warm kitchen, laughing at her daughters' blackberry fingers as they
showed them to her—still stained, even after washing with Castile
soap. Olive stole a scrap of pastry when her mother wasn't looking
and ran off, daring Edie to catch her. But this faded, too, as the
match flickered out.

Edie struck a third time and, going from flame to flame, lit
every candle.

The little grotto filled with brilliant white light. The faint scent
of rose blossomed in the warming air. The robin's-egg blue of Bernadette's gown and Our Lady's cloak began to shimmer. The walls
receded as the light expanded and pushed them back.

On Edie's upturned face, the dark shadows of torment vanished
in the glow. She felt young again, innocent. She brimmed with
yearning and hope. She knew this story.

She *knew* this story.

But this was real life . . . and this wonderful moment would
disappear like the others. She dropped the match and fell to her
knees. She put her hands together in prayer.

She whispered: "I can't go back. I can't go on. I don't know
what to do."

She begged: "Please help me."

She murmured this litany, over and over and over again.

I can't go back. I can't go on. I don't know what to do.

Please help me.

When the Lady finally came in her black gown with the big white collar, her face shining in the warm light like a full moon, she gathered Edie in her ample arms as if she were a baby.

Her voice, so loving and gentle. "My child, my child . . ." She rocked Edie to her. Edie smiled and closed her eyes, sinking into the embrace.

And Edie, blissfully, forgot.

9

❦

MARCH

Lemon and Blueberry

By the time the Professor arrived, I had already been supercharged with my second double-shot latte. I stirred in the extra sugar before foaming the milk. The heart-shaped design I was going for morphed into what looked like a goose. I hoped that was not some premonition of the day ahead.

"Good morning, ladies."

"Well, it's official, Professor. Your good taste has been our inspiration for March." I gestured toward the blueberry-colored curtain that allowed the little lemon goodies on the display table to pop out in contrast. Since we'd opened in January, his default setting for a breakfast cupcake had been blueberry and lemon.

He beamed and watched as Maggie transferred a tray full of birdhouse-shaped sugar cookies into the front case. Our blueberry shirts for this month really suited her blond-haired, blue-eyed coloring. He beamed some more.

"Professor," she said, her voice warmer since he'd given her those flowers for Valentine's Day. "What can we do for you this morning?"

"Just my usual. I can't imagine starting my day any other way."

I'm not quite sure when "Professor" first slipped out, but he seemed to think we were saying it out of respect and not ridicule, which was a little more than half-true by now. The more we called him "Professor," the less professorial he behaved. And the more we liked him.

"You sit down over there and I'll bring it right over." He happily did as Maggie commanded.

I was packaging two rainbow cakes when Stephanie, my sales rep for *Queen City Weddings* magazine, showed up.

"Omigod, it's so great that Millcreek Valley has turned into this huge bridal district—I can call on all my advertisers and not move my car!" Stephanie was always perky. I'd hate to see her on three lattes.

I tried to tempt her with a blueberry-and-lemon baby cheesecake or a package of pastel blueberry-and-lemon polka dots, but she slapped one hip and then pointed one finger skyward. I guessed that was a no.

When Jett came in after her one morning class today in full Goth gear including black nail polish, I began teaching her the basics of the pastry bag. I had made up the meringue mixture already—basically egg whites beaten with hot sugar syrup until white and billowy. I folded a little almond flour in just before I filled the pastry bag.

Not as difficult as macarons, my signature polka dots sandwiched together with a flavored filling were easier for a full-service bakery to do. The more sensitive macarons required a baker's undivided attention—it was no wonder they were expensive.

A touch of color turned this batch pale yellow. I didn't flavor the meringue mixture—that was what the filling was for. The meringue just provided the form and the texture.

Jett was a quick study. She piped out the meringue in a circular motion. We didn't want perky little points that would break off when we packaged the polka dots. Perky also made me think of Stephanie, who had already buzzed off to another client.

When Jett had a whole tray of polka dots piped out, I gave her the thumbs-up. That was her cue to put in her earbuds and zone out to whatever was on her playlist today.

"Just let me know when you're finished with this batch, okay?"

She nodded, starting to move her head to the music. I could just hear a little bit of some guy's deep, spooky voice and electric guitars.

"It's 'Gothic Girl,'" she said, her head bobbing up and down.

I left her to the dark side for a while.

The polka dots went in the old double oven, set at a low temperature, for two hours or so, or until the meringues were light and crispy.

After they cooled, Jett would sandwich them together with seedless blueberry jam or lemon buttercream.

Personally, I couldn't bear thinking about lemon today. No one told you that when you ran a bakery, you could get really, really tired of flavors you seemed to taste all the time.

Later on, when I set out the cellophane packages of polka dots in our seasonal display area, I saw Mrs. Amici walking Barney for the fifth time today already. Maybe Barney had a problem.

As the little dog stopped alongside the pole of a streetlight, I couldn't help but notice Diane Amici staggering toward them with her son, Bobby. He kept trying to pull her arm and turn her back, but Diane swatted him away and bulldozed her way forward.

Until ten years ago when the bridal makeover began, Benson Street sported working men's taverns at intervals like rough-cut jack-o'-lantern teeth. There, shift workers could get a cold one after a long day making lightbulbs or roof shingles or mattresses. Most of those bars closed when the factory jobs disappeared. Or they had morphed into a more upscale sports bar, like Finnegan's across the street. But tucked around the corner was one grubby tavern— Hinky's—that still smelled of cheap beer and cigarette smoke and attracted a clientele that included Diane. Hinky's opened at ten. It was ten thirty.

And Diane looked drunk. This wasn't good.

Bobby's tattoos, inked in brilliant blues and greens down both sausagelike arms, were on display because his jean shirt had ragged, cutoff sleeves. His stubby cargo pants rode so low on his hips that just a tug from Barney could have gotten Bobby arrested, and definitely not for the first time. Bobby's black-tipped blond hair, spiked with some kind of industrial-strength gel to get the natural curl to go straight, made him look like a demented angel or an overgrown teenager. Bobby was only a couple of years younger than me. When was he going to grow up?

I edged closer to our big display window and then pulled away. I didn't want them to see me watching them. I needed to make a special retirement cake delivery to a law office in Fairview. Maybe now was the time to do that. As I went behind the counter to collect the cake box from the order shelf, I could hear Diane ranting.

"You're just an old bitch! An old, dried-up bitch!"

I whispered to Maggie to call the police. I put the cake box in a shopping bag and made my way out of the bakery to the side parking lot. I was not about to get involved, but I had to see how this would play out. Their ugliness in front of the bakery was bad for business, and I felt bad for all of them. Such an unhappy family. I locked myself in the car and hoped the police would get there soon.

Bobby started pulling Diane's arm again. "C'mon, Mom. You don't want to do this here." He kept tugging her arm. As Diane lunged drunkenly toward her mother, he pulled her back.

Diane pivoted around to face Bobby. "And you're no better, stealing from your own mother," she screamed. "You're a liar *and* a thief! I know you took my stuff."

"Me? A liar and a thief? Me?" Bobby retorted. "What about your stash, huh, Mom? If the cops came to our house, they'd arrest your crazy ass in two seconds. And then what, huh? You think you know everything. You think you're excused because you had a shit life. Well, guess what? Other people had a shit life, too!" he yelled.

Diane got right in Bobby's face and shoved him back. "You little jerk . . ." She took a wild swing at Bobby and missed. The effort left her doubled over and winded.

"Ha-ha, Mom. If you think you can take *me* down, think again."

"Bobby," Mrs. Amici started to plead. Barney barked excitably and started to jump up on Bobby. His clenched fists uncurled, and his face softened. He bent down to pet the dog, smoothing Barney's long ears with both hands. "It's okay, Barney. You're a good old dog."

Bobby stood up again. "Not now, Grandma. This is between me and her."

"You little shit," Diane growled again, staggering toward her son. "You ungrateful sonofabitch. After all I've done for you?"

"And what exactly is that?" Bobby wheeled around, agitated, waving his arms as he talked. "Being too wasted to take me to school? Bringing a different asshole home every night?"

They both stopped as suddenly as they had started.

"Diane. Bobby," Mrs. Amici pleaded, "don't do this. You two are all I have left." Barney, as if he could understand, howled.

Diane's shoulders slumped. She began to cry in big, heaving sobs, twisting her face in a bloated grimace.

The Millcreek Valley police cruiser double-parked in front of the bakery, its lights flashing. A uniformed police officer slid out of the front seat, carefully adjusting the brim of his hat.

Good, it's Daniel, I thought. He and Bobby had been in the same class. I remembered Daniel as a calm, methodical, no-nonsense guy who got along with everyone. Even Bobby, I realized.

"Hello, folks," Daniel said, walking up to Diane and Bobby with one hand on his holster.

"Aw, Daniel. We weren't doin' nothin'," whined Bobby, putting his thumbs in his belt loops.

Diane held her breath to quiet the sobs, but one sputtered out anyway.

Barney growled. Mrs. Amici tugged on his leash to pull him closer to her.

Daniel quickly sized up the situation. We all knew that neither Bobby nor Diane was any stranger to law enforcement. Drugs, disorderly conduct, domestic violence—the triple D. "Well, we got a call about disturbing the peace," replied Daniel in slow, measured tones. "If you folks just move along right now, we can all forget about this."

"Yes, Officer," Mrs. Amici said meekly. She pulled Barney away and slowly hobbled down toward the bridge and her home. Barney turned to look back and barked a few times, but the upcoming fire hydrant soon took his mind off the unpleasant encounter. He was back in the moment.

Diane and Bobby walked the other way, toward Millcreek Valley Road, not speaking.

In another thirty minutes, I was back at the bakery after delivering the cake.

"A tempest in a teapot," said Maggie, smiling. "Thank goodness."

Still, I would have to find a way to keep Diane away from Rainbow Cake in the future.

"Good-bye, ladies. I will see you tomorrow," said the Professor. He folded up his laptop and waved on his way out. He had stayed later than usual today, and I couldn't help but think it had to do with Maggie.

She remained up front to check our e-mail. I went back to the workroom to see how Jett was getting on.

Totally into her music, her whole body swayed as she moved the piping bag around, one little mound of meringue after another.

I needed to make more lemon buttercream, but I couldn't bear the thought. When Jett was finished piping, I thought I'd teach her the secrets of buttercream, too. She already had a box full of dark blueberries she had fashioned from marzipan; another of tiny, sparkly sugar-paste lemons; and a third of green-tinted white-chocolate leaves. We were good for March's signature cake decorations.

I walked from the workroom up to the front of the bakery and did a quick visual inventory of the blueberry-and-lemon-colored paper plates and napkins on our display. Almost time to restock.

I heard Maggie's cell phone, then a few moments later her frenzied "Shit, shit, shit!"

"What's wrong?"

Maggie pulled on her jacket and yanked her purse from the cabinet under the cash register. She brushed past me and flung open the door. "Kathy Ervin saw Emily walking home from preschool by herself! Down that steep hill! She's four years old! Her goddamn father was supposed to pick her up."

"Stop, Maggie." I ran after her. "You didn't drive today, remember? I'll have to drive."

"You can't. Who will watch the bakery?"

"Jett."

I ran back in to the workroom and grabbed Jett by the shoulder. She screamed, dropped the piping bag, and looked at me like I was about to hit her.

"It's okay, it's okay." I tried to calm her, holding up my hands as she pulled out her earbuds. I explained what was going on. "We'll clean that up later," I told her, pointing to the mess on the floor.

By the time I grabbed my keys and ran out to my car, I was just in time to see Maggie climbing into the passenger seat of a strange silver SUV and roaring off.

I stopped in my tracks and threw my head back. What a day. And people thought a bakery was all sweetness and light.

There was nothing to do now but text Maggie and hope for the best. So I sat down on the bench in front of Rainbow Cake to await her reply. At the twelve-minute mark, the silver SUV pulled back into the side parking lot, going a lot slower this time.

"No, you have to come in," I heard Maggie say to the driver. "At least for a few minutes. Please?" The driver must have agreed, because

Maggie nodded and went to unbuckle Emily from the backseat. As mother and daughter walked toward me, I could see that Maggie's face was a study in conflicted emotions: relief, anger, frustration, love.

"Hot chocolates all around?" I asked as I opened the door of the bakery for them. Maggie lifted the booster seat down from above the coatrack and sat Emily in a chair so she could reach the top of the table.

"Oh, can I, Mommy?" Emily piped up in her sweet little voice.

"Okay, honey." Maggie turned to me. "How about Irish coffee for the grown-ups?" she asked drily.

"We've got the coffee, but not the Irish." I smiled back at her.

"Better make it decaf, then. My heart has gotten enough of a workout today."

While I was making Emily's drink, the Professor popped back in.

Just great, I thought. This will put the cherry on top of Maggie's day.

"There you are!" she exclaimed.

He looked flustered and slightly embarrassed, but the added color in his face made him look a little younger.

Maggie pivoted toward me, gesturing at him. She said, brightly, as if she couldn't quite believe it herself, "The Professor here just saved the day."

"That was your silver SUV? I thought you drove a Prius."

"It's a courtesy car—my other car is in the shop today. I was having a helluva time trying to turn on the darn radio and then I saw Maggie run out," he said. "I guess I was just in the right place at the right time."

We all beamed at him, like three spotlights searching and then finding something in a darkened sky.

Did my dad ever save the day for me? I wondered. *For anyone?*

"Anything to meet Little Miss Emily," the Professor added, making a courtly bow to her.

Emily looked up at him with her big blue eyes—so like her mother's—and giggled.

Maggie sat with her arm around her daughter while I brought a tray with mugs of steaming hot chocolate, each one topped with tiny marshmallows.

Emily stirred her marshmallows and watched as they melted into sweet white goo. "Look, Neely," she squealed. "A goose!"

DECEMBER 8, 1941

The train lurched forward. With a sudden click, the handle finally moved and the frosted glass door swung open.

Caught in the no-man's-land of the train coupling, Shemuel followed the momentum of the door and leapt into the last passenger car. The door slammed shut behind him.

Edie had to be here.

He walked down the wood-floored aisle, holding on to each row of upholstered seats, looking to the left, to the right, just to be sure.

She wasn't there.

But he could see where she had been.

A ticket to Chattanooga, already punched, caught in the crease between a cushion and a seat back. Something wrapped in a twist of embroidered handkerchief on the floor.

The door to the passenger car opened again. "Ticket, please," the conductor asked wearily, trudging back to Shemuel.

Shemuel sat down and quickly put the small bundle in his breast pocket. He handed the ticket to the man.

"I don't remember punching your ticket," the conductor said, looking at Shemuel with narrowed eyes. "And where is the girl who was here before?"

"I don't know."

"We're not in the business of giving free rides, you know," he said, eyeing Shemuel's shabby clothing and worn boots.

"I'm not in the business of taking them," Shemuel replied with a flare of anger.

"We'll see what the police at Queen City Terminal have to say about that," he said, turning to limp heavily back the way he came.

When the conductor was gone, Shemuel cried out in frustration. He jumped out of his seat, pacing back and forth in the empty car, trying to make sense of the nightmare that had become his life. He thought Edie was his friend, but she had left him, too. He had no money. Everything he thought he could count on was gone. And now he was in more trouble. At seventeen, he could be sent to a juvenile home or an asylum, and he'd heard stories of what happened to boys who went there.

He wasn't going on to Chattanooga; that much he knew.

When he calmed down enough to sit, he remembered the handkerchief in his breast pocket, rolled up and twisted on the ends. He fingered the fine white lawn, embroidered with tiny daisies. It was older fabric. Washed and starched and ironed countless times, maybe by Mrs. Habig, who had always been kind to him. He held the little bundle to his nose and sniffed. It still smelled like laundry hanging outside on the line—fresh air and sunlight and cotton— and something else. Lilies of the valley. Mrs. Habig. Edie.

There was some kind of jewelry inside; he felt the hard lines of the metal. But when he finally unrolled it, the ring took his breath away. He had never seen anything so beautiful—the dark blue stone, the pearls, and the fine workmanship. How did Edie have a ring like this? He had never seen her mother wear anything but a thin gold band.

Even more important, what was *he* going to do with a ring like this? If the police met the train in Queen City and found him with it, he'd be arrested first, questions asked later, if Lockton police were anything to go by.

He couldn't let that happen.

Before the train came to a full stop at Queen City Terminal, Shemuel jumped off onto the platform and ran a few steps into the crowd, as though he were in a big hurry to catch another train. But he needn't have worried. No one looked his way.

He straightened, then walked to one of the cast-iron structural pillars and found a foothold. He climbed up so that he looked over a banner strung between two pillars. Partially hidden, he felt safer. He watched the other passengers disembarking. Maybe Edie was up in the front engine car, for some reason, or in the caboose, the private quarters for the train crew. Maybe it wasn't too late.

The big station clock ticked off fifteen minutes, and more passengers got on. The whistle blew, and the train headed south on its way to Tennessee. No Edie. No police.

He climbed down from his perch and walked with his chin tipped into his chest. His situation must be written all over him— a poor kid getting into trouble and running away. But nobody gave him a second glance. He walked from one end of the terminal to the other, trying to figure out what to do next. There was so much commotion, so many people, that it was hard to think.

Maybe he could ask someone. But ask somewhat *what*? Shemuel looked up and noticed the newsboys on each side of the tracks. People were practically tearing papers from the stacks, throwing their coins onto the pavement.

He felt like he was drowning in noise—the shrill train whistles, the huffing and puffing of steam engines, the echoes of passengers that reverberated through the high dome of the terminal. Suddenly, it all seemed to part like the Red Sea for Moses.

A woman was wailing. For a moment, he froze. She sounded like his mother.

"Johnny!" the woman cried, and then whimpered. "My boy! My boy . . ."

He walked quickly toward the sound. Closer and closer.

When he found her, she had fallen to her knees with the front page of the *Queen City Star* clutched in one gloved hand. Her plum hat with the bronze feather trim had been knocked askew. She seemed to shrink inside her well-cut wool coat, her private grief now made very public.

A man in a gray tweed overcoat and a fedora tried to raise her up by one arm, while another man stepped in to lift her other elbow.

"Now, Marjorie, just calm down. It will be all right. John can take care of himself," the man in the overcoat said, but he looked anything but calm.

The two men guided her, sensible black heels shuffling, over to a bench where she collapsed to her seat, then started to keel over again. The man in the overcoat sat down hard beside her, catching her fall with his shoulder before he put his arm around her, and she leaned against his neck, almost knocking her hat completely off.

"Johnny!" she wailed again.

"Where's a radio?" the husband suddenly asked in a loud, strained voice, looking around. "It's about our son. We have to know. . . ."

"The coffee shop," someone yelled.

But the couple didn't move from the bench. She began to sob and he distractedly reached into his breast pocket for a handkerchief.

"I'll go." Shemuel ran, looking for signs to the coffee shop, just off the grand hallway.

"What's going on?" he asked one of the people crowded around the soda fountain counter, six or seven deep.

"He's speaking at twelve thirty."

"Who's speaking?"

"Shhh. It's coming on."

"Louder!" someone yelled, and the radio blared out from somewhere along the back wall of the counter.

"We interrupt this program for a special news bulletin," the announcer intoned in his sharp, dramatic style. "We take you now to Washington, DC, where President Roosevelt will be speaking to a joint session of Congress."

The static in the background lasted for a few seconds, and then they heard papers shuffle.

The president began by addressing the Speaker of the House and members of Congress.

Then his cultured voice:

"December seventh, 1941," he said, "a date which will live in infamy—the United States of America was suddenly and deliberately attacked by the naval and air forces of the Empire of Japan. . . ."

For several minutes, as the president spoke, no one moved in the coffee shop.

When they heard "state of war," several in the crowd gasped.

Abruptly, the speech came to an end, and the announcer resumed.

"That was President Franklin Delano Roosevelt, speaking to an emergency joint session of Congress after the Japanese attack on Pearl Harbor, Hawaii, yesterday morning. We will bring you more information as it comes in. And now back to our regular programming."

There was a scratchy pause, the static of the broadcast at high volume. No one moved.

The local announcer smoothly continued, "Back at the WLW studios, we're going straight to the top of the charts. The first movement of Tchaikovsky's *Piano Concerto in B-Flat Minor* with that big band swing in 'Tonight We Love' from Freddy Martin and His Orchestra."

As if nothing had happened, Shemuel thought, backing away.

Should he go back to the wailing woman and her husband? They already knew it was bad for their son. If anyone asked, they might recall the tall kid who ran to get the news.

He couldn't afford that.

He ran out of the station. Once again, he checked the inside breast pocket of his jacket. He couldn't be absolutely sure the silk lining didn't have a hole, as his trouser pockets had. But the ring was still there.

There was only one person who could help him now.

10

Sleep? Who needed it?

I was on a voyage of discovery. You'd never know the surprising places that were open at four a.m. if you were slumbering away like normal people. Who knew you could get a gallon of milk at the twenty-four-hour Valu-Save, drive through White Castle for cheeseburgers, or fill up at the gas station at the intersection of Millcreek Valley Road and Benson Street?

Or visit Mount Saint Mary's memory care wing.

That was a very unlikely place, I had to admit. But I was restless and didn't want to go into work just yet, even though Norb would already be there.

If you were a family member who knew the security codes of the entrance and the memory care wing, you could visit at any time, even now. I wouldn't go in and disturb Gran, but just being near her, knowing she was close by and still there, was comforting. In her lucid moments, she understood better than anyone else the turmoil in my life—and not only the fact that her son, my father, had been missing for years.

She knew firsthand the baggage that went along with being able to "read" people. How sometimes you wished to hell that you could get rid of a bad flavor that lingered. When good flavors went bad, it meant that something was also turning negative for someone connected to you. So you suffered, too, without really knowing why.

Before Dad left, Gran told me she kept tasting something dull and muddy like yesterday's cold coffee. And we all knew how that situation turned out.

I was fairly sure that the corrosive flavor I kept tasting didn't come from Maggie, Jett, or anyone I saw at the bakery. I was even more certain it didn't come from my family.

I didn't think it was reaching me from Luke, either. To my mind, *he* didn't have anything to be angry about. After all, he had been the one who was caught, literally, with his pants down. And I had given him fair warning the last time that if it happened again, even one more time, I would leave.

It happened.

I left.

End of story.

Okay, so maybe I didn't take his calls or answer texts or e-mails or respond to the flowers or perfume or anything else he had sent. I had told him I wouldn't until I had decided what I wanted to do about our relationship. For the moment, he didn't exist for me—and believe me, he understood why. For all his attempts to break through my vow of silence, I found it tough to believe he was doing

so out of ill will. It just wouldn't be very Luke-like to be so calcu-
lating.

Because one of Luke's great abilities as a quarterback had always
been to shake things off. An errant throw, a bad offensive series,
even a string of losses. He would shake this off, too. He didn't want
to feel bad for even one second longer than absolutely necessary.

This persistent, escalating, angry flavor couldn't come from
Luke.

I parked the car at Mount Saint Mary's. When I left the house,
I could still see the evening stars. Now low clouds were scudding
in, and I could smell snow.

I let my mind drift with the clouds. And then it came to me.

It must be something to do with me. The changing patterns in
the latte foam were trying to tell me something, but as usual, I was
much better at intuiting someone else's life.

Maybe stress had caused this terrible acidic taste that lingered
no matter what I tried—mouthwash, sweeteners, incessant tooth
brushing, acid reflux tablets. Better get that checked out first.

I sat in the car and quickly texted my cousin who worked at my
doctor's office. Maybe they could squeeze me in today. Maybe she
was up already. She always was a morning person. Okay, maybe
not this much of a morning person, but you never knew.

Sent.

I relaxed back into the seat again and put the mobile device
down.

I looked around. I was parked right in front of the path that
wound gently down the hill, to the right of the nursing facility
where Gran lived. The path led to Bernadette's grotto, where someone had left candles burning. Weren't they worried about fire?

If they weren't, I was. I left the warmth of the car and tiptoed down the lighted path.

The small, eight-sided chapel, built out of those old concrete bricks that were made to look like real dressed stone, had been there when Mom and Aunt Helen were in grade school here. It looked even older than that.

I had visited the grotto with Mom, sort of her trip down convent-school memory lane. It was one of the few old buildings still left.

Yellow light shimmered through the blue, rose, and gold stained glass panes in the small Gothic window.

Maybe a little divine intervention wouldn't hurt.

I opened the door to the grotto.

A statue of Our Lady of Lourdes, with a long rosary over her right arm, looked down from an alcove made of dark, rounded river stone. She had a long white veil and a gown of pale rose sprinkled with little golden stars. Her blue cloak stood out a little from her body and I could see faint colors of pink, lavender, and gold—like a sunset—in its lining.

A statue of Bernadette, the French peasant girl who first saw this apparition of Mary in 1858, knelt before her.

It was damp and chilly in the grotto, and I could see my breath. But the flowers in a vase at the statue's feet were still fresh, so it couldn't be as cold as I perceived.

A stone balustrade with a padded kneeler enclosed the tableau. Wrought-iron risers filled with white pillar candles flanked either side of the kneeler. Several white candles still flickered in their tall glass containers.

I lit a few more candles, put money in the donation basket, and watched as the candlelight softened the blue walls to the color of our bakery boxes. Maybe that was a sign.

I knelt and said a prayer for Gran, for Dad, and even for me—all the souls who were lost in different ways—and just breathed in the peace.

Before I left, I blew out all the candles, just to be safe.

When I walked back up the hill, the snow was falling in thick clumps. It covered the roof of Bernadette's grotto like lamb's wool, then slid off the candle-warmed windows in thick sheets.

Back in the car, I was amazed to see that it was six thirty already. It felt like only a few minutes had passed.

At the bakery, Norb had finished the coffee cakes and was making a batch of sugar cookie dough. Jett would roll and cut the dough into bunny shapes later this morning after her classes were done, then ice them. I would also have her make the Easter basket cupcakes—yellow cake frosted with a lime buttercream and topped with sweetened flaked coconut tinted green. She'd use a green pipe cleaner to make the basket handle, then scatter a few jelly beans on the coconut. These cupcakes had been big sellers so far, even with Easter two weeks away.

The big thing today, however, was the Whyte-Schumacher wedding. Again, I consulted my spreadsheet. Wedding cake layers—baked. Blood-orange mousse filling and the buttercream frosting—prepared. Wedding cake sugar cookies—packaged. Sugar-paste blossoms for the cake decoration—done. Silver cake stand and cake server—packed and ready to go.

All that was left on the to-do list was to take everything to the reception at the country club and assemble the cake there.

French silk ribbon in midnight blue would form a band around the bottom of each layer. The coral sugar-paste blossoms and pale green leaves would cascade down the layers in a meandering swag. Classic and chic, just like the bride.

Ben said he would help me deliver it. Norb's back was acting up again, or maybe Bonnie had had a fit about him working later than usual.

Ben's company had been hired to do security at the wedding. Even with an early-afternoon reception, one out-of-control guest could ruin a gathering like that, so the Schumachers chose to ward off the possibility. Prominent families like the Whytes and Schumachers often took similar precautions for parties and galas, Ben had told me.

Mrs. Amici and Diane came in, blinking like they had come from a cave into bright sunlight.

"Do you want takeout?" I sincerely hoped. But Diane shook her head.

They had been coming in every morning for the past two weeks, but with Diane, good behavior was only temporary. I didn't want today to be the day she fell off the wagon yet again.

"There's room over here." I motioned to Diane. She took her mother's arm and moved toward the table farthest away.

I walked over to their table, as Diane stage-whispered to Mrs. Amici, "I don't know how much more of this I can take, Mother. This stupid stakeout was a dumb-ass idea. We're not getting anywhere."

Mrs. Amici tried to give Diane a "zip your lip" look.

"What? What?" Diane flung her arms out, knocking another woman's coat off her chair.

Stakeout? What on earth were these two investigating? Our

black-market cinnamon roll operation? Our high-stakes poker games in back? "I'll raise you a sugar-paste rosebud and see you this stack of puffy thingies. . . ." Plus, I never saw two people who were more ill-equipped for surveillance work. If they had their own TV series, it could be called *Sloven and Snark*.

But that didn't mean they couldn't cause problems.

"Just a reminder that we don't want any trouble," I whispered to them. Diane narrowed her eyes and was about to snarl at me when Mrs. Amici handed her wallet to her daughter. "Get us both something."

I took their order, and then delivered two coffees with cream and two breakfast cupcakes.

Maggie rolled in a little after eight looking livid.

"You won't believe this," she cried. "They've sunk to a new low." She threw what passed for an alternative "news" tabloid on the counter with all the contempt she had in her. *The Valley Voodoo*. She leafed through to a middle page and pointed emphatically.

"Look at this!"

I read the headline: "Whyte Trash Wedding." Oh no.

My first thought was that Aunt Helen had somehow been interviewed—that was her kind of humor—so I nervously read on.

Samuel Whyte III, the grandson of Whyte Trash Hauling and Salvage founder Samuel Whyte and his late wife, Vera Cohen Whyte, will marry Ellen Schumacher in a morning ceremony at Plum Street Temple in Queen City.

The elder Whyte started the business after rising to the rank of Army sergeant in World War II.

Now the business has skipped a generation and changed its name to Whyte Industries. Whyte III, following in his grandfather's footsteps, has taken over after the arrest of his father, Samuel Whyte II, on federal charges of tax evasion last year. Although no tax fraud was found in connection with the business, several municipalities told the "industrious" Whytes, "We don't want your trash, er, hauling." Whyte lost Fairview, Riverdale, and Jamesville within the past several months. Whyte III has been quoted in the *Queen City Star* saying that there has been no business fallout, nuclear or otherwise, from his father's personal financial issues.

Can the bride save the day?

Miss Schumacher, the daughter of Steven and Rachel Goldfarb Schumacher, comes from a family of attorneys and is a partner in the firm of Loggins, McCardle, & Fulmer. She couldn't be joining the Whyte family at a better time.

Let's hope everyone will "compost" themselves at the afternoon reception, to be held at the Carriage Hill Country Club after the ceremony. Millcreek Valley's own boutique baker Neely Davis is making the cake.

"This reads like a Groupon ad." I threw the paper down on the counter.

"And it's a hell of a thing to read on your wedding day," Maggie added.

"Maybe Ellen will be too busy to see it. They don't seem like people who would read the *Voodoo*."

"Hand me that?" Diane gruffly asked, pointing to the *Voodoo* on the counter.

"Sure. It's a free paper. Take it with you if you want." *Please take it with you.*

The next time I looked up, they were gone, without incident, thank the Lord.

We got pulled back to bakery business by a group of young women who ogled and then ordered the vegan cinnamon rolls, while I manned the Marzocco to get their coffees, with soy milk, of course.

The Professor got his usual, specially delivered by Maggie, who chatted with him like an old friend.

When an appointment cancelled, I managed to nab a slot with my physician. It paid to know people.

With the breakfast rush over, I put Maggie in charge and drove to their office in Kenwood.

After the height and weight, blood pressure, and general health questions, I put on a stupid butterfly gown and waited for Dr. Bryant in the exam room.

When he came in, I gave him the shorthand of what was wrong with me, the lingering bad taste that got worse, day after day. My sleepless nights. He checked all over the inside of my mouth with a wooden tongue depressor. He listened to my heart, thumped my lungs, looked in my eyes and ears. "I can't find anything wrong,

Neely. I think you're probably just stressed and overtired, especially since you aren't sleeping. Are you working a lot?"

Well, that was an understatement.

"Are you eating right?"

Sure, I eat from all of the major food groups: bakery, five-way chili, pizza, Chinese takeout, and Mom's home cooking.

"When was the last time you went to the dentist? Have you had recent surgery? Have you hit your head on anything? Been in an accident?"

He evaluated my answers, then looked at me sternly. "You might have a mild case of dysgeusia."

"Dis-goose-iya?" That was an actual medical condition? How did he know? Yes, I probably did have a mild case of that. I was seeing imaginary geese. "'Goose' as in honk-honk?"

"No, Neely."

I wasn't sure it was strictly professional for a physician to roll his eyes at a patient.

"Dysgeusia is a disorder with the characteristics you describe, usually some kind of a foul taste in the mouth for which there is no medical explanation," Dr. Bryant told me. "It's more common in middle-aged women. But it has probably been exacerbated by the fact that you are also experiencing insomnia. Your body is trying to tell you something, Neely, so pay attention."

Besides the reminder to take a multivitamin, he gave me two prescriptions. One for sleep, another for a dietary supplement, which was supposed to help banish the sour taste brought on by stress and a compromised diet.

On the way back to the bakery to load up the cake, I picked up the prescriptions that Dr. Bryant had phoned in.

I had a hopeful thought that my sleepless nights and one-track taste would all be over soon.

When I got back, Ben was there, chatting with Maggie and drinking an espresso. Roshonda was draining the dregs of her caramel Americano.

"So what's the verdict, Neely? Rickets? Malaria? Beri-beri?" Maggie asked jokingly.

"Maybe it's all of the above," Roshonda teased. "Because I won't lie—you look pretty terrible. I think you need at least two lattes this morning. Maybe three."

Ben smiled and scanned my face with obvious concern. I must have looked tired.

I held up my prescription bag and gave it a shake. "Not to worry, friends. All I needed was a little something to help me sleep so it's not *Night of the Living Dead* around here anymore."

"Just don't take that sleeping pill now," said Maggie. "You have to call Miranda back at Carriage Hill Country Club about the Schumacher wedding."

"You know I'm ready to help," Ben said, rising and walking over to me. "Just text me when you're leaving here."

"That's great," I said, smiling, wanting to stay close to Ben. I felt better already, I realized. Whether it was the promise of sleep or the presence of Ben—or maybe a little of both—I didn't care. Then, of course, the damn phone buzzed again.

"Later, Neely." Ben nodded to me and took his coffee with him out the door.

Maggie, who took everything at face value, went back to the counter. Roshonda gave me one of those "hmmm" looks she was so good at.

And so I answered the call without looking at the display until it was too late.

A 212 area code. I heard the bluegrass music and a clear female voice singing. I had to give Luke credit for good taste in music. I love Sarah Jarosz' "Come Around." But I wasn't coming around. I was almost sure.

DECEMBER 8, 1941

It was a long way to Izzy's from Queen City Terminal in the early December dark.

Shemuel crossed part of the old canal, the water oily-black and choked with debris, past neighborhoods of brick tenements peeling paint. He sidestepped the broken furniture left out on the curb.

His thoughts outpaced his footsteps, looped back, started again. So much had happened in such a short time.

We're at war, he thought. *War.*

Yet to Shemuel, the fire was still far more real. His mother's death. Locking up the burnt-out salvage yard. Leaving Mishka and the cart behind. Losing Edie.

His old life seemed to consume him—fill him—somehow, and at the same time, it felt so long ago, so little, so gone.

The ragman's son saw the red, white, and green painted sign for the outdoor Lincoln Market on the side of a building. It was not far now.

He turned left at the corner and saw the line at the German butcher that sold fresh mettwurst and pickle loaf to department store salesladies, clutching their worn shopping bags on their way home by streetcar. In the next stall, a man stuffed a bunch of dark leafy greens into a bag for a Negro woman, still in her maid's uniform.

Across from the market and down a side street, the pickle barrel on the sidewalk told him he had arrived in front of Izzy's.

I did remember, after all, he thought.

This was where his father used to take him to buy corned beef, a distant memory of an unusual time when his father was not angry and they all ate well. A memory surfaced—Izzy reaching a meaty hand into the green brine to pull out a crisp sour dill as a treat for him, then a boy. Nine, ten years old?

He almost tripped as he crossed the brick street, the pothole hidden by a wooly covering of snow.

He opened the door and stepped into the warmth. He heard Izzy's old Victrola in the back, scratchily playing a 78. He looked around. The store was empty.

"Do you like Tchaikovsky?" asked the burly proprietor jovially, putting his apron back on as he walked to the front of the store.

The tall young man with the stooped shoulders and the face that looked like the end of the world didn't answer.

"It's my favorite. The Pathetique, especially the last movement, the Adagio lamentoso. Do you know it?"

The young man removed his cap. No.

"It's what I listen to when I think the world has gone completely *meshuggenah.* Which is a lot of the time, I have to admit."

Izzy studied the young man's face as if something about it was familiar.

"But especially today. Maybe that's the problem with people today," he said. "The war."

"The war," Shemuel tonelessly repeated.

"Come in and warm yourself and then you can tell me what you need to tell me," Izzy said, continuing to study the young face. "I always stand over the heat vent when I have cold feet."

Shemuel shuffled his frozen feet toward the rectangular grate in the wooden floor and stood over the vent.

They both looked down at Shemuel's boots with the notch cut out in the corner of the big toe.

"You are not the first man to wear those boots," Izzy observed, giving Shemuel an appraising look from his feet on up to his face. "Your feet must be freezing."

The young man nodded, almost swaying from fatigue.

Izzy's wife, Rosa, a trim dark-haired woman, was wiping her hands on her apron as she click-clacked her way on the old wooden floor toward them. "Isador," she said sternly, "the potato pancakes aren't getting any hotter." She barely raised an eyebrow at yet another surprise guest at their table tonight. "It's a good thing I have made plenty."

"First things first." Izzy clapped his stubby hands together, reached his arm up to put around the young man's shoulders, and led him back to the stairs in the storeroom.

"I think I knew your father, my son," he said. "He used to wear those boots when he worked in the garment district, right over on the next street. A hard man. Didn't get along with people. His own worst enemy. But one thing he liked? My corned beef. You will, too. It wouldn't be easy having such a man for a father," Izzy added, looking at Shemuel closely.

No more needed to be said for now. They both understood.

"A full plate of food makes everything seem better," Izzy

reassured him. "Rosa makes the best potato pancakes you've ever had, my boy—and my corned beef is so tender you can cut it with a fork. Plus, all the kraut you can eat!" he exclaimed heartily.

Shemuel attempted a smile.

"That's a joke, you know," Izzy said, and clapped him on the back. He gently pushed Shemuel toward the back of the store and up the stairway.

"Do you have any luggage, a satchel that you've left somewhere?"

Shemuel tiredly shook his head no.

"I heard all too many stories from my grandparents about getting out before the Cossacks came," Izzy said. "You stay with us tonight, and tomorrow we go to the rabbi at the Russian temple. And we will fix what needs to be fixed."

The young man's eyes widened.

"I know, I know, you're not Russian. But believe me, those stuck-up German Jews will turn their noses up at you. And that's not a pretty sight." He clapped the ragman's son on the back again. "That was a joke, too. Maybe after a full stomach, you will feel your funny bone again," he said lightly.

On the landing, Izzy started humming "Second Hand Rose."

He guided Shemuel to the left, into the dining room with windows that overlooked the street below.

"Remember that song, Rosa, my love?" he called out as she returned from the kitchen with a towel draped over one arm and three full plates of food.

"That's my Rosa." He wagged his eyebrows at her as she set the plates on the table. She made a show of rattling around in a drawer in the built-in corner cabinet for more silverware and a third napkin.

"'That's why they call her *so stuck-up Rose*,'" he sang to Rosa, and kept humming the tune.

She flicked her kitchen towel at him. "Isador Kadetz, you behave."

He made a show of kissing her hand. "You're so lucky to have me."

"So you always say," she said, finally smiling. "Now, let's sit down and eat."

11

By eleven a.m., Ben was waiting for me at the loading area of the Carriage Hill Country Club, outside the kitchen entrance in the back of the rambling structure. Built in the Tudor style with a slate roof, the club exuded an aura of old money. The open-air facilities were groomed to perfection: manicured lawns, clay tennis courts, a swimming pool, an eighteen-hole golf course. A club-wide dress code had recently been instituted to mitigate any vulgar influence of the nouveau riche, however badly these members might be needed for the club's bottom line.

Inside, a dark wood-paneled gathering area with a huge fireplace encouraged quiet and discreet conversation, while the dining room and event spaces were open and airy with French windows leading to the formal garden.

It was true that people with money didn't always display good taste, but at Carriage Hill, even the food was noteworthy. The chef had worked at Chez Panisse in Berkeley as well as several Mario Batali restaurants in New York. When she came to a special Rainbow Cake tasting in January, she loved my work, so I knew she understood what I was trying to do. She'd already ordered from Rainbow Cake several times for private events at the club.

When I texted her from the van, she sent the banquet manager wheeling a large stainless steel cart to open the double back doors for me. Ben helped me shift the large, bottom cake layer onto the cart—it was the heaviest and most crucial—and off I went while he stood guard at the van.

I was glad it was a cool day so I didn't have to worry how the buttercream frosting would do in the heat. The nonskid mat in the bed of the van had kept all the boxed cake layers from sliding around. "Prevention" was the key word when hauling expensive wedding cakes.

I went back three more times for the other layers, doubling up on both shelves of a taller wheeled cart that could hold rows of full sheet pans, like the cart I had at the bakery. The last trip I made by myself, putting the extra containers of buttercream, mousse, sugar-paste decorations, the cake stand and server, and my cake decorator's toolbox on the cart. Ben departed to do his security detail.

I already had my white chef's coat on over my clothes. I'd learned from my apprenticeship with Sylvia Weinstock that not only does your cake have to look good, but you do, too. No jeans, no messy hair, no dirty chef's jacket; you always presented a tailored, professional appearance and, above all, clean hands, to your client.

Sylvia's trademark look was her sleek chignon, large black-framed glasses, and a Chanel suit. Mine? Under my chef's coat, I wore a simple navy lace sheath dress and low nude heels, channeling Kate Middleton. I would be as ready as the cake for the big reveal.

Quickly, the banquet manager wheeled the round cake table into the prep kitchen. I reached under the table's damask cloth and locked the brakes. I didn't want this table going anywhere without me.

Ellen and her mother had chosen an antique footed silver cake stand, so I placed it on the cake table. The bottom and heaviest cake layer was on a heavy cardboard round, so the sous chef helped me center that on the silver stand.

I worked quietly, gently pressing the dark blue ribbon around the bottom of each frosted cake layer so it would stay in place.

Layer by layer, the wedding cake took shape. I used a step stool to arrange the sugar-paste blossoms and leaves on the top of the cake, then worked down and around, so wherever you stood to look at this confection, you could see part of the meandering cascade.

I finished just before noon, a relief. I stood back and smiled. My first official wedding cake! I reached in my pocket and took a few photos with the digital camera I had brought. I asked one of the servers to stand by while I cleaned up. I had heard too many horror stories of clumsy servers with big trays, tottering guests, kids playing tag, and collapsing tables. I wouldn't breathe a sigh of relief until the cake had been cut, the photos taken, and the cake wheeled back to the kitchen to be portioned, plated, and served. Nothing soured your reputation like an expensive wedding cake disaster.

My standard fee included my staying to make sure everything went as planned. With the server on guard, I wheeled all my gear outside and put it in the back of the van, throwing my chef's jacket on top of it all. I wouldn't need that anymore.

I went to the restroom for a quick touch-up—hair, makeup, hands.

About thirty minutes before the reception, the banquet manager and I slowly—very, very slowly—wheeled in the cake, just as the chamber music quartet was tuning up on the other side of the room.

Ellen and Sam had met in their professional lives rather than in college, so they wanted a more refined affair. A silver champagne bucket, ready with ice and a bottle of bubbly, was positioned at the side of each six-top table. Midnight blue sashes tied around the ivory chair covers complemented the coral and green floral arrangements, low on the tables to allow conversation. The cake table, between the two sets of French doors, helped pull the fresh and formal look together.

Guests started drifting in to find their name cards at the tables. From my vantage point by the cake and French doors, I watched the bridal party, the mothers, and a tall, rather elegant old man gather outside in the formal gardens for a few more wedding photos before the reception officially started.

I sighed. They all looked so happy. With all my heart, I wished them well. But you had only to look at their group to know that happily-ever-after wasn't always in the script. Both mothers were alone: Ellen's father had passed away; Sam's father was in prison. And the older man with them, whom I recognized from photos as Samuel Whyte, Sam's grandfather, had probably lost a spouse as well.

I thought of my wedding day, when I had felt like the luckiest person in the world. I was marrying the man I loved and who loved me and I imagined that our future life would play out under blue, blue skies. Back then, I could see only one ghostly cloud on that sunniest of days: my own absent father. How naive I had been.

I shook my head slightly, as if to dislodge these memories. Would I do this at every wedding and spoil my enjoyment? I had to think of something happier.

And then Ben was by my side. "The wedding planner needs to talk to you, Neely." He gently pressed his hand in the small of my back to guide me in her direction, and I felt a surge of warmth that made my cheeks flush. I turned back to him in surprise and our eyes locked. I didn't want to move.

"Don't worry. I'll guard this cake with my life," he said with a wink, and then nudged me toward the woman with the notebook computer.

A quick conversation with the wedding planner, and we agreed with the change of plans—Ellen and Sam would cut the cake first and then the sit-down lunch would be served.

I walked back to Ben—and the cake.

"Before I forget to say it, you look fantastic. Those anti-fungal pills must be working already," he teased.

I jabbed his arm and whispered, as this wasn't professional wedding behavior, "Smart-ass. You know they're sleeping pills. And I haven't taken them yet."

But I linked my slender arm through his big one all the same.

The chamber music quartet began playing "A Little Night Music." Mozart. Perfect.

I smiled. This was going to be wonderful.

I took it all in, standing arm in arm with Ben like we were the bride and groom on top of the cake. More guests walked in, and we watched the kaleidoscope of colors as women in spring pastels and men in well-tailored suits moved from group to group, table to table, to greet the ones they knew.

If only I could have frozen that moment in time.

"Where is she?" someone growled from the doorway. "Get out of my way!" Like a bolt of acid lightning, something scorched down my throat, and I started to choke and stumble.

"Are you all right?" Ben grabbed a glass of water from a nearby table. "Here, drink this." Despite the commotion by the entrance, his entire focus was on me.

I gulped the water down. But my mouth felt blistered, and I motioned for another glass. He handed one to me.

When I straightened up to drink again, I knew we were in big trouble.

VALENTINE'S DAY, 1942

"We'll meet again, don't know where, don't know when," Peggy Lee sang with the Benny Goodman Orchestra, her voice as smooth as Pond's cold cream.

Olive hummed as she slow-danced with Frank Amici in the middle of the Friendly Café, their sodas and shared plate of French fries temporarily forgotten in one of the booths that lined three sides of the room. Frank smelled like Ivory soap and the starch his mother had used to give his old shirt some life.

"You're leading again, Olive," he muttered. "The man is supposed to lead." Olive rolled her eyes and they broke apart, then started over.

It was not too bad letting Frank take the lead, just not something that came naturally to Olive. Give a little here, give a little there, and before you knew it, you were as soppy as milk toast. Yet she couldn't deny that it was nice to have someone to lean on for a little while.

Just an hour ago as she and Frank were walking to Friendly's, Olive noticed how much darker it was outside with the hulking mattress factory blocking most of the moonlight. The streetlights seemed dimmer, too, in the frozen fog. Crossing the bridge into Lockton, Olive thought she had heard someone carousing on the frozen creek banks below, but it was too dark to see. Who would be out in this cold, anyway? She had slipped one arm through Frank's, but she balled the other fist and hid it in her coat pocket, all the same. Nobody was going to get the better of Olive Habig, not if she could help it.

Here, as they swayed in a warm haze of cigarette smoke, Olive caught a reflection of herself and Frank in the mirror at the back of the lunch counter. Olive had lost weight. Her new shorter hairstyle, with a flat crown and soft curls all around her face, made her expression seem less sharp. Her shirtwaist dress with a covered fabric belt and wide padded shoulders—a dress that Edie had made—looked good. Even the seams in her stockings were straight.

When they turned, she spotted Frank's cowlick, which no amount of Brylcreem could ever keep down.

Some Romeo.

Frank was a careful dancer, not like that Johnny Giraldi, who could really move. Olive sighed. Frank held her like Mama's dressmaker's dummy, not a real, live girl. But at least Olive had a date. Every day, some new boy was leaving for the war. Soon there wouldn't be anybody left her own age.

We'll meet again.

Would she ever see Edie again? Was Pickle gone for good?

Don't know where, don't know when.

Why did her sister, the only family she had left, disappear like that? Olive wished she could stop thinking about it.

Edie hadn't been well. She'd seemed scared all the time. Something had happened, but nobody else cared. It was all war, war, war. Olive was sick of it already, she thought, then was suddenly ashamed of herself.

"Pickle probably ran off with the ragman's son," that old idiot policeman Tom Mooney had told her the last time she had gone to the police station. "You said he left her a shoe. Maybe it was a secret message or somethin'. Like one of them codes. Nobody's seen him, neither."

Olive snorted at that idea. Why would Shemuel run off with Pickle? They hardly even knew each other. Sure, Olive had teased Pickle about Shemuel being her boyfriend, but they both knew how ridiculous that was. Usually, if you ran off, you joined the circus or went someplace that offered a better life. Shemuel was poor. Why would Pickle want to be any poorer than she already was? They'd end up as hobos, begging for food. No, that idea was ridiculous.

"It's not a crime to leave home, you know," Mooney had added. "Half our department has signed up. Now the few of us old guys who are left are supposed to identify these German and Jap planes if they fly overhead." He had showed Olive the pamphlet with illustrations of the undersides of American, British, Italian, Japanese, and German planes.

"We have to scan the sky with these binoculars and write down if the plane is single- or multiple-engine. Whether it's a bomber or fighter or transport. Friendly or enemy."

"Who's going to fly all the way over an ocean and then over Millcreek Valley?" Olive had asked.

"Them Japs flew all the way across the Pacific to bomb Pearl Harbor, and nobody expected it. They can fly here, too," he said. "Or the Krauts. We have to be ready."

"But if you're all looking up in the sky," Olive had countered, "who pays attention to what's down here on the streets?"

Mooney had started to grumble, then shook his head. "What I'm tryin' to tell you is that we just don't have the manpower to go looking for trouble in every hot sheet place from here to Chicago. There's no evidence of any crime, Olive."

Other than my sister is gone, and I am all alone.

Olive straightened herself up, suddenly, and Frank looked down at her. She was getting good at twisting some kind of internal faucet, shutting off the cold emptiness, turning on the hot anger.

"Damn it, isn't anybody going to keep that jukebox playing?" she complained a little too loudly as the song ended. The other dancers turned to look at her, moving aimlessly in the silence.

"What do you want to hear next?" Frank asked distractedly, searching through his trouser pockets for change.

"You pick," Olive said, and waved him away.

But when the next song came on, it was Peggy Lee.

We'll meet again.

Olive raised her hands, perplexed. "What are you doing?"

He stared at her, his expression serious. "I signed up today, Olive. I'm going to war."

She gave him a long look, then walked into his arms, and they swayed again to the music.

She was leading, but Frank didn't seem to notice.

"What will your dad do at the store?"

"He's going to get old Mr. Handorf to help him at the meat counter and a new kid to deliver the groceries."

"When do you leave?"

"Next week."

"Oh, Frankie. Are you scared?"

"A little bit. And you have to call me Frank now. I'm a soldier."

Olive leaned in closer, laid her head on Frank's thin chest. She heard his heartbeat, steady and quiet.

They finished the dance and slowly walked back to the booth, holding hands.

"I got you something, Olive," he said, handing her the white Rexall Drug Store bag. "Sort of a going-away present."

Olive took out a small bottle of L'Aimant perfume. The price tag was still on it—$2.50—more than Frank made in a day. She opened the bottle and took a whiff. It smelled soft and round and full of love, like how she wanted to be. She brushed away a tear, embarrassed, because feisty Olive Habig, the other half of Pickle and Olive, never cried.

"I don't have anything to give you."

"Yes, you do," Frank said, taking her hand.

12

I gulped down more water. It seemed to help. The blistering acid taste went away as suddenly and mysteriously as it had begun.

"Something must have gone down wrong," I gasped, then gave a deep sigh of relief.

"You're sure you're okay?" Ben looked worried.

"I'm fine now, really. Maybe it was just nerves. My first big wedding cake . . ." I managed a *whew* as if I were a runner who had just finished a race.

When I stood up straight, I gestured toward the double doors at the front of the reception room. "But we have other issues. I don't think those two were on the guest list. I'm worried they might be crashing," I said.

At least they had cleaned up a bit. Mrs. Amici was in a floral dress and a white crocheted sweater. Diane had on a sparkly tunic top, a long skirt with an uneven hem, and what looked like knee-high boots in some shiny material. Ben knew them, of course. He just didn't know that Diane had caused a scene in front of the bakery, and that it had involved the police.

"I don't understand how they got past my guys. I'll take care of this," said Ben, and moved toward them.

I reached for his arm to make him stop. "Let's try the diplomatic approach first," I suggested. "Maybe they're here for some other event. They've become regulars at Rainbow Cake, so maybe I can talk to them. You stay by the cake."

"Thanks, Neely. I don't want to lay hands on those sad old ladies—not if I don't have to. But promise you won't let things go too far. If they give you any trouble at all, you just give me a sign and I'll be by your side before you can blink. Okay?"

I stared at Ben for a second after he stopped speaking, wondering why I had been such a fool for so long. Rugged, handsome, oh-so-solid Ben offered the comfort and support I needed. With a reassuring nod to me, Ben stepped back and resumed his sentry duty, keeping one eye on the would-be wedding crashers and the other on the bridal party still outside in the garden.

I plastered on a smile and walked to the doorway where the two were standing, looking again as if they had just landed on Earth from Mars, winking, blinking, and unsure of how to act in an alien environment. Had they never been to a wedding reception before?

"Diane, Mrs. Amici, can I point the way to the room you're looking for? This is a private wedding."

"We're family, too," Diane said.

I raised an eyebrow.

"Well, sort of," she said, swaying backward a little bit. "Just stay out of this, Neely."

"Yes, let's stay out of this," Mrs. Amici said to her daughter, trying to pull her away.

"Noooo-hoooo, Mom," Diane said. "How many years have I heard about how your life is crap? I would have ripped that damn thing off her finger, asked questions later. But not you. You had your chance after she'd stuffed herself with cake, and you just walked away. You'd rather bitch about it and get someone else to do your dirty work. We won't get another chance like this, Mom. The *Voodoo* led us here and we're not leaving until we get it back."

"What are you talking about?" I asked.

"None of your business." Diane squinted and peered around the room.

"Let's go, Diane," Mrs. Amici pleaded.

"Yes, maybe that's best." For once, I agreed with Mrs. Amici.

Diane's eyes widened as she looked toward the cake, Ben, and the garden beyond. What was she looking for?

She got a crafty smile on her face. "Maybe the direct approach is not the way to go here. Hell, I'm flexible, aren't I, Mom?" She raised the toe of one boot and spun around on the heel of the other boot to face the other direction. "That was damn flexible, wasn't it?"

"Diane, please," Mrs. Amici said.

"Okay, Mom. You want to wimp out. I get it. I can see this was a big mistake. Point us to the ladies' room, Neely. We need to make a pit stop before we leave." I gave them directions to the restroom in between this reception room and the one right next door. Diane grabbed her mother's arm and tugged her back out into the lobby. I watched as Diane pushed open the restroom door. She gave me a smart-ass salute.

Mission accomplished. I quickly walked back to Ben.

"Another crisis averted," I said when I reached him, "but you should probably make sure they really leave."

Ben discreetly used his walkie-talkie to alert his team, then hurried to station himself outside the ladies' room door, waiting to escort Diane and her mother out to their car.

I resumed my place by the cake, which was still in pristine condition. Not a sugar blossom out of place.

The formal garden, visible from the French doors, looked lovely, too. Aged stone urns spilled over with colorful spring blooms, the trees blossomed in delicate pinks and whites, and daffodils and jonquils popped up amid the ivy ground cover. In the brick courtyard, the photographer was posing the bride and groom in front of a fountain. The two mothers and Sam Whyte's grandfather stood off to the side. The uncle who had walked Ellen down the aisle, the bridesmaids, and the groomsmen stood closer to the French doors, waiting for their photo call, but also partially blocking my view.

But I still saw something sparkly to the right of the courtyard, out of place in the English garden. Diane, dragging her mother by the hand along a narrow brick pathway. *Oh no.*

I texted Ben, gestured for one of the waitstaff to babysit the cake, then went out into the courtyard.

I had to give Mrs. Amici credit. She was keeping up pretty well as Diane tugged her along. It must have been like Barney pulling her when he found a new smell to investigate.

I had to stop them from making a scene. They had no business here, and Diane was under the influence of something, judging from the almost-over-the-edge look in her eyes. I stood, blocking their path, my arms crossed.

"I think I know that man," I heard Mrs. Amici say as they approached.

I turned quickly to look. She was pointing to the older Mr. Whyte.

"He used to come to our house for fabric scraps. He was friends with my sister."

"Oh, shut up, Mother. Forget about Pickle. We're here to . . . whoops!" Diane waved her finger at me. "I'm not going to tell you why we're here."

"Maybe he knows what happened to Pickle," said Mrs. Amici.

"Screw that. We're going to get what we came for and then you're going to shut the fuck up, once and for all."

I took a step forward. Maybe diplomacy would work better the second time around. "Look, Diane. You can't stay here; you—"

"Don't tell me what I can't do!" Diane elbowed me aside and I had to hop backward over the boxwood border on my side of the brick path to keep from falling.

Diane bulldozed their way back up onto the brick path, past the mothers and the old man. When the photographer turned to see what the ruckus was all about, Diane gave him a one-armed shove, sending him reeling backward. Luckily, he kept his balance and a firm hold on his camera.

As Diane careened forward, Mrs. Amici tripped on a tangle of green ivy. She snapped loose from Diane's grip and fell hard against a stone urn. Almost in slow motion, she straightened to an upright but tilted standstill, then crumpled to the ground.

I ran to Mrs. Amici. She lay there, moaning softly, looking like a doll that had been left outside and forgotten.

Diane lumbered on toward the bride and groom.

I texted Ben again. *Courtyard. Now.* I was torn between leaving Mrs. Amici and running to Diane, but Mrs. Amici was hurt and needed me more. Someone else would have to deal with Diane.

I quickly checked Mrs. Amici. She was breathing. She had a heartbeat. As I stroked her hand, I could see Diane, looking back at her mother on the ground. Her face red and eyes bulging, Diane twirled around to confront Sam and Ellen. "Give me the damn ring!" She grabbed for Ellen's hand.

Ellen shrank back and her new husband pushed in front to protect her.

The next thing I knew, Ben and the club manager hurdled over the beds and tackled Diane to the ground. Ben turned Diane over on her stomach, grabbed her neck with one big hand, her arms with the other, and forced her face into the mulch; she turned her face sideways in a grimace.

"Damn it," she said through gritted teeth. "Shit, shit, shit." Ben pressed more firmly on her neck and planted a knee in her back. She stopped cursing.

"I've called the police and an ambulance," Ben said calmly, looking up at everyone. "It's all right now. You can all go back inside. We'll get this cleared up."

The photographer recovered first. "Let's come back out and take more photos a little later," he suggested. "Just a slight change in the schedule. Every wedding has one," he added brightly. "Won't this be a story to tell in years to come?"

He shepherded the bridesmaids and groomsmen, who had luckily been shielding this scene from guests, back into the reception area. The sound of sirens got louder.

"I'll keep the other guests inside," the club manager said. He pulled the drapes over the French doors to block the view of Diane on the ground.

"Let's touch up your makeup in the powder room, honey," Mrs. Schumacher said to Ellen. "Or get a glass of champagne. I definitely think we could use one." They went back indoors.

The younger Sam knelt down beside me. I gently brushed off the bits of cedar mulch that stuck to Mrs. Amici's face and hair. He took off his jacket and draped it over her legs to protect her from the chill. Then he looked at me questioningly.

"I'm Neely. I made your wedding cake. I'm sorry we had to meet like this," I said quietly.

"Everybody says that weddings are crazy. I just didn't believe them," he said. "I hope she'll be all right."

The tall old man made his way over to us and stood stiffly, looking down at Mrs. Amici.

"Pickle," she moaned. "Pickle."

The old man stood with his head cocked to one side. "I haven't heard that name in years." Sadly, he said, "Olive Habig. Well, what do you know? Did someone get help for her?"

I nodded.

Sam looked questioningly at his grandfather. "Do you know her, Grandpa?"

Mrs. Amici moaned again. I squeezed her hand.

"It will be all right. You'll be all right," I said, looking up at the groom and his grandfather.

Two emergency technicians hurried up the path, carrying a stretcher. The Whytes moved aside as a tech bent down to take

Mrs. Amici's pulse. The other man handed the groom his coat. Sam shook it out quickly and put it back on.

The EMTs carefully placed a padded red collar around the old woman's neck to stabilize it before they lifted her onto the stretcher and carried it back to the waiting ambulance.

"We should go back inside," said the elder Whyte. "There's nothing more we can do here."

The groom put his arm through his grandfather's and they slowly walked back toward the French doors.

I saw Mrs. Amici's handbag under the boxwood and picked it up.

I followed behind them.

"I used to call on their mother years ago," the old man was telling his grandson. "Mrs. Habig was always good to me. Olive was the older daughter and sort of chubby. Edie was younger, but taller. People used to call them Pickle and Olive."

"Who was that other woman, the one who tried to grab Ellen's ring?"

"I don't know. I don't understand any of this."

"But you think it might have something to do with you?" Sam still looked questioningly at his grandfather.

"I don't know. Maybe. Olive's sister and I were going to run away together the day after Pearl Harbor."

"Together?"

"Together, but not *together*," Samuel Whyte tried to explain. "We were friends, sort of. Misfits. A lot of bad things had happened to me. But something bad had also happened to Edie. She would never say what it was, but you could tell it had broken her. People probably thought her disappearance had to do with me. Nobody has seen Edie—Pickle—since that day. Maybe Olive blames me."

"But this happened—what?—over seventy years ago?" Sam said, trying to understand. "Olive could have found you pretty easily, if she had wanted to. You live in town. Why wait all this time, then show up at my wedding?"

Samuel Whyte just shrugged.

"What happened to the sister?"

"I don't know. She left me a train ticket and the engagement ring I gave your grandmother, the one your wife wears now. Then I never heard from her again. I tried to trace her whereabouts many times over the years, but she just disappeared."

He paused on the walk to catch his breath, and I had to stop behind them.

"It must have been very difficult for Olive, but I assumed she got over it. She always was as tough as an old boot, and I know quite a bit about old boots," he said with a wry smile. "We'll have to get to the bottom of this incident, but not on your wedding day."

A few feet from the door, the old man paused again. "I've always thought of that ring as my good-luck charm. A rabbi helped a young, scared Shemuel Weiss leave it with a banker until a battle-tested Samuel Whyte came back from the war. Because of that ring, I had collateral to start my business and ask your grandmother to marry me. And then I was lucky enough to become your grand-father." He patted his grandson on the shoulder.

Sam looked over at Ellen waiting for him at the center of the long table. "I think your good-luck charm worked, Grandpa."

Back inside, while they sat down and the reception officially began, I still stood sentry by the cake, trying to make sense of what I had just witnessed. So, Ellen's beautiful ring had originally belonged to the Habig family, to Edie and Olive. Edie had left it for Shemuel when they were running away together the day after Pearl Harbor, before she disappeared.

And then one day, out of the blue, Mrs. Amici saw that same ring on Ellen Schumacher's hand. It must have been after the cake tasting when we all tangled with Barney's leash out on the sidewalk. I remember now that she seemed stunned to see it when Ellen held out her hand. I had attributed it to the beauty of the ring, but it must have been shock.

If I had lost my sister seventy years ago and suddenly there was a clue to her disappearance, I'd want to know. Now it made sense that Mrs. Amici and Diane had started frequenting the bakery, probably hoping we'd talk about Ellen's wedding or that Ellen would come in again. And it probably solved the mystery of the missing trash. They had been looking for answers in their own inept way, not for my electric bill.

When they heard Maggie and me complain about the Whyte Trash story in the *Voodoo*, they had Ellen's name and where the wedding would be held. If they found Ellen, they would find the ring, and they had to get it back.

But did Mrs. Amici recognize Shemuel as Samuel before she fell? Did she understand that he was the last person to see Edie? Maybe he knew something that could shed light on Edie's disappearance. Hopefully, it would still be possible for Mrs. Amici and Samuel to reconnect.

And then there was something else. I wasn't so sure that Edie was missing so much as *hiding*. When I thought about Edie, I tasted lemon meringue pie, the sunny counterpoint to the caustic lemon flavor I had been experiencing. But what did that mean?

I sighed. My work was not yet done, neither in Olive and Edie's troubled past nor in the bridal couple's happy present.

The champagne toasts and the cutting of the cake passed by in a happy blur, with that buzz of delight that I wished I could put on my playlist and listen to as a wedding cake meditation for a stressed-out baker.

As soon as the banquet manager wheeled the rest of the cake back to the kitchen to be cut and served for dessert, my duty was done. I breathed a sigh of relief and satisfaction combined.

I packed up the van with the few things I had left—the tub of buttercream and a couple of tools—and wheeled the cart back to the service kitchen.

Ben came out to see me off, and I plucked a stray bit of mulch from the shoulder of his suit coat.

"Do you have any plans for later on?" I asked him. "I think we could both use a drink after this. And Finnegan's happy hour goes until eight on Friday evenings."

He smiled. "I thought you'd never ask. If I can escape early from my second gig, I'll join you. I'll text you later."

On the way home, I tilted the rearview mirror up and caught myself smiling, which made me smile all the more.

Was it just my imagination, or did the sky look bluer, the sun brighter, the trees greener? Life in general looked better, I decided, when you had good friends and maybe the promise of more with one man in particular. It didn't hurt to have a two-hundred-dollar tip in your purse, either. Courtesy of Sam Whyte, Senior.

"Mr. Whyte wanted me to thank you for being so kind to Olive

Habig," the wedding planner said when she discreetly handed me the envelope before I left, "and the groom said that was the best cake he had ever tasted."

MAY 1955

Olive wrapped the meat in white butcher paper, taped the package shut, then used her red grease pencil to mark it with "cottage ham" and "2½ pounds."

"You'll need green beans, potatoes, and an onion with that, too, won't you?" she asked Mrs. Schramm. "Maybe a jar of horseradish?" Everybody knew that you simmered the cured and smoked pork shoulder with the beans and onion until it was all tender, then added the potatoes to cook for the last fifteen minutes or so. Some people liked their cottage ham with yellow mustard, but Olive preferred horseradish. It livened things up.

"Oh, no. I got all of that at Alberino's yesterday," Mrs. Schramm said. "They were out of cottage ham."

Olive wanted to leap over the butcher counter and smack that woman in the head with the package, but instead, she passed it across the high counter without comment. Alberino's. That big new grocery store south on Millcreek Valley Road. You had to have a car to get there. It was too far to walk from here, then haul your groceries back.

She and Frank didn't have a car. They didn't need one. Everything they wanted was right here. And if, by chance, they had to go somewhere farther, they took the bus or a taxi.

Mrs. Schramm looked around the store absently, then back in the meat case. "But I do need some goetta. Maybe a pound?"

Olive took out the loaf pan of goetta. She placed a waxed paper on the scale and expertly cut the breakfast pork loaf out of the pan in one piece. "It's just a little over a pound; is that okay?"

Mrs. Schramm nodded.

Olive knew that very few people objected to just a little over a pound. It was a way to get more from every sale.

"And does your husband like ketchup on his?" Olive asked as she wrapped up the goetta. "My Frank likes his goetta sliced thin and fried really crisp and then puts on lots of ketchup."

"My husband likes his with extra salt," Mrs. Schramm replied. "It's probably not good for him, but you can't tell him that."

"Are you all fixed up for Friday? Maybe a tuna noodle casserole? We've got all the makin's for that, too, and nothing to go bad in a few days."

"No, I think this will be it."

Olive painted a smile on her face as she handed Mrs. Schramm her change and heard the bell clang on the back of the door as she left.

Olive barrelled out from behind the meat counter, grabbed a feather duster, and furiously attacked the tops of cans and boxes on the shelves. Some of their Kellogg's cereal boxes were so old, they still had Singing Lady stories printed on the back. Olive moved them to the front of the shelf. Maybe they should have a sale on cereal and get rid of these. She didn't want any more reminders of Pickle than she already had.

If only Frank were here. Frank was nicer to customers, but they didn't sell as much when he was in the store. He didn't have the same knack as his father, God rest his soul. Frank was just plain nice. And Olive was grateful she didn't have to carry the burden of their little store alone.

But it was better if Frank did the school run. He didn't seem to mind the endless repetition, the monotony of small children. How Diane dawdled on the walk to and from kindergarten, noticing every pebble, every stray cat, every crack in the sidewalk. He didn't seem to care how much time it took to do a simple thing like find her socks or tie her shoes. And the questions. Always questions.

Olive had about an hour before Frank brought Diane back to the store after feeding her lunch at home. It was hard to keep Diane occupied in the store. She didn't like coloring books. She couldn't read yet. She was always messing up Olive's displays or getting in the way of customers. But what else could they do? Olive couldn't wait for September when Diane would be in school all day. Then she would get the business moving again.

Since that new Alberino's opened, Olive had noticed a drop-off in sales. Leaving Frank in charge of the store one morning, she'd taken a taxi to check out the competition.

Alberino's was huge. At least five times the size of their corner grocery. Alberino's had wheeled carts to get about the store, not just baskets you carried. They had a bigger selection of almost everything. Housewives with cars looked like they bought enough to last them a week. They weren't just buying enough for a day or a meal, like Amici's customers.

When there was no more to dust, Olive made a list with her grease pencil on butcher paper, then tacked it up in the storeroom.

Under "More Selection," she detailed "sliced white bread" and "hamburger buns" from Oster's. Customers couldn't get Oster's bakery goods at Alberino's, and having them for sale in the store would save them an extra trip. Another item on the list said "Advertise Free Delivery." Why not remind people?

Taking stock and facing facts usually made her feel more in control. But Olive couldn't shake the feeling that a big boulder was rolling down Benson Street hill, gathering speed, coming right at her.

13

"Drinks are on me!" I told Roshonda.

We were sitting at the bar at Finnegan's, across the street from Rainbow Cake. It was the start of Friday night happy hour. It was also the end of my long, long day, but Roshonda was just getting going. She actually had a date afterward. Lucky her. Ben had texted that it was unlikely he would get away from his second gig in time to meet, so I had a date with an early night and my first sleeping pill. Lucky me.

When I caught our reflection in the mirror behind the bar, I had to say we looked pretty good. I was still in my "wedding cake lady" navy lace sheath dress with the long sleeves. Roshonda's sleeveless dress was in that chartreuse green called "lemongrass" that looked so good against her skin. Roshonda caught me looking at us.

"You know, I could pass for Kerry Washington in this dress

and you for one of those skinny women anchors on *The Today Show*. We're gorgeous, I hope you realize."

We both laughed, and when our glasses of wine came we clinked our "cheers."

"So Ben had to tackle Diane Amici at the reception?" Roshonda asked, her eyes squinting as if this would make the story more believable. "At that Whyte Trash wedding at the country club," she went on in that "just confirming this" tone she had.

I had told her all about it when I called her on the way home from the Carriage Hill Country Club.

"People have been talking about how unfair that *Valley Voodoo* story was," Roshonda said. "People in the community genuinely like old Mr. Whyte. He's always giving money to some cause or other."

"Well, I know for a fact that he was generous to me today. I guess he knew Mrs. Amici's sister a long time ago." I didn't explain about the ring Diane had come looking for or that old Mr. Whyte and Mrs. Amici's sister had tried to run away together. It seemed like unnecessary gossip. And I didn't go into my growing feeling that Edie was hiding somewhere.

"I didn't know she had a sister. I'm sure there's a story there, but you and I both know Diane doesn't need any special excuse to go all unhinged like that. She's happy to oblige for no reason at all. I swear, there's a picture of that woman in the dictionary next to the entry for 'menace.' And speaking of menaces . . ." She took another sip. "Wait till you hear about my new tech entrepreneur bridezilla." She took a longer sip. "I'm going to need a whole bottle just thinking about that girl."

"Well, spill," I said, laughing.

Roshonda sort of rolled her shoulders and wiggled a little bit, like she always did when she couldn't wait to tell you something really juicy. "I'm calling her 'Twitter,' because she spends her entire day texting me dozens of crazy wedding ideas, each one more indecipherable than the last and all of them less than one hundred and forty characters. Her latest thing is that, instead of using boring old names on the place cards, we're going to use selfies! So, not only do I need to collect a photo from each of the two hundred fifty people this insane person has invited to her wedding, but then, at the reception, I have to help each guest locate her own tiny face on a two-by-two card so that she can, at some point, find her table and eat her meal. It's going to be chaos."

"Ugh."

"I've tried to explain to Twitter why this is a terrible, terrible idea, but she won't listen to me. Maybe I should send her to you for the cake and you can text some sense into her."

Just then, I saw another woman come in who put Roshonda and me to shame—Roberta Canfield. She sat down at a small table in the bar area. When I caught her eye, I raised my glass to her and she smiled. I hoped everything was all right. Maybe she was just getting out again after breaking up with her fiancé at the wedding cake tasting last month. Whenever I thought I had it hard in the relationship department, I thought of Roberta. How would she ever find someone? It would take an exceptional man to get over "baggage" like that.

As I smiled at her, I saw Thomas join her. He turned and looked at me, smiling nervously. I still hoped that he would find the strength to truly love her for the amazing woman she had become.

"You're not listening to me, either," Roshonda said.

"Sorry; I just saw somebody I knew from the bakery."

"Here we are, out for fun, and we're still talking about work," she said. "For the rest of this evening, we are only allowed to discuss our personal lives."

We clinked glasses yet again to seal the deal.

Forty-five minutes later, just as we finished our wine, Roshonda's date showed up and she introduced us. Tall, good-looking, and dressed to impress. My, my, my.

"Remember, her curfew is midnight," I said as I waved them off.

As I was waiting for my credit card receipt, I got a text from Ben confirming that he wasn't going to make it. *Just as well*. I yawned.

I kept my phone with me. This was Roshonda's first date with this guy, whose name I wouldn't even try to remember until she had gone out with him a few times. Roshonda was picky. I had to call her in an hour to make sure everything was okay. My call would be her excuse to leave if the date had gone south.

Since I wasn't meeting Ben, I decided to go back home.

As I rose to exit, I happened to walk out with Roberta and Thomas, who were holding hands.

"I'm so glad to see you two together again," I said warmly.

"I was miserable without her," Thomas confessed, bringing Roberta's hand up to his lips to kiss it, and I saw the sparkle of a diamond ring again. "And I got to thinking that every relationship has its issues—maybe not quite like ours," he said with a wry expression. "But we love each other and want to be together."

"Well, come and see me again for a little cake therapy," I said, smiling, and we agreed to set another tasting date.

The March winds had picked up and I shivered as I ran across the street. Because the day had been so cool, I had left my gear in the van parked in the bakery lot. I quickly unlocked the back door and started toting. The buttercream tub was still cold to the touch, so I put it back in the walk-in refrigerator.

I locked up the bakery and the van, then unlocked the gate to my backyard next door. Maybe if I unpacked my tote bag right away, I could hang up my chef's jacket and it would miraculously unwrinkle. Or I could just throw it in the dryer with a damp cloth tomorrow.

At the bottom of my tote, I found an extra purse. I recognized Mrs. Amici's handbag that I had found at the scene of her accident. In all the excitement, I had forgotten about it.

The beige leatherette pocketbook had seen better days. The metal clasp had tarnished and the corners of the purse were peeling. It looked like it was from the 1960s. Vintage, but not good vintage. Most people would have thrown it away. Nevertheless, I would have to get this back to her somehow. Ben would probably know which hospital she had been taken to.

I opened her purse to see whether she had a cell phone or her wallet inside. She would need her insurance card at the hospital. But her purse was empty except for an embroidered handkerchief, a ballpoint pen, and a distinct aroma of vinegar that made me wrinkle my nose. What had she been carrying around in there?

That simple question opened the door in my mind that I had kept firmly locked against Mrs. Amici and Diane. Unlike my wedding cake customers, whom I tried to get to know at a deep level, I had kept those two from getting in. What could be the harm in opening that door now? I wanted to know why Mrs. Amici and Diane wanted that ring so badly that they would try to tackle a bride at her own wedding. And maybe there was a reason, lodged in a story long ago, that explained why Mrs. Amici was so angry with the world. Maybe I could do something about that.

I turned on the gas fireplace in my parlor, kicked off my shoes, and wrapped the cashmere throw around me. I curled up on my comfy sofa with the phone in my lap and just watched the flames. I had to call Roshonda in forty-five minutes.

I felt myself get drowsy. I was in that half-conscious state where you're dreaming but awake as I saw an old-fashioned gentleman who reminded me of plum and port. I saw two little girls who looked like they were from the 1930s in an old mom-and-pop grocery store. I felt a man's hand over my mouth and the cold stones of a creek bed against my back on a dark night. I smelled a fire in a junkyard. I heard the noise of the Queen City terminal. I felt the peace of Bernadette's grotto. None of it made much sense, but I'd learned to trust these sensations. To know they would lead me to the full story eventually.

And then I tasted the rest of the story that had been hidden in plain sight all along—one with the sour flavor of anger.

MARCH 1964

"Damn it, Diane, get down here. Your dinner's getting cold."

Diane heard her mother perfectly well from her bedroom upstairs. But she chose to ignore her. She'd rather listen to the Beatles' "I Want to Hold Your Hand" for the umpteenth time.

It wouldn't matter if she ran down the stairs as soon as her mother called her to dinner. It wouldn't matter if she didn't come down at all. The scene in the kitchen would play out the same way.

Her mother would be standing by the small kitchen table, hands on her hips. Her father would be sitting meekly, fork in the air over his plate of minute steak and peas—this was Wednesday, after all, not meat loaf night—waiting for the signal that he could start.

"Oh, go ahead, Frank. At least *your* dinner won't be spoiled," Olive would say acidly.

And then there would be the day's special complaint. Maybe it was "What a mistake to finish the upstairs for that ungrateful lump of a teenager. All that beautiful white Formica with the gold flecks, the built-in shelves that took you forever to finish, even her own bathroom, goddammit. We scrimp on ourselves and spoil that girl."

Or maybe it would be her lack of success in school. "Does that kid ever pick up a book unless I stand over her and make her read?"

Or how her father couldn't do anything right. "It's all down to me, all of it," her mother would say. "Your father can hardly even do the books at the store, Diane! He gets orders screwed up when someone calls in. He gives people lamb chops instead of pork chops. He overcharges or doesn't charge enough. And when he tries to make a delivery, he gets lost. He can't find his ass with both hands."

Stoop-shouldered, his eyes perpetually blinking behind his glasses, her father had faded, no doubt about it. He hardly resembled the young soldier in the black-and-white photograph.

"I wanna hold your hand. . . ."

Diane couldn't imagine her father and mother holding hands. They could barely coexist in the same room.

"Diane!" Olive yelled again and thumped the ceiling with the stick end of a broom. "I'm on my feet all day and I can hardly get rid of the stink of meat by the time I get home," Diane heard her mother rant. "I keep the house clean. I put a meal on the table. And Little Miss Priss thinks she's too good to come down and join us."

That was Diane's cue. She galumphed down the stairs. Still in her light blue shirtwaist dress and saddle shoes from school, her short curly hair pinned back on both sides with bow-shaped barrettes, Diane quickly plopped down in her chair without looking directly at her mother.

"So glad you could join us." Olive plunked down a plate in front of her daughter.

"I didn't hear you, Mom."

"Didn't hear me!" Olive sputtered, pushed to the limit. "Well, you can hear me now. I'm leaving the dishes for you and your father. I'm going to bingo. I can't stand it anymore."

Olive stormed out of the kitchen. The front door slammed.

Diane started to cry. Frank patted her hand. "It's okay, honey. Your mother has just had a bad day."

"She's always having a bad day," Diane sniffed. "She doesn't think I do anything right."

"I know the feeling," Frank said with a weak smile.

"She hates me."

"No, she doesn't, Diane. She loves you. We both love you."

Frank finished his dinner, wiping his plate clean with a half slice of Roman Meal bread, then folded the soft bread in half, then in half again, and gently stuffed it all in his mouth.

He chewed for a few seconds, then pushed back a little bit from the table. "Do you want some lemon pie?"

Diane gulped down her dinner and a big slice of pie. She and her father cleaned up the kitchen together, enjoying the temporary calm. He washed; she dried. But even now the anger still hung in the air.

"Do you want to watch the six o'clock news with me? Topo Gigio is on *Ed Sullivan*. You always liked that little Italian mouse," Frank asked her, turning on the television. He walked over to the worn purple chenille armchair and sunk down into it. He picked up his pipe from the end table.

"That's okay, Dad. I'm going over to study at Helen's house."

Frank raised his eyebrows as he lit his pipe tobacco with the silver-plated cigarette lighter that Olive gave him long ago. "Helen O'Neil?"

"We've got a big geography test on Thursday."

"Well, be home by nine, honey."

Diane threw on her sweater and grabbed her book bag—to make it look good. She put a stick of chewing gum in her pocket for afterward. She ran the few blocks to the O'Neil house on Benson Street.

Diane knocked on the door of the house with the big front porch next to the library. Helen's older brother, Jack, answered.

"I'm going to study, Mom," he yelled back into the house. "Be home later." He quickly shut the door before she could answer.

"Pattersons'," he whispered to Diane.

They ran around the side of his house and cut through the small, narrow backyard, ducking under the clothesline, to a house on the back street. They let themselves in the side door of the old wood-framed garage that smelled of old leather seats and gasoline.

They sat on the old metal glider that Mr. Patterson had been meaning to fix for years. Jack took a pint of Wild Turkey from his inside coat pocket, unscrewed the top, and passed it to Diane.

"How'd you get it this time?" Diane asked. She took a little swig, made a face, and passed the bottle to Jack.

He turned the bottle up and swallowed the cheap bourbon, wincing. "Hinky's. When nobody's lookin,' I top this up with whatever I can sneak from behind the bar when I'm doin' dishes. Just makes life easier." He took another swig and passed the bottle back to Diane.

Before she took her turn, Diane looked at Jack. "Does your mom know?"

"Hell, no. She's usually in bed by the time I get home. And I keep a bottle of Listerine under the front porch. I can swish and spit before I go in the house."

"Listerine would kill anything," Diane snorted.

They sat side by side, quietly sharing the bottle. Diane couldn't believe that a handsome senior like Jack O'Neil, with his auburn hair and green eyes, would want anything to do with a freshman like her. Diane hoped that Jack would kiss her one of these days, but he had shown no sign of that.

Ever since that party over Christmas break, when everyone else was drinking 3.2 beer from the keg in the basement, she and Jack had passed the bottle. That night, they had a special, unspoken understanding. They both needed more.

Plus, as Jack had explained to her at their last secret session, it was drinking alone that turned you into an alcoholic. That was what his mother always said about Jack's father: *He took to drinking alone.* And then he got really sick, and then he died.

If you drank with other people, you'd be okay, Jack said.

"I wonder if we'll have better stuff than this in Vietnam?"

Diane didn't quite know where Vietnam was, only that it was far away and that was where Jack was going after graduation.

But that was way far in the future. It was only Wednesday, with two more long days of school left this week. She took a gulp, then another, and waited for that warm, woozy sensation that would start to set in soon. It made not being a good girl feel better.

14

"My dad has had a drinking problem since high school," I blurted into my phone. "*That* must be why he left."

"Thank you, but I already have life insurance."

I looked at my phone, puzzled. "Ro, you know this is your 'get out of date free' call, but I'm also serious." I hoped her date couldn't hear me. "I just dozed off and when I was in la-la land, that's when it came to me. My dad was an alcoholic who kept trying to hide it until he couldn't anymore. That must be why he always smelled like Listerine."

"I understand what you're saying, but can I get back to you on that?"

"I get it. Glad your date is going well." Roshonda had heard all my previous theories, including my dad being abducted by aliens, being on a secret spy mission, or being in the witness protection program. But this one rang true.

"I'll talk to you tomorrow, later in the day," she said.

"Woo-hoo. Must be going really well. Have fun."

There was Ro with this gorgeous guy at a fancy restaurant. I could just picture it.

Here I sat on a Friday night, wrapped up like an old lady in a shawl before a fire. But I had just received incredible insights into my own family as well as Mrs. Amici's. I felt like a guitar that had just been played and was still thrumming with energy. I had to get outside and burn some off.

I turned off the gas fire. Upstairs, I took off my navy lace dress and put on yoga pants and a T-shirt. I added socks and running shoes. Downstairs, I got my puffy jacket, keys, phone, and wallet. I saw Mrs. Amici's handbag on my nightstand, right next to the latest Maisie Dobbs mystery I'd been meaning to read.

I was a big fan of that 1930s English detective who did New Age things like meditate and revisit all the people and places she had contacted during a case to clear up any bad energy.

That was it. Revisit.

That was what I needed to do: Make the disparate pieces of this story fit together, and maybe understand what happened to Edie. Perhaps then the terrible sour flavor would stop plaguing me. Some inner force propelled me out of the house, carrying Mrs. Amici's handbag.

The first stop was just next door. My bakery, which had been the library when Mrs. Amici and her sister—Olive and Pickle— were girls. It had been a place of stories, of letting the imagination soar. It was still that kind of place, but in a different way. No unfinished business there, so I walked the few blocks to Mrs. Amici's house.

The house was dark. I heard Barney barking. Barney! I called the police department from my cell phone and told the dispatcher to contact Bobby—hopefully at home in the trailer park—and let him know that his grandmother was in the hospital and her dog needed to be taken care of. I looked for a key under the front doormat, and found one. I let myself in. The house had a mild odor of vinegar, just like the inside of Mrs. Amici's purse, but it didn't choke me like it had before.

Barney barked furiously, growled, and backed away from me as I put her handbag on the little hall table. In a few seconds, he caught a whiff of cake, and it was all good. I petted him, rubbed his ears, and let him sniff around a little more. I checked his food and water in the kitchen. As I walked from room to room, I spotted Frank's faded purple armchair, Mrs. Habig's dressmaker dummy, and the old kitchen table I had seen in flashes of story. Time had stood still here, but not Barney.

I found his leash by the front door and took him for a much-needed walk. I would check back with him again in the morning, unless Bobby was here by then.

When Barney and I were finished, I locked up and put the key back under the mat. I walked to the corner of Benson and Church, the old location of Amici's. Over time, the little store, once at the corner of a long brick row house, had been absorbed by the big sprinkler company where Aunt Helen worked; it was now office space.

I walked to the middle of the bridge to Lockton and looked over the side. The Mill Creek was just a trickle, but the banks were still steep. I could see upstream to the oxbow bend, but it was too shallow for any message to echo down the water. I hurried away.

The old mattress factory was being dismantled, brick by brick, one of the nineteenth-century factory sites that had been declared a brownfield. An early-evening moon cast a chilly blue glare on what had been the Friendly Café, now a thrift store.

I picked up the pace and jogged onto a back street, through the alley, to where Shemuel's salvage yard was enclosed by a corrugated aluminum fence with a sign painted on it: *Whyte's. We Pay Cash for Recyclable Materials.* The piles of old mufflers, factory fan systems, and copper pipe that peeked over the top must be valuable for them to keep the yard lit up like a baseball field.

I jogged back to where I felt safer on the main street and then the overpass where the traffic on I-75, the old canal, thundered beneath. Lockton had always been a place cut in half, first by the canal, then by the highway. Now that the factories had closed, both sides had withered, leaving a tannic flavor like dried tea leaves.

The answer to the mystery I was seeking wasn't here, although I wasn't sure what I was supposed to find. The only place left was the train station, where Edie's story had ended. But she had to have gone somewhere from there. She didn't get on the train. She didn't go back to town. The only other direction was up the convent hill. Maybe Edie had found the same peace that I had experienced in Bernadette's grotto. But what difference would that make to Mrs. Amici's situation now?

I licked my lips and noticed my mouth was starting to feel parched. That told me there was still unfinished business, a worry— somewhere. When anxiety came through, it revealed itself as salty and dry rather than as an actual flavor, because it was fear that kept repeating itself.

I walked the few blocks back from Lockton, passing all the

colorful bridal windows along both sides of Benson Street. I debated whether to stop off at my house and get a bottle of water, but I needed that parched sensation, as unpleasant as it was, to direct me.

I also debated whether to jump in my car and drive up to the hilltop, but no, this felt like something I needed to do on foot, perhaps retracing Edie's steps from the train station to Bernadette's grotto.

When I got to Vine Street, I remembered that the train station had been torn down last year. There was no building now, just an open grassy area, although the tracks still ran parallel to Millcreek Valley Road.

I crossed over the tracks to where Vine Street dead-ended into the old convent entrance. The tall, ornate wrought-iron gate was still padlocked with a loop of thick chain, but I was able to squeeze through the opening. I got out my cell phone and found the flashlight app that I turned on to guide my way.

The left side of the circular drive had not been cleared in a long time, since no one used this entrance anymore. Concrete had come loose from the old brick paving underneath it. I stepped over downed tree branches and shuffled through patches of old, wet leaves, climbing toward the grotto. This could have been the path that Edie took all those years ago.

I heard the raucous call of a wild goose flying overhead, probably a straggler. Maybe this one was joining the other geese camped out around the convent fishpond farther up the hill. A light came on in a window at the back of the nuns' residence. I saw a woman's silhouette. Maybe she had heard it, too.

In a few steps, I reached the upper section of the old drive that was indirectly lit by the nursing facility and the parking lot, so I turned off my flashlight. As I approached the grotto, I heard glass breaking, as if someone was angrily sweeping glasses off a table. The sound echoed in a weird way.

And there was no light in the grotto. The salty bile rose in my throat.

I called 911.

I texted Ben, so someone knew where I was.

Help was coming, but I couldn't wait. I put my phone in my pocket, picked up a sturdy stick, and opened the grotto door.

My heart thudded. My mouth was so dry it felt like my tongue would split open. But I had to go on.

It took a moment for my eyes to adjust to the darkness inside. As the moonlight flooded in and turned the dark to gray, I could see the head and shoulders of a body curled in the fetal position on the stone floor, shards of broken glass and bits of white candle everywhere.

I bent down and felt the neck for a pulse. It was weak.

When I straightened up to get my phone out of my pocket again, a dark shape lunged forward from the grotto's dark recess. I screamed as it knocked me over.

I fell hard against the half-opened door, then flat on the cold ground. I yelped as a heavy workman's boot trampled my left arm as the man ran away.

I heard his heavy breathing and his footsteps as he lumbered up the path to the parking lot. Cradling my injured arm and tingling hand, I pulled myself up to a sitting position. My head was spinning, but I could still hear a truck revving up and roaring off, the pings of gravel spitting out from its wheels—the same sound from the January night I had rescued Jett.

Oh, God, no.

With my good hand, I found my phone and turned the flashlight app on again. Its bright white light made everything look even more surreal. I maneuvered myself up on my knees and shuffled closer to check the body. Spiky dark hair. The eyes bruised and puffy, a cut over one eye, mouth bleeding, but I recognized the dusting of freckles and that nose ring.

Oh no.

I aimed the flashlight down the side of her body. Her jeans and panties had been pulled below her hips. I saw a dark stain that could be blood. Oh no. Please, no.

I placed the lighted phone on the floor and held Jett's limp, cold hand with my good one.

"It's okay, sweetie. It's all over. You're safe with me. Help is coming. They're on their way."

She was still unconscious, but I kept repeating those words, squeezing her hand, as much for my benefit as hers.

I heard a police cruiser screech to a stop.

In the time that followed, I told my story over and over again. To Daniel, who had also responded to Diane's tantrum in front of Rainbow Cake. To Sister Josepha and Sister Agnes, who were in their robes and slippers; Josepha had her arm protectively around the older nun. To Ben, who took off his coat and put it around my shoulders. To Jett's mother and brother, who came after I called them.

"I'll get that no-good bastard," Jett's mother growled, and then howled in frustration. "Who would hurt my baby?"

For all her bravado, she looked scared, too, an older biker-babe version of her Goth daughter, with mascara running down her cheeks. She brushed tears away with the backs of her hands. Jett's junior high brother, pimply and underweight, shrank behind his mother.

An ambulance took Jett to the hospital. Jett's mother and brother followed in their car.

"I need to go, too, see if Jett is all right," I told Ben.

We were sitting in Ben's SUV while the police crime-taped the grotto and shepherded the nuns back inside with an admonition to lock up tight. They waved us on as well.

"He didn't . . . touch you . . . did he?" Ben asked carefully as he drove me home.

"No, no. But, Jett . . ."

"I understand, Neely. Of course I do. But there's nothing we can do to help her right now," he said. "She's getting the care she needs, and her mother and brother are there for her. It would be better to see her when she's conscious and you feel better. To-morrow."

I nodded, closed my eyes, and said a silent prayer that Jett would wake up and be all right.

"Why were you at the grotto? You shouldn't be walking around by yourself in the dark."

I bristled at that.

Okay, Ben was just being Ben: good-hearted, concerned, pro-tective. Would it be so terrible to have someone watching out for me for a change? No, it wouldn't. But I had to make myself clear to Ben. I wasn't the resident ditso. I had lived in New York, for God's sake, and managed to get around when Luke was away, which was most of the time. I was independent. I refused to be limited anymore—I had to be my full self. The person who colored inside the lines married to someone who didn't recognize them. The dimpled daddy's girl without a daddy. The cake therapist who couldn't figure out her own life. And now was as good a time as any to start.

"I appreciate your concern, but I'm not the victim here," I replied, a little too forcefully. "I was the one who tried to save the day. I'm not some weak, hand-wringing damsel in distress that you had to rescue."

Ben flinched as if I had slapped him. "Oh, no?" He turned to look at me. "Then what am I doing here?"

"Well, I called you *after* I called nine-one-one. I could have had Daniel take me home."

"Right," he said sarcastically. "Daniel." He shook his head. "You won't admit you've had me on speed dial since second grade. *I've* answered every time you called the Damsel Rescue Hotline."

"You act like I'm some flake."

"Well, you've done a pretty good impersonation of that for the past few years."

Now *I* was mad. "How can you *say* that?"

"I can say that because it's true. Guys talk, you know. I probably don't know all of Luke's *adventures*, but I know enough. Why would you put up with that crap? That's not the Neely I thought I knew. When you really needed to call me to get you the hell out of there, you didn't."

I turned to face him. "I didn't 'put up with that crap,'" I yelled, angry that I was starting to cry when I just wanted to be mad. I wiped the tears from my cheeks with the backs of my hands. "I wasn't clueless or weak. I was stuck, okay? Stuck. I *hated* being stuck. But I finally did something about it. All by myself."

I turned away from him, looking out the window into the black night, trying to stifle the sobs that came from deep down.

Ben reached in his breast pocket and handed over his handkerchief. "I'm sorry, Neely. I shouldn't have said that. You've been through enough tonight."

We rode in silence for the next few minutes. I dabbed my eyes and took several deep breaths and tried to calm myself. I breathed out a big sigh. When I had settled down enough so my voice wouldn't wobble, I returned to our previous conversation. I had made a start with Ben, trying to let him see the person I was now. But as much as I wanted him to know everything, I also knew I needed to find a better moment than this one to reveal the woowoo of my intuition. For the next few minutes, I needed to sound *not* crazy; so I kept it simple. "You wanted to know what I was doing on the convent grounds so late at night. Well, I was just out jogging and I heard glass breaking and went to see what was going on. I guess it wasn't the smartest thing."

"No. But you probably saved Jett. He could have killed her."

I nodded. "I wonder why *she* was there."

I began to shiver uncontrollably.

"It's the aftershock," Ben said, matter-of-factly. "It will stop in a few minutes. I've got the heat cranked up, and you'll be home soon, safe and sound."

At my house, Ben helped me off with my coat, then up the stairs.

At the door to my bedroom, Ben held me by my shoulders. "That guy is still out there somewhere, Neely," he said. "You're not safe alone, so I'm staying here tonight."

I was too tired to resist. Wordlessly, I led him across the hall to my office with its big leather lounge chair, the Christmas present I didn't give Luke. I got a pillow and blankets from the closet and handed them to Ben.

"Thank you for everything," I said. "And I'm sorry I yelled at you. You were only trying to help. I do appreciate that, no matter how snarly I get sometimes."

He smiled down at me, smoothed and kissed my forehead. "I'm sorry, too. I dunno," he said, rubbing my shoulders. "There is something about you that always gets to me, Neely. Way back to when you were a skinny little girl who got a hundred on every spelling test but couldn't remember to wear your gloves when it was below zero."

I smiled. "I remember that. You tried to give me yours, and I wouldn't take them. But I walked home from school right next to you, with both of my hands in your coat pocket. I had creative solutions even back then."

Ben smiled and rolled his eyes. "You just keep telling yourself that. . . ."

I wrapped my arms around his middle, tucking my head under his chin. In a perfect world, I would kiss him, tentatively at first, then more and more deeply. We would sink down into the big leather lounge chair, Luke be damned. I'd curl into Ben's lap, getting as close as I could. We would spend delicious time getting to know each other again, slowly, before I led him across the hall to my bed. And there we would finish what we had started years ago.

But tonight was not the night. I couldn't risk hurting him again. When our time came, I wanted it to feel like the most natural thing in the world. It would feel so right, I wouldn't have to think about it. I would just *know*.

Right now, my body was willing, but I was still waiting for my head and heart to catch up.

I pushed back from Ben, gently ran my finger down his arm, and said good night.

"I'll be in here if you need me," he said.

In my bedroom, I changed into my nightgown, took my first sleeping pill with a glass of water, and fell into bed.

15

I woke up a little after six a.m., late for me, but I was happy to have fallen asleep to begin with. My arm was stiff and sore, and that brought back last night's trauma with Jett. I needed to go to the hospital to see her. I needed to know that she would be all right.

And then I thought about Barney. He needed to go out and be fed.

And it was Saturday. There was a full workday ahead at the bakery, minus one employee.

Quietly, I tiptoed into my office. Ben was snoring softly. His blanket had fallen down, so I gently pulled it up to his chin.

In sleep, he looked just like the boy I had known since grade school, if you could see past the not-quite-perfect nose and the scar on his chin. A battle-scarred boy, determined to protect everyone he cared for.

I tried to be as quiet as possible, making coffee downstairs in the kitchen, but I heard Ben push the lounge chair back into its upright position and come down the steps.

"Black? Cream? Sugar?" I asked, pouring him a mug of coffee. Sleepy-eyed, Ben still managed to beam out that strong, masculine, shoulder-to-lean-on beacon in a wrinkled shirt with mussed-up hair. Maybe one day soon I wouldn't need to ask what he wanted in his morning coffee; I'd just know. Maybe one day soon I would walk into his arms and belong there.

"Just a little cream."

I filed a mental note as I handed him his mug.

"Well, it wasn't much of a pajama party," I said by way of apology.

He smiled at me as he took a big sip. "No pajamas, for one thing."

Any other guy, especially those I had come across in the sports world, would have put a leer into that, but Ben didn't need to. He had my undivided attention.

"I'm glad you stayed. I felt a lot safer. Thank you."

"Is that the statement that damsels in distress are required to give in rescue situations, something like 'you have the right to remain silent'?"

"How did you know? You must have done this a time or two."

"Or three or four."

I took a sip of my coffee and grimaced. "Does this taste okay to you?" The coffee seemed weak to me. I hoped I wasn't starting with some new mystery when I wasn't finished with the old one yet.

"Yeah. It's not as good as your lattes next door."

"Well, let's go get the good stuff." I was relieved. I poured out our coffees in the sink, rinsed out the mugs, and grabbed my coat and bag.

We went in the back door. Norb turned to look at us, raised his eyebrows slightly, and went back to baking the two hundred rainbow cupcakes we needed today for a gay pride event. That was another reason I loved Norb. He didn't ask; he wouldn't tell.

Once again, I fired up the trusty La Marzocco for Ben's latte. I tried to guide the foam into a heart, but it spread out into a pumpkin that split apart. When would I get the hang of this? Maybe it was my sore arm.

Ben munched on his second ham and cheese croissant and downed the glass of orange juice I brought him. "Can't say when I've had a better breakfast, Neely," he said, wiping the crumbs from his mouth with a napkin.

There was something about feeding a man who appreciated your efforts and ate every bite. I squeezed his shoulder as I got up from the café table to make my own latte. I was surprised I could be so civil in the morning. Maybe it was the five hours I had actually slept.

"What's your day like?" I asked Ben as I tried to guide the foam into a simple spiral, but ended up with a double helix.

"Going home to clean up. Then we're doing security for a shareholders' meeting in Queen City, which might turn ugly," Ben said. "And then I have another wedding tonight. I can stop by after that, if you want. Shouldn't be too late."

I smiled. "I'd like that. A lot."

"And you?"

"I'll be here most of the day, but I'll sneak out at some point to go see Jett."

After Ben left, I looked at the cupcakes piling up on the cooling racks. Instead of making each one a rainbow, we were doing separate batches of color, so the cake and frosting matched. When they were all displayed, you'd get the full Roy G. Biv effect.

When I checked the walk-in refrigerator, I saw that Jett had filled the disposable piping bags with seven different colors and flavors of buttercream, as I had asked. I lined up three dozen raspberry cupcakes on the work counter and started piping rosy frosting on each one. Orange was next, then lemon yellow, pistachio green, and so on. Whatever I had left over, I'd put out for sale.

As the sun came up, I was packing up the last of the violet-hued blackberry cupcakes.

That task completed, I threw on my coat and jogged the few blocks to Mrs. Amici's house. Her key wasn't under the doormat. I peeped in the front window and saw a backpack on the plum-colored armchair. That had to be Bobby. And no barking, so Barney was still asleep. Good.

Back at the bakery, the morning had begun. The Professor came in at his usual time, had his usual breakfast cupcake and latte, and his usual chat with Maggie that left them both smiling as they parted ways. I briefly wondered how he spent his Sunday mornings, since he was here every other day.

The gay-pride organizer picked up the boxes of rainbow cupcakes. Roshonda stopped by for her caramel macchiato, but she was mum about her date, a good sign. She didn't stay long. We arranged to meet up later at Finnegan's.

By late Saturday afternoon, the bakery had finally gotten quiet.

"Let me know how she is," Maggie said as I left to see Jett at the hospital.

When I got to Jett's room, she was sitting up in bed, staring out the window. She startled at the noise, then visibly relaxed when she saw it was me.

Wordlessly, I passed her a box of rainbow cupcakes.

She opened the box and started to cry.

I sat down on the bed and took her hand. "It's okay. You're gonna be okay." I grabbed a tissue from the box on the side table and handed it to her.

She dabbed her eyes. "I got a mild concussion. My head hurts."

"It's a good thing to be hardheaded sometimes."

She gave me a watery smile.

"Those frostings I made look pretty good," she said, pointing to the cupcakes, then looking down at her hands, which still showed the effects of the food colorings she'd used. "I'm glad I get first pick before my mom and brother come back. She's supposed to take me home when she gets off work," Jett added. "But I don't want to go home if he's still out there somewhere."

"You know who attacked you?"

Jett closed her eyes and nodded. "Crazy Sean, my old boy-friend."

"I thought he wasn't stalking you anymore."

"I thought so, too."

She twisted a lock of hair in her fingers, like Maggie's little girl. My heart ached for Jett.

"You might as well know, Neely. They had to do a rape kit," Jett said. "At least I was out of it for some of what they had to do. And then they let me take a long, long shower."

"I wish I had gotten to you sooner."

We sat quietly for a few moments.

Then her voice dropped to a whisper. "How did you find me?"

I stroked her hand. "I was out jogging and heard glass breaking and the grotto was dark. I knew something was wrong."

She dabbed her eyes again. "After I broke up with Sean in January, he started following me home from school. He works construction, so it was only on days when it was too cold or too wet to work. And then he started following me when I was out with my friends at night. One night I agreed to go out with him again, and we got into another fight. I told him to get a life, but he backhanded me across my face. That's when I stayed at your house."

She blew her nose and got another tissue.

"I thought all of that bad stuff was finally over with. My dad leaving. My mom crying. My boyfriend stalking me. I just wanted it all to go away. I went to the grotto to light a candle—weird, huh? Me, lighting candles and everything."

"Not so weird," I assured her. "I've gone there, too. It's quiet and peaceful and being there just makes you feel better."

"Until he ruined it," Jett said angrily, wiping her nose.

I gathered her into my arms and rocked her back and forth.

When Jett started drifting off to sleep, I gently settled her against the pillow, put the box of cupcakes on the side table, and walked out to my car.

The day had warmed up, one of those quicksilver weather changes March always brought. I threw my coat in the backseat, rolled down the driver's side window, and drove out of the parking lot.

Maybe taking off my coat lowered my carefully constructed defenses, too. There was a smell of spring in the air and that sense of yearning that always came with it.

I want. I want what I can't have. I don't know what I want.

And then I heard that song. The Beatles' "Something" stopped me in my tracks even after the car in front of me had driven off, trailing sound. I sat at the stoplight. That song churned up a depth of yearning that took me by surprise.

"Something" was an unlikely song to pick for a lullaby, but my dad never did things the usual way. No "Rock-a-bye Baby" for him. He just sang me songs he knew and liked. I remembered sitting on his lap in the rocking chair in my little bedroom, a chink of fading light coming through the blinds. I heard the sound deep in his chest, felt the in-and-out of his breath, the warmth of his arms around me. The words lulled me to sleep, but what they really meant was, *Go to sleep. You're safe. You're special to me.*

And who knew that years later, as the college party wound down and people were passed out or pairing up, someone would play "Something" and Luke would ask me to dance, his eyes lighting up in recognition. *That girl from the bakery.* I was more than the girl whose father left her. I could be special in a different way. There was something about me, after all. And I would step away from my old life into his arms, thinking, *This is where I belong.*

At home, I opened the upstairs windows to let the warm, soft air in, but still keep me safe—this part of Millcreek Valley was more urban than suburban. As darkness fell, I paced from room to room, not knowing what to do with the disquiet I felt.

My cell phone rang. It was Daniel. "Just wanted you to know, Neely, that we caught Sean Mooney, the guy who assaulted Jett. He's in custody now."

"Oh, that's a relief," I said, breathing out the tension I had held. "Where did you find him?"

"We located a ping on his cell phone. He was hiding out in an old warehouse being torn down in Lockton. He didn't put up much of a fight," Daniel said. "I was kinda looking forward to rearranging that guy's face without any police brutality involved. His great-grandfather was a cop. My dad knew him. Hate to see his legacy tainted by having a scumbag relative."

"Does Jett know yet?"

"Just coming back from the hospital. They're going to press charges. She's a brave girl."

"Yes, she is," I said. "You need anything from me, you know where to find me."

When it was time to meet Roshonda, I walked across the street to Finnegan's. I looked around the front room. She wasn't there. I walked back to the bar area and saw her talking to a guy. A big guy.

Even in dimmed light, with his back turned to me, dressed in a custom suit, I knew.

Luke.

My heart took an unwelcome plunge.

Better get this over with, I thought and willed myself to be strong. With Luke, I needed every bit of backbone I possessed, even now.

"What brings you here? To Finnegan's, of all places?"

"Great to see you, too, Cupcake."

Roshonda got up from her barstool and stood between us. "I tried to call you, Neely, but you had your phone turned off. Luke and I were just chatting about the TV commercial he's in talks about doing." She looked over at Luke. "Deep pockets, he says." She raised her eyebrows like she was impressed. "They want him to tell his fans how much he loves the food at this chain of *family* restaurants." She looked back at me meaningfully.

I got it.

"If you don't want to see him, you don't have to, you know," she said with steel in her voice.

"You should have been an offensive lineman, Roshonda. You've got what it takes to protect your quarterback," Luke said with a grin. He fanned out his hands in front of him like the peacemaker he wasn't. "I'm just here to talk to my wife. She *is* still my wife, you know," he said with an equally determined smile.

"Not if she doesn't want to be," Roshonda said, pulling herself up to her full height. Even so, Luke could have crushed her like an empty soda can.

I sighed and knew it was time for a decision. "It's all right, Ro."

"You're sure? I'm just going to talk to some people in the other room, but I'm here if you need me." She gave Luke the look she used when Nickel and Dime had asked for a discount—after not showing up for several appointments. You didn't want to mess with Roshonda.

"I'll talk to you later," I said.

Reluctantly, I turned my attention back to Luke.

He did that thing he did so well. He looked deep into my eyes as if I were the only person in the whole world for him. I didn't flinch. I looked back, steady and calm. I wasn't going to be mesmerized this time. *I can do this. I can be strong.*

But my other senses started to betray me. He smelled like Luke. Like clean shirts and that aftershave he had worn since college. He looked good.

He tenderly slipped a stray curl behind my ear. Slowly, seriously, he bent to kiss me.

"Luke," I protested, and took a step backward.

I sat down on the barstool that Roshonda had just vacated,

changing tactics. "I'm serious. What brings you all the way from New York to Finnegan's, of all places?"

"Shhh." He sat down on his barstool, but leaned in and placed a finger on my lips.

"Luke, I'm not—"

"Shhh," he whispered again, stroking my cheek with the back of his big hand that can be oh, so surprisingly gentle. "I need to talk to you, Claire. Okay, Roshonda was right. I am up for this commercial and they do want a guy with a wife and, preferably, a kid or two. But if I don't get it, there will be others. That's not why I'm here."

I crossed my arms over my chest and waited.

"The Whyte Trash Wedding story was in the *New York Daily News* this morning."

"What, in a 'News of the Weird' column, strange goings-on in the hinterlands?" I asked.

"It doesn't matter. What matters is that when I read your name, it hit me. 'Claire Davis. My wife. My wife who is living a life without me. Who is doing things that I don't know about unless I read the goddamn newspaper.' I got the first flight out. And here I am."

Neither one of us said anything for a moment.

Luke's temper always flared hot, then cooled down fast.

The new bartender came back from the kitchen and served a cheeseburger and fries to a customer at the other end of the bar. "Another beer?" he asked the guy, but eyed us.

"Can we go somewhere quiet?" Luke asked, throwing a hundred-dollar bill on the bar.

Somewhere quiet. I wasn't letting him in my house. I didn't want to be alone with him in his car. I just wanted to get this over with. "Let's walk. It's nice out for March."

As we left Finnegan's, I gestured to an alarmed Roshonda that it was all okay.

For two lovers just starting out, the soft air and the moonlight would have worked its magic. But we weren't starting out.

"I can't do this anymore, Claire. It's not working for me," he said, looking at me with that same green-eyed intensity I remembered so well. We had stopped at the corner under a streetlight. I was grateful for the traffic noise and the glare from the headlights.

"It's not working for me, either." Maybe this was going to be easier than I thought.

"I'm sorry I was such a jerk. I'm sorry I caused you pain." He leaned down and tried to kiss me once again, but I turned away. "You're not making this easy. But I probably deserve that."

I was just getting ready to say, "I can't be married to you anymore," when he turned toward me and grabbed me by the shoulders.

"I love you."

Those magic words.

Not "Love ya," the offhand good-bye he usually tossed my way. This sounded serious. This sounded real. I felt myself soften. I tried to put my invisible shield up again, but he got there first.

Maybe . . .

He wrapped himself around me and kissed me like there was nothing else in the world, nowhere else to be. I felt the lean, muscled contour of his body, the passion that had always been Luke. My thoughts looped around again. *I shouldn't do this. I don't love him anymore. I don't. We've been through this before. They're just words to him.*

In the old days, the "no" in my head would have gotten fainter as those old, powerful feelings swept everything else away. This was what love with Luke felt like. We'd back into the indigo shadows, entwined and needy again, just like the first time. And it would start all over again.

But those were the old days.

This didn't feel right.

I pushed Luke away. Now I understood what people meant when they said "estranged." He felt like a stranger to me.

"I can't do this anymore. Any of it," I said.

"But I love you. You love me. We can work this out."

"We can't work it out this time because I don't want to."

"You can't forgive me one last time?"

"We both know it wouldn't be the last time. I just don't have it in me anymore."

Luke crushed me to him, trying to kiss me again, but I moved my head from side to side.

"Stop. Stop." He loosened his grip on me and I pulled away, breathless. "Just stop. I can't do this. I mean that. I don't love you like that anymore. It's over."

He stepped back from me, his shoulders slumping. I saw a look on his face that I had never seen before—sadness.

"I'm sorry," I said. "I'm different now and I can't go back. I'm sorry," I said again as I turned away, running toward home.

I thought he might run after me, begging, pleading, cajoling— all of his old tricks that I used to fall for. I let myself in the front door, locked it behind me, barricaded myself in. I had to grip my phone with both shaking hands to read the text from Ben: *OK to come over?*

Ben. Was it just a few hours ago that I wanted him in my bed?

How could I smell spring in the air, hear an old song, and almost fall for Luke again? What was I doing?

I texted him back: *Luke stopped by. I need to be alone right now.*

Ben replied: *Take care.*

After a long soak in the tub that still left me feeling restless, I thought about taking a sleeping pill and falling into welcome oblivion again.

But I needed some kind of closure.

The old-fashioned way.

In my robe and slippers, I grabbed my iPod from its charging station.

What was on my Spotify playlist that sounded like I felt? I started my heartbreak hit parade with Patsy Cline's "Crazy" and the raw pain in Bonnie Raitt's "I Can't Make You Love Me." I churned up all the old "he done me wrong" feelings.

At my desk upstairs, well after midnight, I took out paper and pen and wrote Luke a long letter, crossing out words, underlining others. I could have used the computer, but I needed the physicality of pressing pen to paper. Tapping on the keyboard was too gentle for heavy-duty venting.

Luke also deserved more of an explanation than what he had gotten tonight. I needed to explain it to myself, as well, and I wasn't doing a very good job. I crumpled another sheet of paper and threw it in the wastebasket.

As the music played, I had imaginary conversations with him, envisioned scenes in a movie with us as characters, he as the charmer, me as the wronged woman.

What it came down to, in practical terms, was this: Luke couldn't be faithful. I couldn't be with a man like that anymore.

God knew, I had tried. But he wouldn't change, and I couldn't. So somebody had to bow out or we'd both continue with this old sad song, this broken record.

I sat back in the chair and sighed. I searched Spotify for "Something" and played it. The memories, the yearning, came drifting back. But I realized something as the song finished. What I yearned for wasn't Luke. *It wasn't Luke.* I didn't want him, but more important, I didn't *need* him.

So, what had I clung to all this time, if it hadn't really been Luke? Why had I let myself get so stuck?

The last question made me think, somehow, of my dad. I rummaged in the desk drawer and took out that snapshot from my fourteenth birthday again, the one with Dad's arm around my shoulders. He had the look of someone pulling away. I could see it clearly now.

My dad hadn't left us all at once, although that was how it had seemed at the time. He had left us by degrees. It had started with the silent treatment at home. He had seemed wrapped up in his thoughts, as if he were miles away. Then he'd had a couple of "lost weekends," when Mom didn't know where he had gone; when he returned, he had acted as if nothing had happened. At first they had argued about it, but then Mom got really scared. She didn't know what to do, so she didn't do anything. Pretty soon, Dad was gone for good.

In a subconscious way, I must have been determined not to repeat family history. I must have dug in my heels to prevent Luke from leaving, as my dad had left. When Luke strayed, it must have brought back all of Dad's lost-weekend stuff. That fear of abandonment. Unlike my mother, I had held on. I hadn't been helpless.

No. That seemed logical, but it didn't resonate.

That wasn't it.

What felt true was this: It had been hard to stay in my marriage, the hardest thing I had ever done. After our head-over-heels court-ship and early married days, it had hurt like hell to be the un-fun person in a romantic triangle, the ball and chain. It had taken everything I had to weather the tears, recriminations, frosty silences, and then the slow thawing and getting back to normal. Three times that I knew about. How many more that I didn't?

The easy thing for me would have been to call it quits after the first, or even the second time that Luke had played around. A clean break. Admit the mistake. Move on.

So why *had* I stayed?

I didn't want to repeat our family story. That felt true.

And then I realized: I had the story backward.

I hadn't been keeping Luke from leaving me. I had been pre-venting *myself* from leaving him. I had been trying so, so hard not to be the one who was gone for good.

But, like my dad, it happened by degrees. First in my mind, when I said enough was enough. Then in body, when I moved back here. And, finally, in my heart.

Whew.

I put the pen down, then sat back in the chair and sighed with relief.

My emotional cupboard was bare. I had cried it out of me, written it out of me. Now I had room for whatever or whoever was coming next.

I was beginning to taste it. Something bitter, but warm.

A flavor that woke me up and let me see things clearly. A flavor that made me feel safe, so I could let those things go. A flavor that held my hand and walked me across to the other side of loss, and assured me that one day, I would be *just fine*. A flavor for a change of heart—part grief, part hope.

Suddenly, I knew what that flavor would be. I padded down to the kitchen and cut a slice of sour cream coffee cake with a spicy underground river coursing through its center, left over from an order that had not been picked up today.

One bite and I was sure. A familiar flavor that now seemed utterly fresh and custom-made for me.

Cinnamon.

The comfort of sweet cinnamon. It always worked. I felt better. Lighter. Not quite "everything is going to be all right," but getting there. One step at a time.

Back upstairs, I texted Ben: *Breakfast? Late morning?* I hoped the ping of my message didn't wake him from a sound sleep.

And there was one more thing before I was finally ready for bed.

I took down the postcard from the memory board above my desk and read it again: "Sorry for all this. Miss you. Love you. Dad." I brushed my fingers over the signature and tried to imagine what my father looked like now. I wondered whether he was still in Kansas City.

Maybe my father had been having a change of heart, and I just hadn't realized it. This was the first postcard from him that had a return address.

He had left a trail that I could follow.

Maybe it was time for me to be the grown-up who reached out instead of the child left behind.

I took out another piece of paper.

"Dear Dad . . ."

16

"Thanks so much for meeting me here. I'm glad Sunday afternoon worked for us all."

I shook hands with Sam and Ellen Whyte, just back from their honeymoon, and old Mr. Whyte. We gathered for a moment near the nurses' station on the fifth floor of Queen City Rehabilitation Hospital.

Since the flood of insights that hit me on the night of Jett's assault two weeks ago, I hadn't experienced the tiniest glimpse of someone's story, an unpleasantly sour taste in my mouth, or a bad night's sleep.

I felt much better. But I was still recovering from an intuitive's hangover. It took a while for the energy overload to dissipate.

Now only one lingering shadow remained.

Edie. The former Shemuel Weiss and Olive Habig needed to

connect again. Maybe something lodged in their memories—or my visions—could provide a clue to her disappearance. And bring them both some sense of closure.

"Marriage agrees with you," I said to Ellen and Sam.

They smiled at each other, then looked at me expectantly.

"I'm glad you all agreed to visit Mrs. Amici—Olive Habig, as you knew her growing up," I said to the older Samuel. "After the disruption she and her daughter, Diane, caused at your reception, I wouldn't have blamed you for saying no."

"I still don't understand what all of that was about," said Sam.

"Maybe Mrs. Amici can tell us," I said. "I spoke with her grandson, Bobby. She is dealing with head trauma and still goes in and out of consciousness. The doctor told Bobby she has delirium—when an older person has been in one hospital after another and is disoriented. But when she is lucid, she can remember the past."

"Maybe we should wait out here, then," said young Sam. "Grandpa was the one who knew her a long time ago."

"No. There are things we all need to get cleared up," the elder Whyte said.

"Let's have a piece of cake together in Olive's room," I suggested, holding up a pale turquoise cake box tied with chocolate-brown ribbon. "And then maybe Sam and Ellen could wait out here until you and Olive have finished."

As we walked to room 522, Shemuel mused, "I've been thinking about Frankie Amici. He was a quiet, unassuming fellow. Pretty shy. I don't think I ever said five words to him the whole time I lived in Lockton. And to marry someone like Olive . . . Opposites attract, I guess."

I smiled wistfully.

I understand that better than he realizes.

In the small, drab room sat a tiny woman with an IV pole and a portable oxygen tank attached to her wheelchair. Olive listed a little to the left, her eyes closed, almost lost in a maze of plastic tubing and a hospital gown much too big for her. She had a thermal blanket tucked around her lap and hospital socks on her feet.

I gestured to a chair for old Mr. Whyte. Sam, Ellen, and I would have to stand. I put the cake box on the rolling hospital bed table. I stacked the pale pink plates, napkins, and forks next to it. Then I pulled the drapes to let in a little more light. With people and color and sunshine, the room became more cheerful.

I knelt down to take Olive's hand, something I never would have attempted before her accident. It felt dry and cool. If I held it up to the light and spread her fingers, I thought I could almost see through her hand, like parchment paper. The line between here and not here was thinning, no question.

"Your old friend Shemuel is here to visit you, Mrs. Amici. We're going to have a piece of cake, and then we can talk."

A tall, white-haired lady in powder blue pants and an embroidered white sweater entered the room with the help of her walker. It took me a moment to realize who it was.

"Sister Agnes," I said, "you're just in time for cake."

"How about that for good timing?" She smiled. "Sister Josepha usually makes the Sunday hospital visits, but she's down with a bug, so I said I'd do it."

"I didn't know Mrs. Amici was Catholic," I said.

Sister shrugged. "I don't know if she is. Somebody must have marked that on her admittance papers. We offer spiritual comfort to Millcreek Valley patients in the hospital, whatever their faith."

I introduced Sister Agnes to everyone, and then offered her my chair.

I opened the box and cut a slice of layer cake for each plate. "I think it might work best if I serve Mrs. Amici last." I gave Sister Agnes and Shemuel a plate, a fork, and a napkin, then Ellen and Sam. And lastly, I laid a napkin over Olive's lap and held a forkful of cake up to her lips.

She couldn't see the homemade colored sprinkles, the tender yellow cake, or the pale pink frosting made with strawberry syrup enhanced with a little rosewater. Although our local strawberries weren't in season yet, I had conjured the aroma and taste of juicy berries warmed by the sun. I hoped this flavor would help the two old people return once more to their youth and the carefree feeling of a summer day.

Slowly, with her eyes still closed, she opened her mouth. She looked like a hungry baby bird, ready for a worm. She took one bite after another, then smacked her lips like the ten-year-old Olive I had glimpsed.

When I looked across at old Mr. Whyte, he, too, was licking the frosting from around his mouth, smiling like the Shemuel who had treasured the few precious minutes he had spent in the Habig home each week.

"Would you like another piece?" I asked.

"Yes!" the older people said.

With each new bite of cake, the more years they seemed to shed.

"Don't let Shemuel eat it all," Olive muttered, and suddenly her eyes snapped open. "He always got the last of the milk."

"Your mother was always feeding me, wasn't she, Olive?" he said gently.

"Peanut butter sandwiches," Olive recalled. "I remember stirring the peanut butter in that tin container it used to come in years ago. The oil always separated at the top and you had to stir it together again. And Ovaltine, lots of Ovaltine."

"I always left your house with a cookie."

Mrs. Amici snorted. "Maybe too many. You grew up to be a lot bigger than me. Doesn't look like you missed too many meals."

They each took another bite of cake.

Sister Agnes' face softened, the years falling away. "There was a bakery when I was a girl—Oster's—and they had the best strawberry cake. Oh, we hardly ever got to have cake. We didn't have any money. But every once in a while, Mama would be paid by one of her Fairview ladies and we'd get a treat," she said in a childish rush.

"You used to say 'true show' and not 'trousseau,'" Mrs. Amici said, matter-of-factly.

Poor Mrs. Amici was really confused. But then I looked at Sister Agnes, and back at Mrs. Amici. I gasped. *Could this be?*

I searched the nun's face for the little girl I had glimpsed reading *The Princess and the Goblin* in the library. There was something of little Edie in her pale coloring, her quiet demeanor. Smiling, Sister Agnes set her plate aside, took off her glasses, and pressed the napkin to her eyes. "It's all right, Neely. I'm sure I said many silly things as a child." She welled up again. "Memories," she whispered. "After all this time."

Shemuel looked at Sister Agnes, too. Did he see what I saw?

Ellen finished her cake and delicately wiped her mouth with the napkin before putting her plate and fork aside.

"I've been thinking, Mrs. Amici," Ellen said, in a kind and calm voice. "Sam and I are so happy together. And I love this beautiful ring that belonged to your family." She twisted the sapphire ring off her finger and held it out in the palm of her left hand for the old woman to see. "But maybe this is not really mine to keep. If this will make you feel better, please know that it is yours. Again."

Sister Agnes leaned forward in her chair to get a good look.

Mrs. Amici stared at the sapphire and seemed to consider it for a moment. "I forgot how beautiful it was." She sighed, then shook her head and said softly, "Keep it, hon."

When Ellen moved to offer again, Mrs. Amici said a little more forcefully, "Keep it." She paused a moment. "And wear it. Wear it every day. My mother didn't wear it near enough."

"She didn't," said Sister Agnes, who began to cry, softly.

I gave the nun's shoulder a gentle squeeze. I wasn't sure how to proceed with someone who was just recovering her memory, so I just went with how I would want to be treated—with kindness and compassion, but without drama. We would take this slowly.

Ellen put the ring back on her finger, cradling it with her right hand. "Thank you," she said, to both Mrs. Amici and Sister Agnes.

"Won't do me any good now anyway," muttered Olive, snapping back to her old self. "What I want, I can't have. Story of my life."

Olive's eyes narrowed at Shemuel. "Diane's in jail." She turned to Sam and Ellen. "It was all her idea, to go after the ring. She dragged me along." She turned toward me. "You talked to Bobby?" she asked. "What did he say about Diane? He hasn't been to see me since Christmas."

Uh-oh. It was April and Mrs. Amici had only been in the rehab hospital for a short while. I wondered if she was beginning to slip again. *I had better move this along.*

"Diane can't post bail," I explained. "Bobby says she could be charged with assault. They have to wait until you are more yourself to decide whether they will press charges or not. Her public defender isn't sure when the preliminary hearing will be. The municipal court docket is pretty full right now."

Olive looked at Ellen. "Wish she had turned out more like you."

"I'm sorry about Diane," said the old man, clearing his throat.

"Well, that's something," said Olive, sarcastically.

"I'm sorry, too, Mrs. Amici," Ellen said.

We reached another impasse in the conversation.

"Ellen and I are going to step out now to give you a chance to talk," said Sam.

Olive watched them go, turning to Shemuel. "Are you happy now? You should be. You got everything."

"Yes, I've been fortunate, Olive," he said gently. "Thanks to Edie."

"Edie?"

"Yes, Edie." He reached over and took Sister Agnes' hand and joined it with Olive's. "Your sister."

"Edie? Is that you?"

The sisters faced each other, trying to see beyond the white hair, the altered faces.

"You came back?" Olive said. "All these years, Edie. All these years." She sobbed.

"I didn't know I had been gone," said Sister Agnes, stroking her sister's hand. "I don't know what's happening." She looked as troubled as Olive.

I firmly but gently touched her arm.

"If it wasn't for Edie, I don't know how my life would have turned out," Shemuel said to the two sisters. "Edie wanted to run away. It just happened to be on December eighth, 1941, when everything changed. That was the day we declared war on Japan after the attack on Pearl Harbor."

Olive nodded.

Edie looked confused.

"Remember how people were running all around, not knowing what to do? President Roosevelt giving his speech? People looking for Japanese planes in the sky?" he continued.

"No." Edie shook her head.

"I remember," said Olive. "It was a Monday because I had to restock all the empty shelves that morning at Oster's. I didn't find out until somebody ran in the bakery late in the afternoon and made me drop a pan of sweet rolls," said Olive. "Mrs. Oster said to just pick 'em up, dust 'em off, and put 'em back in the case. People would want something sweet after bad news. And she was right. We had a lot of customers. I could have eaten the whole pan myself after Edie didn't come home that night." She turned to Edie. "Why didn't you come home?"

"I don't know," Edie whispered.

"Edie was sick," the old man reminded her. "Remember, Olive? She was jumpy. Afraid of her shadow. Skin and bones."

"I wish I had known what was wrong with you. You just clammed up," Olive said.

They all sat quietly.

"We didn't really have a plan," Shemuel explained. "We were just going to let the train take us somewhere far away."

"So what happened?"

"It started snowing so hard, you couldn't see your hand in front of your face. I got on the first train car, and didn't see Edie."

"How could you miss her?"

"It was heavy, heavy snowfall. Like cotton batting dropping from the sky. Like someone holding up a white chenille bedspread to a window and you trying to look through it. I couldn't see outside."

"Maybe you didn't want to see."

"I don't remember any of that," said Edie, shrinking back inside herself.

Shemuel breathed deeply. "I walked through the train, looking for you, Edie. By the time I reached the last passenger car, the train was moving and picking up speed. I found the ring on the floor, wrapped up in that handkerchief you always carried." He took a square of folded, embroidered handkerchief from the breast pocket of his blazer and passed it over to Edie. "It's still smells a little like you, I think."

Blankly, Edie passed it to Olive.

Olive raised the hankie to her nose, closed her eyes, and sniffed. "Lilies of the valley. Our mother's favorite." Her breath shuddered, and I thought she was going to sob, but she held herself stiffly.

"Can I keep this?"

"Of course, Olive."

They sat silent for a moment, lost in their thoughts.

"When I found the ring, I thought maybe you had changed your mind about running away, Edie," Shemuel continued, "but still wanted to help me, just like your mother always did. I thought you left it for me on purpose. But just in case I had missed you on the train somehow, I got off at the Queen City terminal and looked for you, but you were gone."

"I don't remember," said Edie sadly.

"You seemed to do all right for yourself since then, Shemuel," said Olive angrily. "Even a new name. I changed my name, too, when I married Frank, but it didn't change my luck."

"Things switched for us, Olive," he said quietly. "You had what I wanted when I was a boy. You had parents who loved you and a meal on the table every night. You had a clean house and a real bed. You had warm clothes. I never had that. My old name tied me to that old life."

"Didn't you care what happened to Edie? Didn't you ever try to find her?"

"Yes, Olive. Many times. After I got out of the Army and started doing well in my business, I hired private detectives to search for her, but they never found anything."

"They could have found me," fumed Olive.

"They did find you. But I didn't get in touch. I thought Edie might have been running away from you, too, Olive."

Olive glared.

"This is almost too much for me," Edie said, sinking back into her chair.

We sat in silence again.

Now was my time to speak. This was going to sound strange to them, I knew. But maybe something would jog Edie's memory.

"As you said," I began, gesturing to Shemuel, "Edie must have gotten off the train before it left the Millcreek Valley station. But where did she go? She didn't go back home. She didn't walk along the railroad tracks because she couldn't see anything in the heavy snowstorm. But she could have walked up the convent hill," I ventured.

"Why would you do that?" Shemuel asked Edie.

"I don't know," Edie said.

"Maybe you thought you saw something on the train and got scared," I suggested. "You could have jumped off at the last minute and started running away from the train, away from town. Up the convent hill. You might have seen the light through the stained glass window in Bernadette's grotto, and walked toward it. I have done that myself."

"I pray there at least once a day," Edie said. "Something about being there keeps my mind from racing. I can slow down my thoughts and just breathe."

"Yes," I said. "It has had that effect on me, too." I gently nudged her back in time. "That day after Pearl Harbor, you might have stayed in the grotto to get out of the weather. Do you remember being there?"

She shook her head no.

"Maybe you felt safe there," I continued, "safe from something bad that happened to you. From what Shemuel and Olive have said, you might have had post-traumatic stress disorder."

"Edie?" exclaimed Olive. "Post-traumatic stress? I thought you only got that in war."

"You can get that after any sudden trauma," Shemuel said. "War. Natural disasters. Domestic violence. I've known men who had 'shell shock,' they used to call it. And one of my employees developed PTSD after her husband beat her and her children. We tried everything we could to help her, but she eventually had to go on disability. She wouldn't leave the house."

"You wouldn't leave the house, either," Olive said sadly. "Do you remember that, Edie? You locked us up like we lived in Fort Knox. I just didn't know why."

"Maybe what happened to you was so painful, you had to shut down in order to keep going. Maybe you kept reliving this *thing*, like a terrifying nightmare. A nightmare you couldn't fully wake up from. Maybe you had to forget everything in order to get over it."

Edie just shook her head.

"How can you forget everything?" Olive asked.

"I knew a guy who never drove a car again after he was an ambulance driver in the war. I knew another guy who never spoke after he got home. You see stuff. You do stuff. And it gets to you. Losing the past doesn't sound far-fetched to me," said Shemuel. "You do what you have to do to survive."

"Maybe she collapsed and someone found her in the grotto," I continued. "A nun, perhaps, since she was on convent grounds. I don't know. That's all I've got."

"Well, that might explain how Edie became a nun," said Shemuel. "But why didn't anyone know that?"

We sat in silence again.

Olive's frail fingers curled around her sister's hand. "You're here now and that's all that matters to me." Tears rolled down her wizened cheeks. There was something about tough old Mrs. Amici crying that got to me more than her sharp words ever did. I took a clean napkin and reached over to gently dry her tears, sparing the precious handkerchief.

"Where's Barney? Where's my dog?" she wailed. Olive's eyes fluttered and then closed. "Pickle and Olive," she whispered. "Pickle and Olive," she repeated, getting louder.

Shemuel pushed himself forward in his chair. "Don't worry, Olive. I'll post Diane's bail. I'll see that she gets a good attorney. Don't worry about that. Don't worry."

But Olive didn't seem to hear. She started rocking back and forth. "Pickle and Olive. Pickle and Olive. Pickle and Olive . . ."

I pushed the call button by her bed, then knelt by her wheelchair. Edie and I both stroked Olive's hand until help arrived.

MARCH 1964

Sister Agnes climbed the big staircase of the academy, pausing on the spacious landing for a moment to admire the towering oil painting of God the Father high up in the clouds with the sun streaming behind Him.

She loved the colors—blue green, salmon, gold. Not at all what you'd think the God of Abraham would favor. She would have guessed a dark, thunder blue and lightning-bolt yellow—sort of like an atomic blast. She squinted to read the artist's name in the bottom right corner and said a silent "hello" to her friend and mentor, Ethel Parsons Paullin.

When Agnes was working with textbook illustrators in New York, she had met Mrs. Paullin on a visit to the Church of Saint Vincent Ferrer on the Upper East Side. Mrs. Paullin was giving a walking lecture on the series of fourteen oil paintings, representing the Stations of the Cross, which she and her late husband, Telford, had completed in 1918. After the lecture, Agnes and the older artist had struck up a friendly conversation, for it turned out that Ethel had grown up in northern Ohio and had worked on a project in Lockton.

Agnes remembered her delightful sense of humor as the older woman talked about her varied career designing mattress covers, playing cards, stained glass windows, and religious art. "From the profane to the sacred," Mrs. Paullin had joked. "I do it all. In fact, the subject matter of the work matters little to me. Instead, I have only one test for my designs. If they give me a feeling of restful happiness, I know they will please other people."

The benefactors of the school had certainly been pleased when, a few years later, Mrs. Paullin had donated the massive oil of God the Father to Mount Saint Mary in honor of her dear friend Sister Agnes—a woman who, like Mrs. Paullin, had defied expectations and achieved creative success.

On the third floor, Sister dipped her long, slim fingers into the holy water font attached to the wall and made the sign of the cross. She always bowed her head to the framed black-and-white print of Blessed Julie Billiart, as if the French founder of their order could actually see her.

Sister Agnes looked a little like Blessed Julie. Her black veil was neatly pinned to her face-framing headdress. A white linen wimple curved around her face, while a stiff white bib reached from shoulder to shoulder of her black long-sleeved gown. Strands of wooden rosary beads tied at her waist jostled with each step.

The long hallway had tall windows on the left that looked down onto the circular drive and the town at the bottom of the hill. On the right, dark oak doors opened to classrooms.

In the alcove on a window wall stood a favorite of nuns and students alike. A lifelike statue of the Infant of Prague—Jesus as a princely toddler holding an orb and scepter—reigned atop a plaster pillar. Every month, the nuns changed the handmade mantle and gown on the Infant. Today, the Infant was dressed in Lenten violet. Two weeks from now, the nun on the rota would change the gown to white for Easter.

The original McCall's pattern had gotten a lot of use over the years, thought Agnes, who remembered stitching an alb or undergarment out of white dimity for the Infant when she was in the infirmary here. *The Infant has more clothes than I do now,* she thought.

When she first came to the convent, she had been so exhausted that she couldn't sew or read. Her eyes just couldn't focus to thread a needle or read the small print of the only book she had brought with her. There was so much else going on with the war, the nuns had just given her the rest she needed. When they kept asking questions as she got better, Agnes was afraid to admit she no longer had a clear picture of what her life was like before. She knew she had to have a story for the sisters, so she stitched one together from tiny scraps of memory. Caroline Edwards—the signature in the book she had brought with her, *The Princess and the Goblin.* Chicago. She loved to read. She was good with a needle. Lemon was her favorite flavor.

"What about your family, Caroline? Is there anyone we should contact?" the kindly nuns kept pressing.

Trying to remember had brought back that cold weight, the darkness pressing down on her. There was something hovering just beyond the reach of allowable memory that still came up in dreams. A silhouette. A shadow. A feeling.

Caroline couldn't go there and Agnes wouldn't. "All my family are gone," she had finally told the nuns. That was the truth, at least—she couldn't recall who her parents and siblings were, if indeed she'd ever had any. Or the place she had called home when she was a child.

Although she had lived and taught in many places, when Agnes came back to Mount Saint Mary's, she felt at home. The nuns here sent her to college in Boston during her novitiate, taught her how to manage a classroom when she began teaching, cheered her on as she wrote and published stories for primary school readers and then became the editor of a series. They welcomed her back when she needed quiet time to write and edit another book, as she was doing now. They gave her the balm of uncomplicated companionship and daily structure.

She had been happy here, as she told Mrs. Paullin the last time they met in the artist's New York studio.

Yet some things could come only from the children. Agnes opened the door and stepped into the large, high-ceilinged room of second-graders. The classroom featured one wall of large, south-facing windows that looked out onto the fishpond and garden. A bitter wind flung tiny ice pellets against them.

The bulletin boards on either side of the front blackboard were almost completely covered with colorful construction paper baskets, partially filled with cut paper flowers, as the students added blooms to mark each step toward their First Communion in May. The baskets added the only extra color, except for the globe on Sister Josepha's desk.

Thirty-four children—girls and boys in navy wool and starched white cotton uniforms—all rose together when their teacher signaled with her wooden spindle "clicker." The racket of their wooden chairs sliding back from their wood-topped metal desks was as familiar to Agnes as the peal of the convent bells that rang the Angelus at six, noon, and six every day.

She smiled and rubbed her hands together. She couldn't wait to get started. It was story time.

17

~❧~

The *beep-beep-beep* of the security code announced entry into the memory care wing at Mount Saint Mary's.

Sister Agnes slowly glided into the ward with her walker, wearing her usual blue fleece and the medal of the Blessed Mother on a silvery chain.

"Couldn't sleep again," she explained ruefully to the staff nurse. "Arthritis acting up."

"You know you're always welcome, at any time, Sister. And you're more awake than I am."

"If you want to get a cup of coffee, I can hold down the fort."

"I'd love to. I'll just run down to the break room and be right back. You know where the call button is if you need me?"

Agnes nodded with that quiet assurance that always made everyone feel more peaceful. Few people knew her unusual story, and Agnes preferred to keep it that way. Only Shemuel, Neely, and

Olive knew that she had been Edie Habig, not Caroline Edwards, before she took her vows. When Agnes tried to remember her past, she could recall only her childhood. If this was what God chose to return to her, Agnes would be grateful and not ask for more. Reuniting with her sister was gift enough.

The nun wheeled her slow, deliberate way down to Olive's room. After sustaining a concussion, Olive had been diagnosed with dementia. Sister Agnes had helped arrange for the rehab hospital to send her here.

Outside each patient's one-bed room, a glass shadow box held precious photos and mementos that showed the person that dementia had stolen away. A yellowed newspaper clipping of Mr. Patton playing baseball in college, a few poker chips, and a Salesman of the Year plaque. Photos of Mrs. Foster on her wedding day, holding her baby daughter, then with her grandchildren on a picnic— and a tea towel she had embroidered. Mrs. O'Neil's was so crammed with mementos, it was difficult to take it all in, but Sister Agnes' eye always went to the photo of the granddaughter, Neely, the one who had brought that delicious strawberry cake. Olive's shadow box had not yet been filled, but her grandson, Bobby—the great-nephew that Agnes hadn't known about—said he'd bring some things in this week. Of course, he had said the same thing last week when he visited, but then they'd all had a lot to deal with recently.

Agnes slowly wheeled herself into Room 7.

She looked at the small figure with the sparse, cotton-candy hair and the faded pink nightgown, the distress etched on her face even in sleep. Olive tossed her head back and forth like she was having a bad dream. Her weak moan sounded like a kitten mewling.

Poor Olive, Agnes thought. *She must be terribly frightened to be in strange surroundings, even this kind and caring place. At this age, we don't adjust too well to anything new,* she mused, *even with all of our wits about us.* Olive always was a fighter, not a peacemaker. Agnes would have to help her calm down.

Bending over Olive's bed made Agnes' back hurt even more. *I'm going to have to sit down,* she thought. But she knew she couldn't grip her walker and move the room's only chair closer to the bed at the same time. She would simply have to sit on the bed. Agnes pressed the button and lowered the bed rail. Slowly, she eased her right hip down to the edge of the bed and faced her sister. She took her hand and whispered the universal words of comfort. *It's all right.*

A new story came to her, as a story still did, sometimes. Little children and old people seemed to find her stories soothing. With her left hand, she touched her talisman, the Miraculous Medal with the image of the Virgin Mary, the lining of her blue cloak radiating those beautiful colors, and gave a silent *Thank you.*

Agnes whispered, "Once upon a time, there were two little girls who lived in a little house by a creek. In their kitchen was a big bowl of yellow lemons because their mother made lemon cake every week. Their house always smelled wonderful."

Olive lay still as if she were listening.

Agnes continued. "One fine day, their mother opened all the windows in the little house. The delicious smell of lemon cake drifted out the windows and up in the air."

The sleeping woman stirred and turned abruptly on her side, knocking Agnes off balance. Awkwardly, in slow motion, she fell on her side and rolled over to face her tiny sister.

Well, I didn't expect that, Agnes thought. *But what's the harm?* Sometimes people needed basic human touch more than a story. This must be what the Blessed Mother wanted her to do.

Olive draped her arm, light as a dried husk, on top of Agnes as they lay together.

"Pickle," she sighed. "Pickle." A ghost of a smile flickered on her face. "Pickle," Olive breathed again.

Agnes smiled.

She felt her own eyelids get heavy, and, surrendering, she let herself drift off to sleep.

But gentle drifting quickly turned into frantic falling. For the first time in a long time, Agnes spiraled down into the black whirlpool of nightmare, the one with the faceless man chasing her around and around, and when she tried to scream, nothing came out. She felt that same heavy weight as she sank to the bottom of the vortex.

Help me. Please, help me.

Just before the dark waters overwhelmed her, Agnes found herself in a place where lamplight flickered on a wall.

She *knew* this place.

She was a little girl again, lying beside her sister on a cool cellar floor, with the sounds of summer cicadas and the low murmur of a bedtime story.

At last, they were home.

Two cheese coneys sat in front of me, piled with tangles of shredded cheese, in our old wooden booth at the House of Chili. The lunchtime crowd had started to thin. I was starving, but the chili dogs could wait. I couldn't get enough of Ben sitting across from me. Maybe it was because he had been out of town for more than a week. Maybe it was his navy blazer or his crisp shirt, and the slight tan he had picked up on a job in Dallas.

Maybe it was realizing that what I, too, had been searching for was right under my nose the whole time.

"I have so much to tell you," I began, and then filled him in on Jett, who was healing and back to work, and whose stalker ex-boyfriend, Sean, was still in custody awaiting trial. On Diane, who was out of jail on probation. And on the long-separated sisters Pickle and Olive, who were as reunited as Sister Agnes' limited memory and Mrs. Amici's dementia would allow. At least they could see each other every day at Mount Saint Mary's.

Ben listened with raised eyebrows. "Whoa. Things were never this interesting before you moved back," he said, taking a sip of his iced tea. "We went years without this much drama."

Then he got serious, reaching across the table to take my hand. "It was like these problems we didn't know we had were just waiting until you came back to fix them."

"The power of cake," I said with a smile.

"If you say so." He withdrew his hand. "But how about the power of chili?"

Ben tore open a small bag of oyster crackers and sprinkled them over his five-way—an oval plate of chili spaghetti with red beans, chopped raw onion, and cheese.

"Since when did you start putting crackers on top?" I asked.

"I've always liked my five-way like this."

Another mental note.

He swirled this Queen City favorite on his fork and took a satisfying bite.

He waved his empty fork at me. "Eat, woman."

I took a bite of my chili dog, and it tasted *just right*.

Readers Guide

THE CAKE THERAPIST

DISCUSSION QUESTIONS

1. Claire admits that she is better at intuiting someone else's life rather than her own. Why do you think this is the case? In what ways did helping others allow Claire to realize more about herself?

2. Do you think Claire's ability to "taste" feelings is a blessing or a curse? Would you want her power to read people?

3. From Ethel Parsons, the textile designer in the 1908 flashback, to Claire O'Neil, who owns her own bakery in the present day, the expectations and roles of women in this novel drastically change. Compare and contrast how the women in *The Cake Therapist* fit in their respective time periods. What positions do they occupy in the workplace and at home? Do any of these women defy society's limitations or, alternatively, succumb to them?

4. The novel revisits the evocative time period of World War II, including the infamous attack on Pearl Harbor and the

involuntary draft. Did reading about this era evoke any memories for you regarding your own family's history?

5. Claire originally thinks of Jett "as 'the Goth Van Gogh' on a good day or 'Vampira' on a bad one," but by the novel's end their rapport has significantly changed. How does Claire and Jett's relationship evolve throughout the novel? If you were Claire, would you have handled Jett differently?

6. In the beginning of *The Cake Therapist*, Maggie holds a lot of disdain for the Professor, but she gradually grows affection for him. Have you ever experienced a similar change of heart in your own relationships? What spurred the transformation?

7. In a twist of fate, Shemuel becomes a self-made man and achieves the American dream. Do you think the American dream is attainable in today's world? Does this freedom to prosper also mean there's an equal possibility for failure? How do the events in *The Cake Therapist* support or debunk this?

8. Were you surprised by the true identities revealed at the novel's end, or did you suspect any of these alter egos earlier on? If so, what hints helped you come to these revelations?

9. Claire struggles with her strong but uncertain feelings for Luke and softer but consistent affection for Ben. Were you frustrated with Claire's indecision regarding the men in her life or sympathetic? What did you think of her revelation about why she stayed with Luke for so long?

10. Rainbow Cake very much becomes a safe haven for the characters in the novel, particularly for Claire and Jett. Do you have a place like that, or your own comfort food or flavor?

11. Edie and Olive have a tenuous relationship at times. When Edie is attacked, she does not tell Olive and, moreover, assumes her sister's reaction would be unsympathetically harsh. "Olive would be mad—and ashamed of her. Olive would say it was all Edie's fault. . . . Olive would tell her to stop being a baby. To stop being scared." Do you agree with Edie's perception of young Olive? Why or why not?

12. By the novel's end, Claire starts to find peace with her dad. What emotional hurdles did she overcome throughout the novel to reach this point? If you were Claire, would you be willing to forgive her father?

Turn the page for a preview of
the next book from Judith Fertig

THE MEMORY OF LEMON

Available soon from Berkley Books!

Prologue

LATE MARCH

The spring blizzard had blasted down from Canada, covering everything in sparkly white. That may have been bad news for commuters and daffodils, but it was good news for Jack O'Neil.

Jack's buddy Marvin was doing the rounds of the parking lots on old Route 40—fast-food drive-ins, no-tell motels, and porn palaces—with the snow plow hitched to his pickup, making a little extra money. Marvin took the dog with him. He said he'd bring back a pizza and some soda.

Jack stayed behind for his tour of duty at the beat-up desk in the motel office.

The "No Vacancy" sign was crooked in the City Vue's window, but he wasn't expecting any travelers in this weather. I-70, which ran parallel to Route 40 a little ways to the north, was closed.

Most of the City Vue tenants were on welfare and rented by the week, so there was little need for hospitality. But you never knew what might happen. The numbers he needed were right by the old push-button phone: the Independence, Missouri, police department; the ambulance service; and the fire department. If you called 911, you got all three and a lot of flack afterward. It was better to be particular and ask for only what you needed in the low-rent district.

Jack had worked some construction last year so he would have a warmer place to stay in deep winter. Ever since he got frostbite on one of his toes—it looked like freezer burn and hurt like hell—he didn't sleep rough when it got too cold.

Yet it wasn't like he had the TV on and a weather report he could check. Hell, he didn't even have a cell phone. In Kansas City, the temperature could plummet fifty degrees in twelve hours. Despite the layers of sock, plastic bag, sock, plastic bag, then boot, he almost lost that toe and could have lost others during a cold snap last year. No way was he going to be a cripple.

So when Marvin, another regular at the nearby VA Hospital, had offered him this temporary gig, Jack took it.

By April, it should be okay to go back to his old place.

Here at the City Vue, where it was warm and dry, he could keep things safe. Like the letter from his daughter that the guy from Project Uplift, the nonprofit group that fed the homeless, had brought by. Jack kept the letter in his shirt pocket, which he patted from time to time to make sure it was still there.

He sat back in the swivel chair that didn't swivel anymore and looked around the room.

A rack of Technicolor postcards of the Kansas City skyline was furry with dust. Fake paneling peeled off the walls. The dropped-down ceiling tiles were yellowed with nicotine, even though Marvin had stopped smoking years ago.

Jack opened the desk drawer and drew out a sheet from a stack of stationery so old, there was no zip code. The paper smelled musty.

But it was free.

One of the perks of the job here, along with a room for him and the dog.

In the back of the drawer, he found a ballpoint pen almost as old as the postcards. Amazingly, the darn pen still wrote.

He opened with *Dear Claire*, then put the pen down, unsure what to say next. He had left when she was fifteen. He hadn't spoken to her since, barely able to send a postcard from wherever he landed over the years.

There was so much, he didn't know where to start. *Better keep it short this time,* he told himself. When he finished, Jack put the letter in a City Vue envelope and wrote out the address he knew by heart in Millcreek Valley, Ohio.

He leaned back in the chair, just to rest his eyes, and fell into that old dream again.

He's dangling by strings like a marionette, his arms and legs in a silky fabric, jerking at some invisible puppet master's whim. Abruptly, the strings go limp and Jack collapses in a heap.

He wakes up in the dark, in pain, a smell of woodsmoke in the air. And piss. A girl with blue hands reaches down to him. She's trying to tell him something, but he can't understand her. Her round face glows red.

When Jack woke up, a blue light was seeping through the opening in the sagging draperies. Jack looked down at the floor and shook his head.

More than forty years of this same goddamn dream. Wasn't it time for it to make some sense?

Or for Jack to quit searching for clues? Or to stop dreaming it?

In the old days, this would have made him turn to the bottle.

But he was learning to feel his feelings. And now he was goddamn hungry.

Where the hell was Marvin?

1

APRIL

Lime and Coconut

This was not the way I wanted to start the week.

Lydia, the twentysomething bride-to-be, sat stony-faced on the settee in my front parlor.

Since I opened my bakery in Millcreek Valley's bridal district in January, I had learned a lot about wooing, in the business sense. When I did wedding cake tastings, I took potential clients out of Rainbow Cake next door and into the more intimate setting of my home. Here, I hoped they would be charmed by the French gray walls, the glint of heavy hotel silver serving pieces, the fire in the Victorian hearth, and the little cakes, buttercream frostings, and mousses I had made for them.

But this bride was unmoved.

When we first opened, Lydia's mother had put a substantial deposit down and reserved the date for her daughter's July wedding, but trying to find a time when her *wedding team* could meet with her had been problematic. The bride had kept putting us off. And now this.

As a new business owner, I could not afford to have high-profile, unhappy clients. Word of mouth was everything to wealthy mothers and brides. *Who did your flowers? Where did you get those pashminas for the bridesmaids? Don't use so-and-so.* You never wanted to have your business name fill in the blank for *so-and-so.*

I refilled Lydia's teacup with a chamomile blend and poured more French press coffee for her mother and the other wedding team members, who must feel like I looked. My reflection in the silver teapot cast back my auburn hair tied up in a knot, wide green eyes, and a now-familiar Claire "Neely" O'Neil expression—a duck seeming to stay afloat effortlessly while paddling furiously underwater.

Roshonda Taylor, wedding-planner-to-the-stars, was gorgeous as usual in her salmon sheath dress that showed off skin the color of her favorite caramel macchiato. Gavin Nichols, gifted interior designer and space planner, sipped his coffee, careful not to spill on his pristine starched shirt, navy blazer, and khaki pants. If someone had told us back in our blue-collar high school days that as thirtysomethings, we would be planning a high-style wedding together, we maybe would have moved our prom from the rickety but cheap Fraternal Order of Eagles hall to somewhere more expensive and glamorous. But probably not. We learned early: You have to work with what you've got.

And what we had here was a crisis. Somehow we had to navigate the choppy waters between what the mother wanted and what the bride envisioned.

They had sampled tiny browned-butter yellow, classic white,

devil's food, almond, and Grand Marnier cakes with a variety of pastel mousses and gossamer-textured buttercreams.

Usually, by this part of a tasting, I'd be casting images of wedding cakes on the smooth plaster walls with my laptop, casually dropping a few celebrity client names from my New York days, and my current clients would be choosing a design.

But we weren't there yet. And I was beginning to fear that we wouldn't get there. I looked over at Lydia again, who sat, stiff and silent.

"Sweetheart, what do you think of the lemon with the lavender? For a hot summer night, that might be very refreshing," Mrs. Stidham asked. Her expensively cut and streaked hair and the whiff of $350-a-bottle perfume from Jean Patou were at odds with her too-tight, too-short leather skirt and the animal-print top. Her French manicured nails were immaculate, if impractically long.

The mother had remarried, I assumed, as Lydia's last name was Ballou.

Lydia crossed her arms in front of her chest. Where her mother was groomed and flashy, Lydia looked like a sixties folk singer. She wore no makeup and her long, curly, mouse-brown hair was parted in the middle. She had on a shapeless lace dress that hung on her thin frame, and a short-sleeved beige cardigan. Her beautiful, big gray eyes could probably look soulful when she wasn't being obstinate.

"Mother," she finally said. "I told you I didn't want cake. I want wedding pie."

Well, I can't help you there, I wanted to say. My bakery was called Rainbow Cake for a reason.

Roshonda jumped in.

"I think what Lydia is trying to say is that although Claire's cakes were delicious, maybe we've strayed too far from the Appalachian theme we talked about," Roshonda said, giving me the eye.

Appalachian. Hmmm.

Bourbon and branch water. Dulcimer music. Wildflowers in jelly jars. Biscuits and country ham. That did have a certain charm.

"I know you've talked this over with Roshonda and Gavin, but why don't you tell me about the kind of wedding you want," I said to Lydia with a smile. "What is your inspiration?"

Lydia sat up straighter, unfolded her arms, and put her hands in her lap. "Some of my happiest memories growing up were the summers I spent with my grandmother in northern Kentucky," she said.

Her mother reached over and took her hand.

"Mom worked two jobs to support us," Lydia said, looking sideways at her mother and then back at me. "We lived in a crappy apartment. The neighborhood wasn't safe, so I couldn't go outside if she wasn't at home. At my grandma's in Augusta, it was like paradise. I would spend hours in the woods, by the creek, in her garden, in her skiff on the river. And that's what I want for my wedding, that simple paradise," Lydia said.

I nodded and gave her those few moments of silence that always prompted more of the story.

"I loved taking the little ferry near Point Pleasant. As it went across the river, getting closer to old buildings along the waterfront, you felt the wind in your hair and the pull of the river under your feet. It was like stepping back in time and going home, if that makes any sense."

Simple paradise. Stepping back in time. Grandmother's garden.

Going home. So why was I suddenly getting the taste of Christmas? Of evergreen and spice together?

Usually, if I focused on a client and then let myself open to her, I sensed a flavor that usually became the link to a meaningful, personal story. This is how I got to the heart of my client, flavor *and* story. With that signature flavor and the understanding I received from her story, I could craft a wedding cake that would fit her like a couture gown.

As I liked to say, there was a flavor that explained you, even to yourself. There was a flavor to help you move on, mend your broken heart, help you start over, or begin a new life. Gavin once called me a cake therapist, but as any kind of therapist knows, you need information.

I had a perplexing flavor. *Christmas*. But no story yet to help me interpret what it meant. Maybe I was pushing myself too much. Maybe if I just relaxed a little bit, the story would come.

Spice usually indicated grief, a loss that lingered for a long time, just like the pungent flavor of the spice itself, whether it was nutmeg or allspice or star anise. The more pronounced the flavor, the more recent the loss and the stronger the emotion. But the puzzling thing was that evergreen, a taste that was new to me, came through just as strongly.

Lydia was staring at me, and as I looked around the room, everyone else was, too.

Somehow, I would have to figure out what to do with evergreen and spice. And pie.

"So, it was just summers that you spent with your grandmother in Augusta? Did you ever go there for the holidays?" I asked. *Maybe that was the link.*

"No. Grandma came to us then because Mom always worked at the restaurant on Christmas."

"And is there a special reason you'd like pie instead of cake for your wedding?" I asked her.

"Grandma was the one who taught me how to make pie. She made the best pies."

I nodded. "Well, I don't have pie today, but see what you think of this," I said, and passed her a sugar cookie, which she—thankfully—took and began to nibble.

I had to think fast.

"Let's start with the little things and then we can work up to wedding pie," I suggested. "We can do these sugar cookies in virtually any shape and flavor you want for a bridesmaids' luncheon and wedding guest favors or simply as part of the wedding dessert buffet. I have these wonderful edible transfer wafer papers that you can apply to a sugar cookie so it looks like a vintage postcard or a perfume bottle or a china pattern."

Lydia scowled.

"But I don't see those designs for you," I quickly added. "I see botanical prints of Kentucky wildflowers or woodland plants like ferns on these cookies. We put the cookies in handwoven baskets so the guests can gather them for themselves."

"Yes!" Lydia said, suddenly animated.

"And maybe the flavoring for the cookie could be a Kentucky flavor, something that could have come from your grandmother's garden. We can figure that out later."

Lydia beamed and turned to her mother, who looked crestfallen.

Uh-oh.

"You have to understand, Claire, that this wedding is for Lydia and Brian, first, but it's also a big social occasion for my husband," said Mrs. Stidham. "He has been very good to Lydia and me, and I don't want to disappoint him," she said, twisting her hands together in her lap. "He has so many friends and business associates he wants to invite, but . . ." She trailed off, looking miserable.

"Almost all of my weddings feature signature sugar cookies," I explained. "It's just a question of what you do with them."

But we were back to the classic standoff: Bride versus Mother.

When Lydia got up to use the restroom, Mrs. Stidham whispered to us, "Isn't it funny? I've spent most of my life trying to get as far away as I could from the backwoods, and now my daughter wants a hillbilly wedding."